PRAISE FOR
THE ALPHA PACK SERIES

Hunter's Heart

"In the rapid-fire fifth Alpha Pack novel from Tyler (after *Black Moon*), a psychic wolf shifter meets a wildlife biologist who captures his heart. As the Alpha Pack—a group of former Navy SEALs turned shifters—races against time to catch the killer, Daria and Ryon's romance turns red-hot, even though they're fighting to stay alive. An unexpected concluding twist provides a little edge and neatly sets up the next entry in the series."

—*Publishers Weekly*

"Fast-paced with a great sense of adventure, as only sexy psychic Navy SEALs turned wolf shifters can provide. The characters have a complexity that brings depth to the story, but the passion between Ryon and Daria makes for a particularly hot read."   —*RT Book Reviews*

Black Moon

"I loved every single minute of [*Black Moon*], every event and every twist. This book was action-packed and smexy-packed. You will fall in love with Kalen if you weren't already."   —Under the Covers

continued . . .

"Tyler brings more intense romance and danger to this third entry in the Alpha Pack series. Werewolves and Marines are a heady combination, making the men of the Alpha Pack exciting and passionate. The women in this series are strong enough to stand up to the men without losing their feminine edge, and Mackenzie definitely lives up to the standard." —*RT Book Reviews*

Savage Awakening

"In a genre with werewolves aplenty, *Savage Awakening* leads the herd with its strong character development and intensity. . . . It's hard not to fall in love with the Alpha Pack." —*Romantic Times*

Primal Law

"With *Primal Law*, J. D. Tyler has created a whole squad of yummy shifter heroes whom readers will fall head over heels for. . . . I can't wait for Tyler's next Alpha Pack adventure!"

—*New York Times* bestselling author
Angela Knight

"Tyler has set up an intriguing premise for her series, which promises plenty of action, treachery, and scorchingly hot sex." —*Romantic Times*

"Sizzling and interesting, *Primal Law* pays homage to Lora Leigh's Breed series while forging its own paths. The characters are likable, and the work speeds along."
—Fresh Fiction

"In a genre where the paranormal is intense, J. D. Tyler may just be a force to be reckoned with. The book kept me riveted from start to finish." —Night Owl Reviews

Also by J. D. Tyler

Cole's REDEMPTION

AN ALPHA PACK NOVEL

J. D. TYLER

A SIGNET ECLIPSE BOOK

SIGNET ECLIPSE
Published by the Penguin Group
Penguin Group (USA) LLC, 375 Hudson Street,
New York, New York 10014

USA | Canada | UK | Ireland | Australia | New Zealand | India | South Africa | China
penguin.com
A Penguin Random House Company

First published by Signet Eclipse, an imprint of New American Library,
a division of Penguin Group (USA) LLC

First Printing, March 2014

Copyright © J. D. Tyler, 2014
Excerpt from *Raw* copyright © Jo Davis, 2013
Penguin supports copyright. Copyright fuels creativity, encourages diverse voices, pro-
motes free speech, and creates a vibrant culture. Thank you for buying an authorized
edition of this book and for complying with copyright laws by not reproducing, scanning, or distributing any part of it in any form without permission. You are supporting
writers and allowing Penguin to continue to publish books for every reader.

SIGNET ECLIPSE and logo are trademarks of Penguin Group (USA) LLC.

ISBN 978-0-451-41723-7

Printed in the United States of America
10 9 8 7 6 5 4 3 2 1

To my dear friend Melody Walker. There is no greater joy than a friend and sister found again and a heart made whole. The day you came back into my life was one of the happiest ever, and my soul was set free.

It is only fitting that Zander's story is for you.

I love you, my friend.

"Hell is empty and all the devils are here."

—William Shakespeare

One

The white wolf scented the air, searching for her prey.

The commander hadn't ventured into the forest lately, but that would change. Sooner or later, the traitorous bastard would come out of his stronghold, venture beyond the protection of brick and mortar, past the magical boundary erected by the Sorcerer.

He'd put aside the shadows on his soul, even if temporarily. He'd forget that his ability as a Seer was severely hampered when it came to his own impending death. Longing for solitude, to feel the wind in his face, his toes digging into the soft earth, he'd let his wolf loose. Go for a run.

And if all went as planned, he would never return.

Settling in, she watched. Waited. She burned to

see the expression on his face when he realized his past had finally come to call. That, in a great twist of irony, he had sired his own executioner, and his sins would be paid for with his blood. It was all that mattered, all she lived for.

Soon, her father would die.

"The vampire problem is becoming increasingly unstable," Nick Westfall said, face grim as he studied each member of his Alpha Pack team of shifters. "If we don't get a handle on the rogues, they're going to end up exposing the entire paranormal world to the human race."

Resting his elbows on the conference room's table, Zander Cole struggled to understand his commander's briefing. It wasn't as if he was *completely* deaf anymore. When he was a kid, he and his friends would while away the summer at the local swimming pool. Sometimes they'd entertain themselves by yelling to one another underwater and trying to decipher the messages, to little success and a great deal of laughter. His current predicament was like that—without the amusement.

But over the past few months, he'd gotten better at reading lips. As long as he was looking directly at the speaker and concentrating hard, he could catch most of what was said.

It was a vast improvement over the total deafness he'd been left with after the Pack's Sorcerer had created an explosion of lightning that had literally rocked the earth. Progress, yes—but a long way from being healed.

Because his brain injury had left him to contend with so much more than just his hearing being shot to hell.

Despair swelled in his chest, and he fought it down yet again. The blinding headaches were as bad as they'd been in the beginning. Maybe worse. Every day, the feelings of helplessness, uselessness, got harder to take. He feared he was no longer an asset to his team, but a burden. A waste of space.

Sort of hard to swallow, considering Zan was the Pack's Healer. His Psy gift allowed him to heal everyone except himself, and even that was in jeopardy of failing him altogether.

For years, his Pack brothers and their mission of battling the world's most dangerous paranormal predators had been his whole life, and now his future wasn't looking too bright. His days on the team appeared to be numbered, and rejoining the "normal" human world wasn't an option.

Where that left him was a very, very frightening place in his head.

Shaking himself from his misery, he forced himself to focus again on what Nick was telling them.

". . . capture one of them alive if we can. Find out why there's so goddamned many of them lately." Pausing, he consulted some notes in his hand. "Our latest report cites a rogue problem on a ranch in Texas."

"Texas?" Zan mused out loud. He glanced around and saw the same curiosity reflected in his brothers' faces before returning his attention to Nick.

"Not their usual stomping ground, for sure. They normally keep to big cities, where it's easier to blend in and feed and where one more dead homeless person will hardly be noted. But for whatever reason, it seems we have a group targeting a ranch in East Texas. The owners were shocked last week when a couple of hands found two cows with their throats slashed and only a minimal amount of blood around their bodies when the ground should've been soaked."

There was a murmur around the room as Nick went on. "We know vampires will drink from large animals if they're desperate for food. What's unusual is that the animals were killed during the daytime."

A loud exclamation came from Zan's right, and he needed no clarification to interpret it as a curse. Glancing over, he saw Aric Savage lean forward in his chair and rest his elbows on the conference table. The redhead looked pissed as he pushed his long hair from his face.

"The bastards are walking during the day now? How the hell are they managing that?"

Nick shook his head. "No idea, which is another reason we need one of them alive."

"I doubt this reached your desk because of a couple of dead cows," Zan said, working to enunciate clearly. He hated how his voice must sound to everyone, strange and flat, and tried hard to ignore the gazes that swung in his direction. "There must be more."

"You're right. It wasn't the cows that got our friends in Washington moving—it was the dead cowboy who was found this morning, throat slashed and body drained. He went out early to check the cattle, and his horse came back alone. Our contacts were already aware of the slaughtered cattle, so when this news came over the wire, Grant called me while the government sent in a couple of suits to keep local law enforcement at bay."

General Jarrod Grant was an old friend of Nick's and one of the only allies in Washington whom the Pack trusted. If Grant was involved, the rogue situation was serious.

Zan snorted. "I bet that went over well. When do we leave?"

Nick paused, giving Zan a searching look, and a lead ball formed in his gut. For one excruciating moment, he feared the commander would order him to remain behind at the compound, despite their previous talks. Even Packmate Micah Chase, with his nightmares and heavy meds, was now allowed to join their missions. If Zan had to stay behind, confirming his status as useless to everyone, he'd crawl under a rock and die.

Then the man nodded at him slightly and said, "Thirty minutes. We'll take a couple of the Hueys."

Zan fought to hide his relief. Nick had placed his trust in him, and Zan couldn't let him or the team down. As the team stood and began to file from the room to make ready for the flight, he felt a hand on his shoulder and turned to see his best friend, Jaxon Law, gazing at him with a slight smile on his face, not an ounce of sympathy evident. Thank God. Jax of all people knew that pity was the one thing Zan wouldn't be able to handle.

"You ready?" Jax asked.

"Yeah. As I'll ever be."

"You'll do fine."

"I'm not worried about doing my job," he snapped, then immediately felt bad about it. Especially since that statement was a big lie. And because Jax was simply standing there wearing an expression of patient understanding instead of giving in to the fight Zan suddenly craved.

As though reading his mind, Jax smiled and said, "Good. Save that aggression for the enemy and we'll both be proven right. Come on."

He felt like an ass. His team had been nothing but supportive in the aftermath of his injury and throughout his recovery. They knew how tough these past few weeks had been for him, and nobody gave him a hard time. They didn't dare, considering that if they were truly doing their jobs, every single one of them would end up out of commission sooner or later. The difference was that being shifters, their injuries typically healed within days.

Zan's wounds were severe, possibly permanent.

Giving Jax a grin he didn't feel, he nodded. "Sorry. Lead the way."

They hurried out, taking only seconds to dash to their living quarters and retrieve the new laser guns they'd been issued, along with the big bowie knife Zan liked to strap to his thigh. Unlike Aric, he wasn't a Telekinetic/Firestarter and didn't have the power to hurl objects or set the enemy on fire in a fight—though that would be awesome. Being a Healer was rewarding, but it certainly didn't give him an edge in battle, so he preferred human weapons. Teeth and claws and superior speed were cool when he was in wolf form, but the knife was just as effective in close combat.

Meeting in the hallway, he and Jax made their way through the compound and down a corridor leading to the huge hangar that housed all of the Pack's vehicles. In addition to the helicopters, there were several SUVs, cars, and a jet, along with their personal modes of transportation. Zan's baby, a big, macho Ford Raptor, sat on the far side of the building, and he spared it a longing glance before climbing into one of the Hueys with Jax, Nick, Ryon, Micah, and Phoenix. In the other copter rode Aric, his mate, Rowan, Kalen, Hammer,

A.J. and finally Noah, a nurse who worked in the compound's infirmary. It was quite common for one of them to need patching up in the field, and Noah's presence was a great help to Zan these days.

Zan tried not to think about why. It wasn't like Noah's being around was a vote of no confidence, since one of the doctors or nurses usually accompanied the Pack on a mission. But an insidious voice inside him whispered, *Yeah, but for how long? What happens when you've got nothing left to give?*

Inside him, his wolf growled at the thought.

Once they were in the air, he lost himself to the dull roar of the aircraft and paid no particular attention to the shouted conversations going on around him. That was one dangerous thing about being practically deaf—it was all too easy for him to retreat from the world. If he didn't look, he couldn't participate. Both a blessing and a curse.

Eventually, however, his gaze was drawn to his Pack brothers. Especially Micah and Phoenix. It was strange, getting used to having the two of them with the team again, especially after they'd been believed dead. Zan was glad they'd been rescued from the horrible labs after being tortured for months, and wondered how they were really coping.

One side of Micah's face was ruined, like melted wax, the result of molten silver being poured on him. God knows he had to still be in pain, but Micah claimed that his medications were helping. He'd come out of his shell in recent weeks, had stopped hiding his face. He smiled more, though the expression was still reserved. The man was a walking miracle; so what if his eyes were a bit too bright, almost feverish?

Nobody questioned it, at least not to Micah. No one wanted to risk setting back his progress.

Phoenix was a completely different story. Rescued separately from Micah, the man had come away malnourished but with no physical scars and seemed to be handling the horrors he'd been through with relative ease. Too much so, which had Zan concerned. But if he was hurting inside, he was hiding it well. Nix appeared to be quite happy lately—and even a blind man could see that it was due to his attraction to Noah.

Were those two Bondmates? A betting pool had been started, and Zan hadn't bothered to chip in on what he figured was a *yes*. The great thing was, not one of the guys had expressed a negative attitude about it. In the shifter world, a man's Bondmate just *was*, like the leaves on the trees or the air they breathed. If fate blessed a man with the other half of his soul, he didn't question his good fortune. He simply seized his destiny with both hands and thanked God he didn't have to walk through life alone.

Zan knew he sure as hell would, if he were so lucky.

Dammit. Not going to think about one more impossible dream heaped on the bonfire. The rest will be a pile of smoldering ashes soon enough.

As if to punctuate that miserable thought, Zan glanced over just in time to catch a snippet of conversation between Micah and Nix.

"Don't know, man," Micah was saying. "I'm not one to talk about whether *he's* ready to be on duty. I mean, look at me." He gestured to his own face, but Nix shook his head.

"Your scars don't affect your ability to do your job, buddy. His situation is totally different. Just sayin'."

Unable to bear witnessing another word, Zan averted his gaze and stared at the ugly gray wall of the Huey. Hurt speared him like a lance to the gut, and he rested his elbows on his knees. Was that what all of them were saying? Speculating out loud on whether he was fit to be in the field?

Doubting himself in private was one thing.

But seeing his brothers do the same—in front of him, as if he were stupid as well as deaf—was a whole different level of pain.

Lost in his head, he let the hours roll by, scarcely making an attempt to join in what little talk the guys managed. By the time they landed in a wide, grassy plain in Texas, Jax was gazing at him with worry etched on his brow as he stroked his goatee. The second he saw Zan noticing, however, he put on his poker face. Already on edge, Zan wasn't about to let him get away with pretending nothing was wrong.

As soon as they were clear of the transport, Zan grabbed his friend's arm and held him back as the others walked across the pasture to meet a trio of men in suits.

"Don't do that," he hissed. "Don't pretend to my face that you're okay with me being here when you think the same as everyone else."

Anger flashed in Jax's eyes. "You telling me what I think now? News flash—you're a Healer, not a Seer, so you have no clue what's going on in my head."

"I have eyes. I can tell you're second-guessing whether I can do the job."

"Am I?" He took a step forward, got in Zan's face. "I doubt any one of us could possibly second-guess you more than you're doing all on your own. You saw concern, yes. But that's because I'm your *friend*, jackass. I give a damn about you, that's all."

Put like that, the perspective made Zan feel about an inch tall. Blowing out a breath, he looked away for a moment, scanning the horizon without really noticing much. One of Jax's hands clasped his shoulder, and he returned his attention to his friend.

"The thing is, *your* doubt is the only thing that

matters. Don't you see? When you have your confidence back, when you've lost the anger and fear and you can join the mission knowing you're back to one hundred percent, then what anyone else believes won't amount to shit."

He swallowed hard. "But what if I'm never the same? What if I don't heal?"

"Then you learn to compensate, like I did after my leg was mangled."

"That's different—" he began.

"No, it's not. My leg physically healed, yes, but the strength and agility I used to have in that limb are not equal to the good leg. And it won't ever be the same. But I've learned techniques to help me make up for it in a fight—techniques you and the others helped me perfect, I'll remind you."

"I get it," he muttered.

"Do you? Nobody wants anything but the best for you, Zan," he said, warm sincerity evident in his expression. "The guys are worried, and they may run off at the mouth too much, but every one of them is in your corner. Believe that."

Hey, guys? Ryon pushed into their minds telepathically. *Nick's giving you both the stink eye, so you might want to cut the lovefest short, get your butts over here, and join the party.*

Jax made a face and turned, starting off toward the group of Feds, who appeared decidedly unhappy. With a sigh, Zan followed him, sort of glad for Ryon's interruption. Save for a mated couple, who could speak telepathically to each other, the Channeler/Telepath was the only one who could push his thoughts directly into others' heads. Zan relished being able to hear someone's voice clearly, even if just temporarily.

Those brief periods of contact might be all he had to look forward to.

As they reached the spot where Nick stood in front of his Pack, Zan noted that the meeting between his commander and the Feds looked more like a standoff.

"So, are you guys military or not?" one of the agents asked with a frown, arms crossed over his chest.

Nick had his back to Zan, but whatever the commander said did not go over well with the suits. A second agent, short and stocky, pushed the issue.

"Your outfit doesn't look like any Special Ops team I ever saw. More like mercenaries, if you ask me." This was said with a slight curl to his lips, as though he'd tasted something bad.

Zan got close enough to maneuver around and catch Nick's response.

"Nobody *did* ask you." The commander's stare was hard and flat. "And now that we're here, you all can pull back and let us do what the White House sent us here to do. Unless, of course, you'd like for me to get the president on the phone so he can tell you personally."

The agents froze, and several of the Pack members blinked at Nick in surprise.

"You've got President Warren on speed dial? You're full of shit," the stocky agent sneered, recovering some.

"Try me. But fair warning—you'll be out of a job before I end the call. Up to you if losing your career is worth the attitude."

Way to pull rank, Zan thought with a smirk. *Nothing like the mention of the Oval Office to chap their asses.*

Holy crap. Did Nick really have that kind of clout? The Feds eyed Nick's stony expression for a few tense moments, seemed to buy it, and reluctantly backed off. Once they'd moved off to stand elsewhere and act official—*translation, be completely useless*—the commander turned to a tall, beefy rancher who'd been hovering on the perimeter of the gathering, weathered face grim under the brim of his hat, broad shoulders drooping with the weight of what had occurred on his property. Zan pegged him as either the owner or the foreman.

Taking off his hat to scratch his head, the rancher also looked plenty baffled. "I don't understand why the government sent damned near two dozen people to investigate poor Saul's murder, unless you're looking for a serial killer or something. Whatever the reason, I'm glad you're here."

"We're looking for a specific type of killer,"

Nick informed him, before fudging the truth. A lot. "There have been a rash of cult killings, and this murder fits the pattern. We came as soon as we heard."

"That was damned fast, but I'm grateful. Sure might take a military group to stop a bunch of cult crazies." The rancher eyed Nick, then the team in general. "I'm Tim Edwards, by the way. What do you need me to do?"

"I need use of a couple of trucks, if you have any to spare. We want to look around the area where the cattle and your hand were found."

"Sure. I'll send a couple of my men out to show you—"

Nick shook his head. "Just to tell us. We can find it. I'd rather not put more of your men in un-necessary danger when the culprits are still at large."

Zan tried to imagine what the rancher would do if he knew that the team could simply sniff out the murder scenes with their canine noses when they got close enough. That would probably finish off the poor guy.

Thankfully, the rancher seemed to agree with Nick's plan. "That's fine. I've got three trucks that belong to the Bar K ya'll can use if you promise to bring 'em back in one piece."

"Thank you. We'll do our best."

Zan fell into step with his Pack as they walked the rest of the way to the main house. The mood was somber, rugged-looking men milling around not knowing what to do and clearly uneasy with the recent events. He spotted more than one cowboy with reddened eyes and knew their fellow hand's murder must've hit them hard. Zan could empathize with the horror of losing a close friend to violence.

None too soon, they'd gotten directions, borrowed the trucks, and were on their way to investigate the sites where the bodies were found. He felt a little guilty for his relief at leaving the heavy cloud of grief behind him and getting on with doing what they did best.

The lead truck followed a well-worn dirt road for a mile or so before veering into the pasture. After it had traveled about forty yards, it came to a halt and the vehicles behind it did the same. Everyone got out and trailed Nick to a pair of bloated carcasses on the ground a few feet away. Zan wrinkled his nose at the stench.

"Jesus."

The bodies of the cattle were stiff, getting ripe. Each one's throat was laid wide open, the wound sort of messy, the meat chewed.

Micah pointed. "Not what I'd expect from a vampire bite. They don't typically ravage their victims like that when they feed."

"But I can scent them all over the place," Zan put in. His lupine sense of smell was one of the traits that hadn't deserted him yet. "Definitely a vampire kill."

There were nods of agreement. Nick squatted, his blue eyes narrowed. "These rogues are out of control. Not that we didn't realize that—they've killed a human out in the open—but this is beyond the ordinary. Even for rogues, this shows a lack of control I haven't seen before. A certain amount of . . ."

"Recklessness?" Zan supplied. "Balls?"

"Yes." The commander stood. "There's no thoughtful cunning here. No discretion."

Jax shook his head. "There's almost a sickness permeating the area."

"We have to find out why," Nick agreed. "Nothing else to see here, though. Let's move on to the ranch hand's body."

Just then, Zan noticed Micah wandering away from the group, sniffing the air. He walked toward the back of the property, in the direction they'd been heading before they stopped. Then he crouched and palmed a handful of dirt, inhaled, then dropped it and brushed his hand on his jeans.

"There was a human here," he told them. "This scent stands out because it was joined by at least one vampire, and then both scents head that way." He pointed toward a copse of trees a ways off.

Zan peered into the distance and remarked, "That's where they told us we can find the body.

Maybe he came out here alone to take another look at the dead cattle and they snatched him. A kill of opportunity."

At that grim prospect, they loaded into the vehicles and drove the rest of the way to the murder scene. As they approached, Zan noted that there was a vehicle there and two men in suits standing near what he assumed to be the body, which was covered with a tarp. Made sense that they couldn't leave the body unguarded, though Nick wouldn't like them hanging around.

They must've been informed in advance about visitors, because they stepped aside and moved a fair distance away with a minimum of protest. Still watchful, they leaned against a couple of trees while Zan and the others surrounded the tarp.

Nick pulled it back and Zan grimaced. *God, that poor bastard.*

The victim's head was turned to the side, eyes wide and staring across the field. Like the cattle, the man's neck was savaged, to the point Zan was surprised it was still attached to his prone body. The Pack had seen some pretty disturbing things in their line of work, but this? This guy had suffered before he died. He had blood and tissue under his fingernails, scratches on his arms. He'd fought. Had been desperate as he'd been dragged across the field to the tree line. He must've known he'd end up like those cows.

What a fucking shitty way to die.

Nick motioned Jax close to the man's body, and Zan knew what his best friend would be asked to do. As the Pack's RetroCog, Jax could touch a person or hold an object in his hand and get a reading on past events. Sometimes that event was a movie clip of the last moments of the person's life, or some other significant happening tied to the mystery they were trying to solve. Other times he got only snapshots of the past that didn't make sense until much later.

As Jax laid a hand on top of the man's head, Zan stepped up close to his friend, ready to catch him if necessary. These sessions usually left Jax drained.

Exhaling a long breath, Jax closed his eyes and grew still. Zan pictured how his friend always described the process of reading a body—there were threads attached to every person and object, and those threads led to the memories. Jax gathered those threads and pulled them close to see where they led.

For several long moments Jax was still. Then his body began to shake, and a soft moan of distress passed through his lips. Suddenly he fell backward with a cry, and Zan caught him from behind, steadying him.

"I've got you."

Before Jax could protest, Zan sent gentle waves of healing energy into his friend's system, cleansing the bad remnants of the memories and chasing away the exhaustion. As he finished, a dull throbbing began at his temples and crept to encompass his skull, and he knew it would get worse before it went away. But he'd do it again and again, to take care of his brothers.

Jax pulled away and turned to glare at him. "You shouldn't do that when you don't have to. Save your energy."

"Save your breath," he countered. "The day I can't heal, you can put me in the ground."

"That's not funny."

"Wasn't meant to be."

Looking frustrated, Jax let the subject go for the moment. He hadn't heard the last of it, however. His friend was like a dog with a bone when it came to making sure the people he cared for stayed safe.

"What did you learn?" Zan asked, changing the subject.

"I saw how he died. Lived it." He shuddered. "It was horrendous, what he suffered. They played with him, enjoyed causing him pain and . . . fuck, you don't want to know the details."

"What about the vamps themselves? Did you see any of them?"

"Yeah. There were two who killed the victim, but there were more hiding deep in the woods. Of the two, one was younger, blond, maybe early twenties when he was turned. The other was a few years older, brown hair, tall and slim, sort of dirty. I didn't get names."

Zan helped his friend to his feet. "You did good."

"It's not enough. I don't have a sense of whether they're still around."

Nick made sure Zan was looking at him before he interjected. "They are. I don't know how many, but they're here. Waiting."

"For what?" Zan asked.

"Us, maybe? I don't know. But I do know we have to go after them."

That was creepy as hell. Especially since Nick frequently *knew* things about the future that he either couldn't—or wouldn't—tell them. He didn't believe in interfering with free will or tampering with the future. Rumor had it he'd once tried to change a terrible outcome, with disastrous results.

None of that mattered at the moment. Any of them would follow Nick into hell on his word alone. The Pack waited as he told the disgruntled Feds that he was taking charge of the body and removing it. Unbeknownst to the suits, the dead man would wind up at the Pack's top-secret compound being studied from head to toe for any clues they could glean about the rogues. Eventually, the body would be released to the man's relatives, if there were any.

They split up into twos and threes to search the woods, spreading out. Zan found himself walking with Nix and Micah, which was fine by him. It was good to work alongside his old buddies again. He'd missed them even more than he'd realized.

Keeping a sharp eye out, he studied his surroundings despite his growing headache. It was strange not to hear the birds in the trees, the crunch of leaves underfoot. No wind, no voices. Just the steady presence of his companions. He had his knife and laser gun, not to mention his wolf's teeth and claws. He could do this after all. Be a contributing team member still.

It was that exact moment when things went to hell.

A rush of air and a scrape on his neck was his only warning as a body barreled into him, knocking him to the ground. He had a split second to realize Nix was the one who'd shoved him—saving him just in time from having his throat ripped out by the razor-sharp claws of a rogue vampire.

And now Nix was fighting for his life.

Zander unsheathed his knife and threw himself at the rogue, just as more of them emerged from the trees and flew at them like the hollow-faced horrors they were.

Two

Change was coming.

Nick could feel it all around him. In his bones, seeping into the rapidly darkening recesses of his heart.

Nothing remained the same forever, and today marked a vital turning point. A period of trial for all of them. More than that, he knew death was rushing for him on swift wings, reaching out with cold talons to tear out his heart and bear him away. The end wouldn't come today, or tomorrow. But all too soon.

He wouldn't submit to the darkness without a fight. But even he couldn't see whether he would survive.

A shout interrupted his thoughts, and he glanced in its direction. Beside him, Aric whirled.

"What was that?"

His question was followed by more shouts, and he quickly stripped, leaving his weapons with his clothing. His wolf could cover the distance much faster than his human form. Aric did the same, and they took off.

It seemed to take forever to reach the location of the fight, which became louder and louder as they sped through the trees, but it was probably just a minute or two. Even that was too long.

As he and Aric burst over a small rise, he spotted the onslaught of rogue vamps that had put Zander, Phoenix, and Micah on the losing end of the battle. Nix was lying on the ground, pressing a hand over his bleeding throat, as his companions swiftly became overwhelmed by six of the enemy.

Fuck!

Five against six wasn't terrible odds, normally. But Nix was hurt and these rogues weren't typical. Sending up a prayer that the rest of the team had heard the fight as well, he threw himself into the fray.

Zan grabbed the vampire attacking Nix, buried his fingers in the bastard's greasy hair, and swiped the bowie knife across his throat. He made the cut so deep he nearly decapitated his opponent, then took him down to the ground and finished the job.

There was no time to gloat. He barely had time to take in Nix struggling to get up and failing, before a body slammed into him, knocking him backward. The back of his head smacked hard earth, and pain exploded in his skull. Before he could move, the rogue grabbed his hair and yanked him up, pulling his head back to expose his throat. Zan struggled, trying to break the vampire's hold, but the creature's strength was unreal.

"Fuck!"

He was pinned like an insect to a corkboard. The rogue grinned, showing off bloodied fangs, and then lowered his head. Zan sucked in a breath, fully expecting to feel the razor-sharp teeth ripping out his throat, and suddenly the vampire was jerked away from him.

Aric, back in human form, threw the rogue to the ground, quickly extending a hand. Fire shot from his palm, and the bastard writhed, screaming as he burned. Zan grimaced at the gruesome sight and then turned his attention back to the fight. The rest of the Pack burst through the trees, and the threat was dispatched.

Except for one. Nick shifted back to human form and shouted something at Kalen just as the Sorcerer leveled his magical staff at the last vampire, stopping him from executing the creature. Kalen made a face, clearly unhappy at the order, but raised the staff and made the rod vanish with a flick of his hand. Instead of killing the vampire, he uttered a few words Zan couldn't make out— probably a spell in Latin—and the creature's hands were immediately bound behind his back with a silver chain. For good measure, Kalen added a wide strip of duct tape over the rogue's mouth.

"Can't have him getting anyone with those teeth," he snarled.

Jax gestured to the bodies of the captive vampire's five companions, and Zan caught his words. "They're not burning in the sun like they're supposed to. What should we do with them?"

Nick pushed a hand through his hair and stared at them. "Take the bodies back for study. This one will be our guest in Block R. We'll give him the opportunity to cooperate."

"You really think he can be rehabbed?" Zan asked.

Nick shot the rogue a doubtful look, and the vamp sneered back at him. "I won't hold my breath, but we'll see what the tests show."

Beyond Nick, Zan saw Rowan shouting and waving her arms at them. She was crouched next to Nix, who was sprawled on the ground, unmoving, as Noah examined him. Her face betrayed her panic, and Zan pushed to his feet and jogged over to them. Kneeling, he gazed at the ragged wound on Nix's throat and cursed under his breath.

Rowan reached over their fallen friend and grabbed his arm to get his attention. "Can you heal him?"

Zan nodded. "Yes." Without his full strength, he was walking a fine line, and he knew it. So did

Jax, who skidded to a stop next to them and squatted beside Zan.

"You're not healed enough for this."

Noah's face was etched with fear. "Jax is right," he said, his voice cracking. "You're still recovering and—"

"And he'll die if I don't." Zan met each of their gazes steadily. "There's never a choice for me. You all know that, so let me work."

Noah looked relieved and worried at the same time. Jax's jaw clenched, and frustrated anger clouded his eyes. But then he looked down at Nix and, sighing, moved back to give Zan room. The others did the same, except for Noah, who remained kneeling on Nix's opposite side.

Nix's eyes were closed, long blond hair fanned around him as Zan laid a palm over the torn flesh. If he had any remaining doubts about putting himself in jeopardy to save his fallen teammate, they were dispelled at the sight of Noah mouthing the word "please" repeatedly.

This is my fault. Nix saved me from the vampire because I couldn't hear him coming. The knowledge stabbed him in the gut, urging him on. Closing his eyes, he found his center and set to work.

Nix's throat was a mess. The tissues were shredded, and he had a tear in his windpipe. By some miracle, the jugular had escaped being severed, or he'd be dead already, wolf shifter or not. Still, there were plenty of vessels to repair. Carefully, he drew forth his healing light, sending gentle waves of it into the torn area.

Starting with the man's airway, he closed the hole and was satisfied Nix could now breathe easier. Then slowly, he knitted together the myriad vessels, a tedious task since each one had to be repaired individually.

He didn't know how long he worked. One after another, he sealed the leaking veins and cleaned the area of blood. Another and another, working with complete focus until he was satisfied all of them were sound. All that remained was the outer skin, and that was simple by comparison. Underneath his palm, the flesh became whole and healthy again.

Opening his eyes, he started to say something— but was blinded by agony spearing through his skull. Crying out, he fell backward, warm blood streaming from his nose. The pain was so bad, he couldn't see. Couldn't talk.

Hands were suddenly on his shoulders, urging him to lie still. Attempting to comfort. There were soothing voices, too, but he couldn't make out the words without seeing their lips. But it hardly mattered what they were saying when he was in hell.

Right where I deserve to be. Nix almost died, and it was my fault.

He knew what he had to do. There was no question now. That thought chased around in his brain all during the long trip back to the compound.

He had nothing left to offer the Pack.

Selene Westfall sat in a corner booth in the local bar called the Cross-eyed Grizzly, nursed her beer, and simply watched. Listened.

Humans were fascinating to her, never having been one herself. They might appear to be the same as her kind on the outside, but they were different in many significant ways. Humans were physically weaker, their bodies more fragile. Obviously, they didn't have the ability to shift. And they were mortal.

Another weakness they possessed besides their physical limitations was their tendency to talk *way* too fucking much. Humans ran their mouths off about every damned thing in their lives, and to complete strangers at that. Perhaps a product of a world tainted with the overshare mentality of social media. Whatever it was, however annoying, their stupidity was often her gain.

People tended to gravitate to Selene, looking to be friendly. Score a one-night stand. Whatever. Hell if she knew why, considering her appearance was hardly that of a soft, demure, willing female. At almost six feet, she was as tall as many of the men in her Pack, and she was lean but strong. Short, white-blond hair emphasized her angular cheekbones and large, vivid blue eyes, which could skewer a man at fifty paces. More than one pup had pissed himself at being the recipient of her displeasure.

Maybe that air of danger, not so common in a female, was the honey that drew people. In any case, she was a master at letting them sidle up, thinking they were getting their game on, then gradually turning the tables. She'd let them talk, spilling their secrets, and she'd take it all in without giving anything in return. Her uncle liked to joke that she would make a great detective if she ever joined the human world.

As if. Though her powers of observation were coming in handy at the moment as she eavesdropped without remorse on the conversations around her. One in particular caught her attention, a couple of local guys speculating about "that top-secret research place" in the forest and what the hell really went on in there.

"You don't want to know," she snorted to herself, taking a sip of her beer.

Research. So that was the bullshit Nick Westfall was feeding to the locals? How long could that last? *Until I burn that place to the ground, that's how long.*

The bartender, a pretty woman with long dark hair, was almost at Selene's table before she noticed. She berated herself for the unusual slip in her attention as the woman stopped and gave her a smile.

"Shouldn't you be working behind the bar?" Selene inquired pleasantly.

"Slow day. Most of the servers won't be in until the after-work crowd hits. Can I get you anything else?"

"Still nursing this one, but thanks."

"No food? It's lunchtime now. . . ."

"I'll wait a bit." Pausing, she studied the bartender, puzzling over what had been bugging her about the woman since she'd arrived. "I'm Selene. What's your name?"

"Jacee." She studied Selene in return—and something flashed in her eyes. Recognition, perhaps?

Without being too obvious, Selene inhaled a whiff of her scent and straightened in surprise. Belatedly recognizing the danger, Jacee tried to step back, but Selene's hand shot out to grab the woman's wrist and pull her closer.

"Coyote," she hissed, and the bartender's face registered shock.

"How did you . . . ? Nobody's ever guessed!" she whispered.

Her laugh was low and sultry. "Not even the boys at the so-called research center?"

"Not even them." She hesitated, fearful, and pushed a lock of hair from her face. "So you know about them, too?"

"I know what they really are," she replied, not giving away too much.

"Because you're the same?"

"Not exactly. I scented you and they didn't, remember? But close enough."

"What do you want from me?" The shock was passing, the coyote getting defensive now. She crossed her arms over her chest, eyeing Selene in suspicion.

Best to lay it on the table. "Information on the wolves at the compound."

Jacee shook her head. "I work hard and mind my own business. I don't make it a habit to get into other people's."

"You will this time, unless you want every shifter in the vicinity to know there's a sweet little coyote bitch here, ripe for the picking."

Defensiveness became seething anger. Casting a quick look around to be sure they weren't drawing attention, Jacee snapped, "This coyote bitch doesn't answer to skanky wolves."

Selene gave the bartender a toothy smile as she started to leave the booth. "Oh, but it's not me you'll have to answer to. The other wolves are a different story, though. They're regulars, right? I think they'll be interested to know—"

"What can I possibly tell you? I don't know anything about those guys!"

Gotcha. Selene resumed her seat. "You're aware

of more than you think. How many of them are there? How often do they come in?"

She shook her head. "I don't know how many, exactly. At least ten, I'd say, plus a few others that aren't on the team."

"Team?" That word got her attention. She'd observed them in action from a distance, how they moved as a well-trained unit, but was still in the dark about their purpose. "Elaborate."

Jacee blew out a frustrated breath. "They're some sort of top-secret military unit. I've seen them called away from here more than once, and when they leave, they do it with this amazing calm, organized precision, if you know what I mean. Their leader, or whatever you call him, is usually issuing orders."

Their leader. Nick Westfall.

"What sort of orders?" When the woman hesitated, she pushed. "Come on. I know you pick up things with your preternatural hearing that others don't."

"Stuff about where they're heading, what vehicles they'll take. Sometimes he says to get the Hueys ready, other times they're taking a jet or SUVs."

"And why are they rushing off, Jacee? Tell me." Her gaze pinned the woman. She knew, and Selene wasn't leaving without the answer.

"From what I've heard, sometimes people are in trouble, and they're called away to help."

She frowned. "How so? They're not regular military from one of the four branches, right? They're not cops, either, so what sort of problems do they deal with?"

"Paranormal ones," Jacee whispered, leaning close. Her gaze was intent. "They're not just wolves. They have Psy abilities, every last one of them."

"What?"

"They're called Alpha Pack, and they all had special abilities, like seeing the dead or telekinesis or whatever, even before they were turned into shifters. Now they protect the world from just about every paranormal threat you can imagine—vampires, witches, demons, Unseelie, Sluagh. You name it, they've probably battled it."

Selene's heart thundered in her chest. This was not *at all* what she'd expected to learn. *Her* father, the commander of a team with such a noble calling? No fucking way. Draining her glass, she slid it across the table.

"You know, I think I'm going to need that second beer after all."

Zan was suffering with a pounding head and a terrible ache in his heart.

He'd almost gotten a Pack brother killed, and he knew the horrible memory of Phoenix sprawled on the ground, desperately trying to hold his torn neck together, would stay with him forever. That was his wake-up call. There was only one course of action left to take, as much as the decision tore him apart.

He had to go. Today.

Struggling to sit up in the infirmary's hospital bed, he yanked at the IV in his hand—only to be interrupted by Mac, who rushed into the room, curly dark hair swirling around her determined face.

"What the hell are you doing?"

Dr. Mackenzie Grant, Kalen's heavily pregnant and annoyed mate, pressed him flat onto the bed and frowned down at him.

"I need to leave," he said hoarsely. "I have things to do."

"Are you trying to scare me into early labor?" she demanded. "You're not getting up from here until we run more tests and discuss the results."

"Sorry." The last thing he wanted was to stress out a pregnant woman. Again, he hadn't been thinking. "How long will that be?"

"At least a couple of hours, probably more, so get comfortable."

He couldn't hide his misery. Her expression softened, and he looked away, unable to stand the pity he knew he'd find there. Hatred or disgust would be preferable, from all of his friends, because his decision to leave would be much simpler. Cleaner.

Mac took his chin in her hand and urged him to look at her again. She waited until she had his attention before she spoke. "We're going to find a way to get you better, all right? I promise."

"You said *better*, not healed."

"Zan . . ."

"Too big a promise?"

She hesitated, but to her credit, she told the truth. "For the time being, yes."

"Fair enough." Disappointment threatened to crush him, and he fought it down. "What's next?"

"A new CAT scan, blood work, and hearing tests. Then we go from there."

He understood why his colleagues wouldn't give up on finding some improvement, however slight. Hell, it wasn't like he *wanted* to quit. He couldn't lie to himself, though. His brain was a ticking bomb, set to explode the second the stress of using his healing power became too much. He'd gotten lucky so far.

With a start, he realized Mac was waiting for his response. "Sure."

"Hang in there." After patting his arm, she turned and walked out, presumably to make sure things were ready for his tests.

A short time later, Jax sauntered in without knocking and took up residence in the chair beside his bed. "Came to babysit, since you're such a pussy about being poked and prodded."

Zan rolled his eyes, which was a bad idea since it caused his head to pound harder. "It's the CAT scan I hate. Being stuck in that tube is creepy."

"Want me to hold your hand?" his friend joked.

"Shut up." He managed a smile, but didn't quite feel it.

Jax's humor bled from his face, and he was silent for a long moment. Finally, he took a deep breath and said what they were both thinking. "You're going to run, aren't you?"

"No. I'm going to walk, after I say good-bye."

"You sure that's what you want?"

"Of course it's not. But what choice do I have when I've become a liability? What am I supposed to do if I stay—sweep the floors and clean toilets?"

"What happened with Nix can be prevented. We can work on teaching you to use your other senses, to feel the changes in the atmosphere around you—"

"Why did I just get a sudden image of Obi-Wan teaching Luke to use the force?"

"It can work," Jax insisted, ignoring the bad joke. "Isn't it worth a try? You owe it to yourself not to leave before you've exhausted every possibility."

"And in the meantime, I sit around and be useless? Or worse, get someone else hurt? I can't do that."

"You returned to the field too soon. Give it more time."

Jax looked so hopeful, and what he said made sense. But Zan still saw Nix's body covered in blood.

"I'll think about it. That's all I can promise for now."

"All right," his friend said, not trying to mask his relief. "Thanks."

Mac and Noah came in to wheel him down for his tests, and Zan endured the seemingly endless onslaught of procedures with as much cheerfulness as he could muster. Which wasn't a lot, but he did his best to keep the gloom from suffocating him.

Back in his room, there was more waiting. He and Jax made small talk about everything under the sun, until Mac returned. When she came through the door at last, clutching a large manila envelope, her expression was carefully neutral, and Zan's heart sank.

"It's bad," he said. Not a question.

"I'd hoped for better results." Opening the envelope, she removed a handful of images, stuck one in a clip mounted to a viewing panel on the wall, and flipped a switch to illuminate a colorful shot of his brain. "These are from the CAT scan. See these areas here?"

She pointed to three spots where there seemed to be some sort of fuzziness to the otherwise sharp image.

"I see, but I don't know what I'm looking at."

"These are areas of new damage to your brain," she said grimly. "In layman's terms, the healing you performed on Nix put too much strain on the weakened vessels, and some of them ruptured. They're causing the horrible headache and dizziness you have now."

"Is he in immediate danger?" Jax asked, glancing at Zan worriedly.

"Not if he rests and follows my advice." Mac arched a brow and gazed at Zan pointedly. "If you were human, you'd be flat on your back in intensive care right now."

"But I'm *not* human," he muttered. "I'll be fine."

Mac shook her head. "You *won't* be if you perform any more healing before you're one hundred percent healed yourself. See these areas?" She pointed to five other spots. They didn't look like anything to Zan, but her expression was as serious as he'd ever seen.

"These are vessels that are currently weakened so severely, the chances are high that you'll wind up with serious brain damage if you use your healing ability again too soon. If the slow bleeding becomes outright hemorrhaging, you might not survive."

"Jesus." Hanging his head, he stared at his hands in his lap without really seeing them. Finally, he raised his eyes to hers and voiced his biggest concern. "If I do what you say, remain on the sidelines and refrain from using my gift, will I completely recover? Can you tell me with reasonable certainty that I'll be back in the field eventually, able to fight and use my healing with no problems?"

Her pause was too long, and he knew the answer before she spoke. "I'm sorry. I can't say that for sure. Only what will happen if you *don't* do as we recommend."

"That's not good enough."

"It's all we've got for now."

God. "I want to go back to my own quarters. Please."

"Not tonight. You're staying here overnight. If you're better tomorrow, I'll consider it." Her stance held a certain finality and stubbornness that he knew meant, *Don't fuck with the doc*.

"Fine."

"I'll check on you later." Shooting Zan a look of sympathy, Mac left, closing the door quietly behind her. Jax hovered for a moment and then let out a deep breath.

"Give me your word you won't leave just yet. Give yourself a chance. The team needs you. Shit, *I* need you."

Damn his best friend for knowing exactly what to say. He knew once Zan gave his word on anything, it was gold. Tension hung in the air between them, Zan struggling with saying the words, until he knew it was pointless to refuse.

"You've got my word. And I'm not a quitter, just for the record."

"Nobody thinks you are."

"I just don't want to endanger my brothers."

"Understood. I felt the same way after my leg was injured and I couldn't fight."

"I know." He paused. "And thanks."

"No problem. I'll let you get some sleep." Giving him a pat on the shoulder, Jax left.

Settling in for the night, Zan tried to sleep, but his dreams were uneasy. Filled with blood and death. A battle. Carnage. Horrible sorrow. Zan, trying desperately to heal . . . someone. Who? Then his own screams rang in his ears as his brain finally detonated—

Zan sat bolt upright in bed, gasping, sweat pouring down his face. His heart thudded against his sternum, and his hands shook as he wiped the moisture from his brow.

Over and over, he told himself that he didn't have the ability to see the future. That was Nick's area. It was just a nightmare. Gradually, his pulse calmed and he lay down again.

But his eyes were still wide open as the sun broke over the horizon.

He had to go for a run.

Nick paced his office, then stopped and stared out the window, across the lawn to the forest at the edge of the compound. His wolf strained inside him, always eager for a good run, and he was usually happy to oblige.

But today felt different. The pull was more than

just the desire for earth under his paws. There was a sense that he was *supposed* to go. Destiny was upon him, for good or ill, and today marked the beginning of serious changes in his life.

For however much longer his life might be.

Surrendering to the pull, Nick left his office and walked down the corridors, speaking to a few of the team along the way. Outside, he strode across the compound and into the woods a ways before stripping his clothes and allowing his wolf to take over.

For him, a born wolf with more than two centuries of experience, the change was effortless. In some ways, he'd always been more comfortable in his wolf skin, and there was a time long ago when he'd nearly traded in his human life in favor of his wolf, permanently. A time when the pain of tragic loss was too much to bear. He'd drifted for years, an immortal creature with no future—a great irony if ever there was one.

If it hadn't been for his old friend Jarrod Grant pulling some strings to get him into the FBI, and eventually the position as commander of the Alpha Pack, there was no telling what might've become of him.

Still, each day was a struggle. To find meaning in life where there was none. To wake up one more day and honor his commitments to his men when the weight of all he'd lost was almost too much to bear.

As he stood on four paws surveying his surroundings, he let the memories go and ran. His paws dug into the earth, sending leaves and dirt flying as his long legs ate up the distance. His wolf didn't care about destiny or death.

But as a white blur detached itself from the trees and raced to intercept him, he knew that one of those—possibly both—had found him all the same.

She heard the crashing sounds in the forest a minute or so before he actually came into view.

All of her careful planning, the months of waiting, had come to this moment. She'd make him pay for what he'd done. At last.

Taking off, she ran full-out to intercept the big white wolf streaking through the trees.

He was alone.

And that was the last mistake the bastard would ever make.

"You really shouldn't be out running the same day the doc lets you go," Micah said as he and Nix kept pace with Zan in the hallway leading to one of the exits. Micah kept bobbing in front of him to make sure Zan could see his lips.

Zan did his best to keep from punching either of his friends as he made his escape. "I don't need a fucking nanny."

"You need a keeper."

Nix grasped his arm, urging Zan to stop and pay attention, then took the opportunity to double-team him. "Neither of the docs will be happy to find out you're ignoring orders to rest."

"And you're going to tell them?" He shot them both a sour look.

"Of course not," Nix said smoothly. "But they'll find out anyway, and you'll get benched."

"Mac said *rest*, not crawl under a rock and hibernate. Besides, letting out my wolf is good for the healing process."

They couldn't argue that one, though he could see they wanted to.

"You wouldn't just leave, right?" Micah asked, clearly anxious. "Jax said you promised."

"Is that what's really bothering you guys?" He shook his head. "If I decide to go, I'll be up front about it. I'll put in my notice and say good-bye like a man, not run like a coward."

"That's not much of a comfort," Micah griped.

He sighed. "That's all I can tell you for now. I'm still thinking things over."

Nix shifted in place and looked him in the eye. "While you are, I want you to know how grateful I am for what you did for me. You took quite a risk to put me back together, and I won't forget it."

Zan gave him a half smile. "We all take risks every day. But in your case, I had extra incentive or a certain nurse would've been heartbroken to lose his mate."

Nix gave a laugh, shaking his head. "I don't know that he's my mate, man. I'm not showing any symptoms of being sick like the other guys did before they Bonded."

"Do you and your wolf feel a pull? Like you both need each other?"

"Yeah, but with none of the nasty side effects."

"Interesting."

"How'd you manage to turn the conversation away from yourself?" Nix gave him a playful shove. "We'll let you go for your run, but don't be gone too long or we're coming after you."

"Yeah, I hear you—well, not really, but you know what I mean."

Both of them made faces at his bad joke and moved off, finally leaving him alone. He had no doubt they'd go straight to Jax, and soon Zan would have a trail of wolves behind him who just suddenly decided they needed to go for a run as well.

Idiots, all of them. But he was damned glad to have them in his corner.

Taking advantage of his brief period of alone time, he left the compound, walked into the forest, and undressed. He welcomed the change, and it flowed over him, though not without some discomfort this time. His fatigue and the pain in his head affected his speed and efficiency, but he managed. Once he was on four paws, he shook himself and started off at a leisurely trot.

He really needed some time in wolf form to relax. Enjoy nature, take himself out of his own head and away from the constant challenges for a while.

Gradually, it began working. The tension seeped from his body until he was relishing his time in the forest, taking in all the sights and wishing he could hear the calls of the birds, the breeze through the branches, the babbling creek nearby. Soon enough, he told himself, when he was healed. He'd hear all of those things and more.

He was so lost in his thoughts, it was a shock to come upon a break in the trees—and see two white wolves about forty yards away. The smaller of the two was streaking toward a large one he instantly recognized as Nick.

As the smaller wolf slammed into Nick and sent them both rolling, Zan took off in their direction. Mind going cold, he focused on his commander's attacker.

He had a wolf to kill.

Three

Zan raced for the pair of wolves, heart thudding in his chest.

The smaller white wolf was snarling and snapping, trying to get Nick pinned. Going for his throat. But as he neared, he realized the commander was making only evasive maneuvers to protect himself. He wasn't attacking in return. What the fuck?

Maybe Nick wasn't counterattacking because, despite his opponent's fierceness, the other wolf simply didn't have the size and strength to best him. Unfair fight. Zan, however, had no such problem taking out the asshole.

Rushing in, he hit the wolf from the side and sent them both skidding across the ground. Immediately, he leaped on the intruder's back before he could gain his footing, driving him into the dirt and leaves. The other wolf was no match for Zan's weight and couldn't throw him no matter how he struggled. Blood lust roared through his veins, and he lunged, sinking his fangs through thick fur into the wolf's neck.

Female. The wonderful scent, like cinnamon spice, hit him like a truck at a hundred miles per hour, and he froze, some primal instinct cutting through his fury like a hot blade through wax. Suddenly, he couldn't finish her off. Distantly, he heard Nick shouting, his voice much clearer than it should be, though he wasn't sure how.

Then something strange began to happen. A warmth started in the center of his chest and spread outward, like ripples in a pond. It grew into an intense heat, searing his lungs and stealing his breath and, to his embarrassment, became the fire of arousal. He wanted to let go of her neck, but couldn't.

A thread, bright and golden, seemed to spin from his heart to the other wolf, and he could swear he felt an answering thread from her twine with his. Solidifying and strengthening until there was an explosion of light that rocked him backward, finally breaking his hold.

Immediately, the female shifted into human form, kneeling on the ground and rubbing at the spot where he'd bitten her. Vivid blue eyes flashed cold fire at Zan as she spat, "What the fuck did you just do?"

He was awestruck. She was beautiful, short hair so pale it was almost white framing an angular face. Her breasts were full, waist narrow, and her limbs were long and toned with muscle. He figured she was tall, maybe as tall as he was. She also was beyond pissed, and he couldn't think why. He shifted back as well, finding his voice.

"What do you mean, what did *I* do?" he asked, incredulous. "First of all, you're trespassing, and second, you just tried to kill my commander. You're lucky I didn't rip out your throat."

The venom in her eyes was a little scary—and a lot puzzling. "Why didn't you? That would've been a lot less complicated than the situation we're in now."

"Lady, the only situation here is that you're now in custody. And as a rogue and a hostile unknown shifter, you're going to be locked up for a good while."

Her laugh was sarcastic. With a start, he realized he had actually *heard* that in her tone, and even if he hadn't been able to see her lips, he could've almost made out her next words. "You mean in your top-secret compound everyone in the county knows about?"

"That's the one," he said, ignoring the jibe. Glancing at Nick, he noted that his boss had also shifted back, but oddly enough, he kept his eyes averted from the intruder. In fact, the woman was studiously avoiding looking directly at Nick, too.

That was odd, since wolf shifters were frequently naked around each other before and after their shifts. It would be pretty stupid to be self-conscious about something so natural.

So why were they acting so weird?

"You okay?" he asked Nick.

"Yeah."

The woman shook her head. "You really don't have any idea what you've done? Priceless."

Zan frowned. "Me? I don't have any idea what you're talking about." Off-kilter, he wondered for the first time what she thought of his odd, flat voice. Jesus, he hated being on the defensive.

Nick opened his mouth to say something, but four wolves burst through the trees and crowded in on the woman in a semicircle, snarling at her in warning. And that's when something *really* weird happened to Zan.

His wolf surged to the surface and took over faster than he ever had before, and he was powerless to stop the change. Scrambling forward, he placed himself squarely between the female and his Pack, laid his ears flat against his head, and bared his teeth. A low, ominous rumble sounded in his chest, letting them know not to come one step closer.

What the hell is wrong with me?

In seconds, the four wolves changed back, and Jax, Aric, Micah, and Phoenix were crouched in front of him. His brothers stood, looking as bewildered as he felt.

"What the fuck, man?" Aric scowled, looking past Zan to the woman.

Zan growled louder.

"Oh shit," Jax groaned, slapping his forehead. "I'm not believing this."

Micah's eyes widened. "Z-Man, did you bite her?"

Nix started laughing but quickly put a lid on it when he caught a glare from his commander.

Dread became a lead weight in Zan's chest, and he forced his wolf into submission, shifting back. "Yeah, I bit her on the neck. So what? I would've been justified in killing her for attacking Nick, but I didn't. She's fine."

Everyone looked at the woman, and she in turn leveled Zan with a murderous stare. "I'm anything but *fine* since I'm now Bonded to *you*, genius."

"I—what?" Zan gaped at her. His Pack brothers' faces showed everything from amusement to wariness to stunned disbelief. Nick's expression of grim resignation scared him most of all. "No, that can't be right. All I did was . . ."

Desperately, he tried to think of another reason for his reaction to the bite. The warmth, the arousal, the golden thread. And the ensuing explosion that seemed to have resulted in some sort of connection between him and this unknown female. But the truth of what had happened settled over him, and his gut liquefied.

"Shit," he whispered, then met her gaze. "I'm sorry. I'll find a way to break the bond. Kalen's a Sorcerer. Maybe he can—"

"So eager to be rid of me already, *honey*?" She smiled, but the expression didn't reach her glittering eyes. "And we haven't even exchanged names."

He nodded slowly. "I'm Zander Cole, the Healer of our unit, the Alpha Pack."

"Selene Westfall." She raised one eyebrow. "Congrats are in order, eh? I mean, since your boss just became your father-in-law and all."

Shocked faces met that announcement. Zan swallowed hard and looked to Nick, who nodded.

Oh, fuck.

Zander Cole. My Bondmate.

The man was a walking orgasm, no point in denying it. He had layered black hair that fell to just below his ears and flopped over his forehead into amazing brown eyes. Kind eyes that were portals to a gentle soul, if first impressions could be trusted. He had a strong jaw and a classic handsome face that reminded her a little of Henry Cavill, and he was tall, topping her by at least a couple of inches.

His chest was broad and smooth, his nipples small, brown, and tight, and a gorgeous tattoo of a snarling wolf graced his right pectoral, curling around one taut peak. His muscles were nicely developed but not too beefy, more on the lean side, just the way she liked. Her perusal dipped south to his impressive cock, a good five inches even while lying flaccid, and to the heavy balls nestled underneath. The dark hair at his groin was neat, trimmed. She liked that, too.

Idiot! This man is not kind, and to hell with his looks. He works for my father, and he was going to kill me. He's my enemy!

And yet he'd placed himself between her and the impending threat from his Pack. . . .

Just then, two men with long hair—one blond and the other a redhead—caught her attention. The blond muttered, "Nick has a daughter? Had no freaking clue."

"Nobody did," the redhead whispered back.

Well, that pretty much summed up how much Daddy Dearest had missed her, didn't it? Whipping around to look at him, she kept her gaze on his face and sneered, "Guess you'd better toss me in the kennel with all the other bad pups. Wouldn't want you to have to deal with me like a man or anything."

His blue eyes flashed with what she could have sworn was pain. "Placing you in custody is the last thing I want to do, but I have the safety of my team to consider. You won't remain there any longer than necessary—you have my word."

Her mouth fell open, and she sputtered in outrage. "Your word? Is that supposed to mean shit to me? Giving your word implies you have honor, and you have none!"

"I'm truly sorry you feel that way."

"You're the reason I feel that way, you sonofa-bitch," she hissed.

He shook his head, sadness shadowing his features, and turned away, refusing to be drawn into an argument. "Aric, run ahead and see if Rowan has any clothes to loan Selene. Everyone, let's go."

The redhead named Aric took off. Before she could think of anything else to hurl at his head, Nick changed back into his wolf form. The rest of his Pack followed suit, leaving her no choice but to do the same or fall behind, which they weren't going to let her get away with anyway. They wouldn't risk allowing her to escape.

Nick took the lead, and the others surrounded her. She couldn't help but notice that Zander remained close by her side, as though keeping watch over her, rather than guarding against possible escape. In fact, when one wolf trotted a bit too close, he bared his teeth and snapped, causing his friend to sidle away quickly.

To have someone looking out for her was strange, to say the least. She'd been self-reliant for so long, even among her own clan. She'd almost forgotten what it felt like to have a defender. It was sort of nice. Okay, a lot nice—but she couldn't get used to it. Bonded or not, she and Zander Cole had no future together. She had a mission to carry out.

The Pack kept up a brisk pace, not a full-out run, and within half an hour they trotted onto the property she'd been trying to gain access to for months. Funny—now that she was here, all she wanted to do was leave. That wasn't going to happen anytime soon, if the grim determination of her enemy was any indication.

At the edge of the forest, the men shifted and gathered the clothing they'd left scattered about, dressing efficiently. She was almost sorry to see all of that prime male flesh covered up, especially Zander's. *Beautiful.*

She couldn't stop staring at the man, which annoyed her, but at least the attention wasn't one-sided. He studied her plenty in return, apparently every bit as curious about her as she was about him. She wasn't very happy about having a mate, but . . .

She began to see that it might have a few advantages. For one, her mating would dissuade the advances of a particularly insistent suitor from her clan. Taggart had been a friend since childhood, but he hadn't let up on hopes of a mating with her since he'd hit puberty and discovered what his dick was for. She loved the big, handsome lug to death, but not like *that*.

Having Zander as a mate might also give her a stay of execution, literally. He had prevented her from killing their commander, so she wouldn't face a murder rap. Plus, it was forbidden to interfere with the mating bond—at least, in her world. Once, that world had been her father's as well.

Being reminded of him leaving, and why, was too painful. So she protected herself as she always had—by wrapping herself in a cloak of anger. Rage was the best antidote to pain. Better than food, liquor, sex, or just about anything. That was a sad commentary on the state of her life, but anger was all that had gotten her through for too long.

Aric jogged across the lawn and handed her the clothes. Without a word of thanks, she slipped on a pair of underwear and a bra, stepped into the borrowed cargo pants, and tugged on the black T-shirt. Then she padded barefoot with the group to a side door and straight into what was obviously a recreation room.

She stood, blinking at the spacious room for a moment, trying to make the sight gel with what she'd pictured. There were tables set up for pool, foosball, and Ping-Pong, as well as a dart board and a large-screen TV with a gaming system hooked to it. Two sofas with pillows, several oversized chairs, and rugs made the room homey. Comfortable.

She had expected the inside of the compound to appear stark, more like a barracks. But as they guided her out of the recreation room and into the hallway, she continued to be surprised. The floors were carpeted, and tasteful wall sconces lit the way. The walls themselves were a pleasant, warm cream color.

"You expected a military compound with cement floors and armed guards?" Zander questioned, looking at her.

His voice had a strange flatness. She'd noticed it from the start, and now that the excitement had died down somewhat, she wondered about the inflection that was a bit off.

"Something like that. You all live here full time?"

He nodded. "Makes our jobs easier."

After a few turns, which she memorized, they led her to a hallway marked AUTHORIZED PERSONNEL ONLY. The rest of the party dispersed, while Zander and Nick escorted her through the double doors. Her blood froze as she noted the rows of steel doors on either side of the corridor, sealing off what could only be cells. Her worst fear was confirmed when Nick halted and pulled open one of the doors.

"This area is Block R, named for Rehabilitation."

"I could've guessed that," she said shortly.

"Then you can also guess what Block T stands for." Nick's voice was gruff. "That's the next stop for those who prove to be too dangerous to remain among us."

She couldn't help but laugh, though the sound was ugly. "Really? That's rich coming from the man who killed my mother!"

"Jesus," Zan said, his shocked gaze bouncing between them.

"Didn't know your boss was a murderer? He forget to tell you guys that he had a mate he killed before he abandoned his daughter?"

Her father started to say something, but then he simply shook his head and gestured her inside the cell. "There's a bunk with a pillow and a blanket. You'll be given three square meals a day while you're here. You seem to be in good physical health, but you'll get an exam tomorrow and begin a psychological evaluation."

The last part had her mouth dropping open. "A test to see if I'm nuts? Are you *shitting* me?"

"When it's determined you're not a danger to yourself or anyone else here, you'll be released to join your mate. And not before." To Zander, he said, "I'm sorry."

He slammed the door of the cell, and it clanged with an ominous racket. Then the bastard turned and walked away. Zander's anxious face hovered in the small window for a moment, and she barely heard him say, "I'm sorry, too."

Then she was alone.

As calmly as possible, Nick walked to his office and closed the door. Then he skirted his desk, sat in his chair, and lowered his head into his shaking hands.

She's here after all this time. All these years. Selene. And my baby girl loathes me.

The heartbreak never ended. However, he'd learned one vital piece of information: as much as she might hate him, and even want him dead, his death wouldn't come at her hands. His gift didn't allow him to know much more than that, but from the moment she'd come racing from the trees, intent on ripping out his throat, he'd known.

Her rage might have fueled her attack, but her soul wasn't on board. Deep down, she was still that confused, grieving young girl who'd lost both of her parents in one awful day. Her heart cried out to know why, and she deserved the truth.

But not today. She wasn't ready to accept it. He didn't know if she ever would be.

In the meantime, he had to stay on top of the rogue vampires. With a heavy heart, he opened his e-mail to see if Grant had sent him any more information. He scanned his in-box impatiently, then paused on one e-mail address he'd never seen before: viper@speedymail.com. Curious, he opened it and began to read.

Westfall,

I'm coming for you and yours. Don't think I've forgotten, because I haven't. No matter how long it takes, or how far I have to track you, I'll come. And when I do, I'll make you suffer before you die.

No name at the end, of course. He read the e-mail again, and his skin prickled. Cold enveloped his entire body, and he let out a deep breath, thinking. In more than two hundred years, he'd made a few enemies. Most of them were long dead, though not all.

Who would come after him now? Why?

Could Selene's arrival be a coincidence? She'd obviously been in the area for a while—after all, he now realized she was the white wolf that had pushed Ryon's mate Daria off the cliff. She might have been hanging around town doing some digging, too, and could have sent the e-mail.

That didn't feel right, though.

The e-mail carried the distinct chill of death brushing down his neck that he'd been feeling for days. The bastard behind it was the one he had to fear, not his daughter.

A sense of foreboding in his gut warned him that this was much, much bigger than just him and his daughter. And he had to discover the truth, soon.

Picking up his cell phone, he placed a call that was past due. On the other end, the phone rang three times before a deep male voice answered.

"Mountain Lodge. How may I direct your call?"

Nick almost smiled. The cover wasn't very original, but it was effective in screening wrong numbers and those who might snoop. "This is Nick Westfall, commander of the Alpha Pack in Wyoming. I'm calling to speak with Prince Tarron Romanoff."

A pause. "How did you get this number?"

"Through our mutual friend Grant."

"I see. What type of group is your Alpha Pack?"

"Shifters. We combat all sorts of creatures the world is better off not knowing about, if you get my drift."

The man laughed. "Sure. This is your personal number, Mr. Westfall?"

"It is."

"Very good. The prince will phone you back shortly."

After I've been checked out, no doubt.

"That's fine."

He hung up, settling in to wait, and started playing a new game on his phone. Damn time-wasting crap, but he was as hooked as everyone else. Fortunately, the phone rang, saving him from turning his brain to mush. A glance confirmed it was a different number, but the same area code. Probably the prince's personal phone.

"Westfall."

"Hello, Mr. Westfall, this is Tarron Romanoff, of the North American coven," he said pleasantly. His voice was smooth and warm. Genuine. "Grant had told me you would likely contact me about a certain problem, but I had to be sure your number checked out via a trace. You understand."

"Of course. In our worlds, we can never be too careful."

"True. So, what's this problem you were referring to? Grant simply said he would let you explain."

He got right to the point. "Have you or your coven members noticed a surge in the numbers of rogue vampires?"

"Not really," he said slowly, thoughtfully. "But we're pretty isolated here in the Smoky Mountains. Care to fill me in?"

"We've had attacks cropping up around the country, and the number and frequency of them are becoming alarming. Not to mention a special ability they seem to have developed—they're now able to attack during the day."

"The hell you say." The prince blew out a breath. "How?"

"I don't know, but I think our two groups need to meet in person. What affects my team and the human population will eventually get to your coven. If we work together, we might be able to stop this thing before it reaches the point of no return."

"Agreed. I'll meet with my men and call you back with some possible dates. Will that work?"

"Yes, and thank you."

"No need to thank me. A problem with rogues affects all of us. Talk to you soon."

After they ended the call, Nick sat with his elbows on his desk, lost in thought. Maybe they could find the answer to the rogue issue together, before it was too late.

Before he could fret on the matter further, a familiar buzz started in his head. His skin prickled and his eyesight dimmed, the hallmark of a coming vision.

In the mist, there stood a figure. Draped in darkness, it moved toward him with grace, and surprisingly, he got no sense of fear. No death.

The figure remained shrouded, but the form was slight. A female. She beckoned to him, and where he might have felt trepidation . . .

Joy. There was nothing but pure joy at her presence, and his heart picked up speed, pounding in excitement. He opened his mouth to ask her name, why she was there—

And he was jolted back to reality with sudden force.

"Who are you?" he whispered, sitting back in his chair.

He hoped and prayed he lived long enough to learn the answer.

Selene sat on her bunk with her back against the wall, arms encircling her drawn-up knees. If someone didn't come soon, she was going to lose her freaking mind.

No TV, no books, no window to see outside. Not even the tick of a clock. Nothing to do but watch the four walls and listen to the disturbing noises coming from another cell along the corridor.

All night, she'd heard growling, snarling, and

terrible howling. All coming from a single creature nearby. Her nose scented another wolf shifter, and she wondered what he'd done to deserve the maddening boredom of this prison.

"Hey!" she called. "Is anybody there? Can you hear me?"

The howling stopped, but only for a few moments. Soon it started up again, and she banged the back of her head against the steel panel in frustration.

A flash of blue light startled her, and she bolted upright on her bunk, pulse tripping. When the light faded, a man was standing inside the cell near the door.

A man who looked like a rock star. He had artfully mussed, layered hair that fell to his shoulders and wore black guyliner, which set off amazing green eyes. He was dressed all in black, from his T-shirt to a leather duster that fell to his ankles, to the shitkickers on his feet. Even his fingernails were like polished onyx.

He looked young, perhaps early twenties—but his eyes were ancient.

She hid a shiver. Masking the hammering of her heart, she fixed a look of amusement on her face. "If you're looking for the Mötley Crüe audition, you're in the wrong state altogether."

One corner of his lush mouth turned up. "Really? Damn. Guess I'll just have to stay here and fight vampires."

She frowned. "Vampires?"

"Long story."

"It seems I have time."

He shrugged. "We're having a bit of a rogue problem lately. The assholes are springing up everywhere in the country when there shouldn't be that many."

"I've not seen any rogues where I'm from."

"Good to know."

She studied him, inhaled a whiff. "You're not a wolf."

"Panther. I'm also a Sorcerer and a Necromancer."

She stared at him, fascinated in spite of herself. "I've never met any one of those things, much less all three."

"Well, ain't it your lucky day?" He winked.

"Believe me, this day has nowhere to go but up." She paused, deciding she was starting to like this man. "I'm Selene Westfall."

"Nick's daughter. Yeah, word got around."

"I can imagine."

"I'm Kalen Black."

"What are you doing here, Kalen, besides checking out the new resident of Block R?"

"The medical team is on their way down to fetch you for some testing. I'm here to make sure everything runs smoothly."

"As insurance."

"You could say that."

"Why would they send you and not Zander? I assume you heard about our mating, too."

He snorted. "Who hasn't? You sure know how to make a grand entrance. Good job."

"Funny." She shot him a sour look.

"I thought so." Pushing away from the wall, he stepped right up to her bunk, his expression growing serious. "To answer your question, Zan's been ordered to stay away for now. We may have to do something he doesn't like—say, restrain you—and the instinct to protect his mate could take over. This is an unstable time for both of you, especially given the way your bonding went down and the fact that your wolves are probably crawling out of your skins with the need to get to each other."

That was true, unfortunately, and she flushed just thinking about how badly she wanted the black wolf. "Good point."

"And because my mate is one of the doctors, I'm here specifically to protect *her* from *you*. If you even *think* of hurting her, or anyone else, I'll turn you into a slug and get out my salt shaker." The wicked gleam in his eyes told her the man wasn't kidding.

Before she could reassure him that her problem was only with Nick, voices and footsteps approached from down the hallway. Kalen moved off to the side as two female doctors wearing lab coats and a male nurse wearing SpongeBob scrubs stepped inside. He didn't go far, though. When the Sorcerer kissed a pretty woman with curly brunette hair and then hovered close, Selene saw why.

Kalen's mate was hugely pregnant. She was radiant, too, and Selene felt a twinge of longing. Forcing her attention from the happy couple, she locked eyes with the other doctor. The woman had a short cap of dark hair, shorter than Selene's own, and though she was petite, she had a bearing and coolness that suggested anyone who gave her a hassle would be sorry.

"I'm Dr. Melina Mallory," she said, then indicated the other two. "That's Dr. Mackenzie Grant and our nurse, Noah Brooks."

"Hello. I'm—"

"We know who you are," Dr. Mallory said curtly.

So much for pleasantries.

"We're going to escort you to the infirmary, where we'll give you a general physical and then visit with you a bit before we conduct our psychological evaluation."

"To determine if you've got a crazy on your hands."

"Well, you tried to kill a shifter five times your age and twice your size, so you'll forgive our caution where your sanity is concerned."

"Ooh, ouch. I guess this means we can't be best friends."

The doctor studied her for a good, long moment, as though she were observing some sort of insect. She didn't have to say a thing to make Selene feel two feet tall. Then the woman smiled, and the expression on her small, elfin face wasn't exactly friendly.

"Let's go get started, shall we?"

The entourage led her out of the cell and down the corridor to a connecting one that took them to the infirmary. Once there, Dr. Mallory conducted most of the physical with Noah assisting. The cute blond nurse was wary of her, moving around her with a watchful eye, not that she could blame him.

She was in top shape, so she wasn't surprised that she passed with flying colors. It was the rest she wasn't particularly thrilled about. Noah disappeared, and the other two doctors ushered her into an office. Instead of talking at her across a desk, as she'd expected, they gestured her to a modest seating area with a sofa and a couple of comfortable-looking chairs.

Selene took one end of the sofa, while Dr. Mallory took the other end and Dr. Grant, a chair. She suspected they were doing this so she didn't feel ganged up on—with the exception of Kalen looming in the corner behind the desk—but couldn't fathom why they'd care.

"Why are both of you talking to me?" she asked. "Isn't that unusual?"

"This is an unusual situation," Dr. Grant told her, shifting to adjust her belly. "Dr. Mallory will be your physician, with me consulting. I'm going to be out on maternity leave soon, so I'd have to hand you over to her anyway."

"Congratulations, by the way," she said, surprised at the softness in her own voice.

"Thank you. Do you want children?"

"I'd like them someday. The gods willing."

Melina smoothly segued into the interview. "Where did you grow up?"

"Clear Springs, Colorado. It's a small town two hours north of Denver."

"Any siblings?"

"No."

"Other family?"

"My uncle, Damien. He's my father's brother."

The women exchanged looks of surprise. Dr. Grant looked to her mate, and he shook his head and shrugged, indicating he hadn't known, either. Apparently, her father had been quite secretive about all aspects of his past. No surprise there.

Dr. Mallory continued. "Are you close to your uncle?"

"Yes. He raised me after my father took off."

The doctor's brows drew together. "Define 'took off.'"

"Seriously? He murdered my mother and disappeared. Left me to fend for myself and grow up with the scandal he left behind as my legacy. Is that defined enough?"

Dead silence. More exchanged glances before the doctor went on.

"How old were you when this happened?"

"Eleven."

"Did you witness what your father did?"

She blinked at the doctor. "Excuse me?"

"Did you witness him killing your mother?"

"No," she admitted. "But I know it's the truth."

"*How* do you know it?"

"Because my uncle said so!" she cried, losing her composure. "*Everyone* knew it! The whole clan never let me forget it, either!"

"I'm sorry this is so painful to discuss," Dr. Mallory said with surprising gentleness. "I'm just trying to understand what an eleven-year-old girl saw and heard. What she lived through."

Swallowing against the burning in her throat, Selene looked away. "She went through hell, but never came out the other side. She was never the same."

Never.

None of her clan, or anyone she met, knew the real Selene, that she wasn't such a badass. That she was still just a frightened, devastated girl who'd lost her parents and didn't understand why. A girl who wanted only to be loved.

Maybe it was a good thing she hadn't succeeded in taking out her father. Dr. Mallory had stirred up some questions that were already nagging her like a sore tooth.

And she was going to get them answered if it was the last thing she ever did.

Four

Zan met Nick in the conference room.

His wolf was going bananas, and he was having a devil of a time keeping him subdued. As he took a seat next to the commander, he wondered at his luck, or lack thereof, in accidentally mating with the man's angry, hurting daughter. Zan had been wanting a mate for some time, especially seeing the other guys find happiness one by one, but this wasn't what he had in mind. The circumstances were less than ideal. And right now, he didn't really like her that much, either.

His wolf didn't care. His need to get to his mate, to protect her, was almost overwhelming.

Taking a deep breath, Zan turned to look Nick in the eye. "Is her accusation true? *Did* you kill her mother?"

Nick looked hurt, but the emotion was quickly masked. "Not in the way she means."

"An accident?"

"In that it wasn't supposed to happen, yes." Staring at the table, he was silent for a long moment before he raised his head again. "You know I don't believe in interfering with the future I see in my visions. I try never to influence people to change the outcome, no matter how horrible the event that's coming."

"Yeah. I always wondered about that. It has to do with Selene?"

"And her mother," the commander said softly. "I tried to screw fate, and her mother paid the price."

Oh, shit. "Not just her mother—you and your daughter also."

"All of us. I didn't know what would happen, what my actions would set in motion," he said. Zan had never seen the man show so much raw pain.

"So tell her. She's operating under a terrible misconception."

"I'll tell her the truth, but not yet. It's a hard thing for someone to believe something all their life and then find out they were fed lies. That the person they hate isn't exactly what they thought. She needs time to get to know me, to come to her own conclusions."

"That might make it easier for her to swallow,"

he agreed. "If she stays at the compound for a while, she'll begin to understand on her own that what she thought was true, isn't."

"And then, hopefully, she'll come to me, ready to listen. She won't believe anything I say until then."

"What really happened, Nick? What did you do that cost your mate her life?"

His expression was bleak. "Selene deserves to hear the story first. I hope you understand."

"Of course." Hesitating, he tried to quell his nerves at his next question. "I have to ask. . . . Do you have a problem with me being practically related to you?"

That earned him a small smile. "Zan, I can't think of anyone I'd be prouder to have as a son-in-law. Assuming this mating works out, I'm happy for you."

Relief swamped him, and he blew out a breath. "Thank you. I won't let you or Selene down. Not if I can help it." *Holy crap, did I just say that?*

"I know you won't."

Just then, Ryon Hunter walked into the room with his mate, Daria Bradford. The man guided her to a chair and held it out for her as she got seated, then took his own place. Zan greeted them both, wondering why they were there, until Mac and Kalen escorted Selene through the door. Then he had a pretty good idea what was going on.

Ryon and Daria took seats opposite Nick and

Zan. As Mac and Kalen left, Selene hesitated uncertainly for a moment, and Zan was struck by an image of her being alone like that all her life. On the fringes, never certain where she fit in.

"You can sit over here by me, if you'd like," he offered.

Surprise flitted across her features, and then she took the empty spot beside him. "Thank you."

He gave her a smile, and again she appeared a bit taken aback. Though her sitting next to him would make it harder for him to read her lips while paying attention to everyone else, he preferred having her close. She was tense as a bowstring, but when he touched her knee in reassurance, he felt her relax. Even though he knew it was the mate bond, a purely natural thing for mates to gravitate toward each other, it was still nice.

To his right, Nick began the meeting. Zan noted once again that his hearing was improving, because he actually heard what his commander was saying—distantly, but still.

"Ryon and Daria are here because they have a couple of questions for Selene."

"Yeah," Ryon snarled. "Like why the fuck she tried to kill my mate!"

Every muscle in Zan's body coiled, ready to spring on Ryon's ass if he made one move toward Selene. Fortunately, Daria soothed her mate, taking his hand and interrupting him to address the other woman directly.

"I've done some thinking, and I don't believe you intended to harm me. We just want to know why you pushed me into the ravine that day."

Selene cleared her throat. "I didn't mean to hurt you, and for that I'm terribly sorry." She ignored Ryon's growl and went on. "That morning, I heard the creature that I had been avoiding since I came to the Shoshone. The thing had the most awful roar, like something out of a black-and-white horror movie."

"I remember." Daria shuddered, rubbing her arms.

"I'd had a couple of near misses with the beast, and I knew he was on the move again."

"Did you know he'd been murdering hikers?" Nick asked, interrupting.

"No. If I had, I would've reported something. As it was, I never even actually saw it, other than a brief glimpse of the outline it made as it went past. The beast was almost invisible, but not quite. Like looking through distorted glass."

"Like the creature in the *Predator* movie."

"Exactly. I didn't know what sort of creature it could be, but I was afraid of it. Anyway, that morning, I was hunting for breakfast in wolf form when I saw the beast's shadow moving through the forest. I decided to follow him, and he led me toward a stand of trees where there was sort of a clearing. And in that clearing was a woman examining the remains of a human. Of course, that woman was you."

Ryon's face paled. "You're saying he was hunting Daria?"

"No. I knew in my gut he was returning to his kill, and the woman who'd found the remains was just unlucky enough to be in his path when he came back."

"God," Daria said, eyes wide. "You ran right past him, didn't you? You scared me off, made me run so he wouldn't slaughter me, too."

"I did, and he followed us." Selene's jaw clenched. "He was closing in, and so I pushed you over the side to get you out of his sight. Then I ran back and engaged him in a . . . small skirmish."

"You did what?" Zan's mind brought forth horrible images of his mate fighting the beast. He'd been on vacation, healing from his injuries, while the Pack tracked the beast. But he'd gotten a description from the others.

"It was all I could think to do. There was nobody but me to lure the thing away, so that's what I did."

Ryon still wasn't satisfied. "Why didn't you go back for Daria? How come you didn't let anyone know about her being in the ravine, bleeding to death?"

"I was out of commission myself. The beast's claws raked my abdomen, nearly gutting me, and I had to find a place to hole up and heal. By the time I was well enough to shift into human form and make it back to town, Daria had already been found and the locals were buzzing about her rescue and the murders. I knew the authorities were on it by then. And I watched you all come and go, talking about attempting to capture the creature."

"Do you have any proof of your story?" Ryon asked.

Nodding, Selene stood. Slowly, she lifted her borrowed T-shirt to reveal a pink scar that ran in a slightly diagonal curve from just below her sternum to her belly button. "It didn't completely go away, I'm assuming because of the venom in its claws. I've never had an injury quite like this one."

Ryon leaned forward. "Convincing."

Lowering the shirt, she sat again. "It's the truth. I have plenty of faults, but I'm no liar." At that, she fell silent and waited.

"Thank you for saving my life," Daria said quietly. "You were almost killed trying to get the beast away from me, and I won't forget that."

The tension leaked from the room like air from a balloon. Daria's belief was good enough for them. Selene appeared relieved to have been vindicated.

"No thanks are necessary. My parents raised me to help others if and when I possibly can." She got the strangest look on her face just then and blinked at Nick, seemingly at a momentary loss for words. "Anyway, what happened to the beast? I know that it left the Shoshone, and there was some activity when the team left to pursue it, but I never learned what went down."

Ryon answered. "The creature was actually a human named Ben Cantrell. He'd been subjected to horrible experiments in Malik's labs—"

"Malik?" Selene looked from him to Zan.

"I'll explain later."

"Okay."

"Anyway," Ryon continued, "they tampered with Ben's DNA and turned him into this super-monster, one of many they hoped to control. When we found and destroyed the last of the labs, Ben escaped to wreak havoc everywhere he went. The poor bastard had no idea what he was doing."

"That's so sad." Selene looked upset.

"Yeah, but the good news is that Mac, Melina, and Jax's mate, Kira, developed a serum that counteracted the drugs and returned Ben to human form. Mercifully, he didn't remember much of what he'd done as the beast. He was a good man who was trapped inside the creature."

"Is he doing well now?"

Daria smiled. "Very. He's actually my former boyfriend, and we'd broken up before I met Ryon. The whole reason he came here was instinct—he was looking for me, and the Pack as well. In his lucid moments, he was trying to get help. He went back to his law practice and is doing fine."

"That's great news." Selene returned her smile.

Ryon stood, extended his hand to Selene. "It appears I was wrong about you. I want to add my thanks for saving my mate. I'll never forget what you did. In a way, you brought us together."

"I did?"

"Tell you another time." Daria grinned. "Over a glass of wine or two."

"I appreciate the invite," Selene said noncommittally.

"Soon, then. We'll let you get settled in."

"It's kind of funny, isn't it?" Ryon said, pinning Selene with a piercing look. "I misinterpreted your actions that injured Daria so severely she almost died. Sometimes there are explanations for things we don't understand at first, things that seem unforgivable. You might want to remember that."

Selene stared at him, cheeks flushing, and then looked away.

The couple left, and Selene's discomfort was obvious. "So where do I go from here? What does getting 'settled in' entail? My nice comfy cot in Block R? If so, can I at least have some magazines?"

Zan's heart clenched. He didn't like to think of her in that place, alone. Nothing to do but wallow in misery and listen to Raven, their poor insane teammate, howl day and night. Once again he turned to meet Nick's gaze and made his plea.

"She can room with me. I'll take good care of her. I swear."

"We don't even know each other." She gave him a questioning look.

"That's going to change anyway, whether they let you out of solitary now or next week. At least this way you have some freedom."

"I don't think—" Nick began.

"I'll take full responsibility for my mate."

"And if she tries to slit my throat while I'm sleeping?" He was only half joking, Zan could tell.

"I don't need to resort to dirty tricks—I can take you in a fair fight!" she said evenly.

Zan tried to speak over her. "If she harms anyone, or even attempts it, I'll take her punishment."

Selene gasped. "Why the hell would you do that?"

"It's my job—no, my *honor*—to protect my mate. I'll do whatever it takes to make sure nothing happens to you."

It was a big gamble. He really didn't know this woman at all. If she were a bad apple, he'd pay the price. But he had to take the chance; he didn't know if his wolf could live without his Bondmate.

Her fingers wrapped around his wrist, and sheer pleasure from even that minimal contact had his wolf rumbling, wanting more. He could barely focus on what she was saying. "I can't let you do that."

"Why not? Because you know that your sense of honor won't allow you to stand by and see me take the fall for your actions? I think that says more about you than you'll admit."

"It says nothing except that I don't want your interference."

He didn't agree. A glance at Nick showed he didn't, either. There was more to this woman than blind rage and thoughts of vengeance. She needed a chance to see that for herself.

"It's done," Nick said. "You commit a crime, your mate takes the punishment. Perhaps your time here will bring you some perspective."

She was fuming. No wolf liked having her hands tied behind her back, especially an alpha bitch. She'd decided on a course of action and had been derailed. Now she was lost.

"If we're done here, I'll show her to my quarters," Zan said. He couldn't say *our quarters* yet. They had a long way to go before that day, if ever.

Nick stood, signaling the end of the meeting. "Bring Selene to dinner. Everyone will want to meet her."

She snorted. "I just bet they will. More than likely, they'll want to rip me to shreds."

"Something tells me you can handle it," the commander said with the barest hint of a smile. "You are my daughter, after all."

"Not by choice," she spat.

Crap. Time to go. Zan put a hand on her arm and tugged gently, guiding her toward the door. As he looked back, Nick's expression was composed, revealing nothing.

Until Zan ushered her out the door. When she'd cleared the room, Zan looked back to see Nick's head bowed, shoulders slumped.

This was going to be a bumpy ride for everyone. And Selene was now his responsibility.

It was enough to make him wish he'd never returned from vacation. In fact, if he bought a ticket to the Caribbean right this second, he doubted anyone would blame him.

Zan had been ready to leave the Pack for good until she showed up loaded for bear.

And now he was just as tethered as he'd been to the Pack—for the rest of his life.

Selene's mind whirled in confusion as Zander ushered her through the hallways toward what he called his quarters.

All of her life, she was told her father had murdered her mother.

Is there another explanation?

She was told he had run away rather than face execution.

Yet Nick doesn't seem like a criminal on the run. He's built a life here.

She was ordered by Uncle Damien never to seek out her father. Warned that Nick would kill her on sight.

Instead he's been . . . kind. His men respect him, even like him.

What was the truth? Who was lying and why?

"Have you heard anything I've said?" Zan asked, interrupting her musings.

"No. I'm sorry." She gave him an apologetic look. "This is all a lot to take in."

Reaching a door with a keypad, he stopped and turned to fully face her. "I know it is, but you'll get used to it. Everyone here will be very welcoming if you'll give them a chance. We're like a big family."

She started to retort that she had a family, thanks, but something stopped her. Maybe it was the kindness in his eyes, his sincerity. He'd gone out on a limb for her when he didn't have to. He was trying. She could at least meet him halfway.

"I have no quarrel with you or your Pack. Just Nick."

"That's where your thinking is wrong. If you intend one of us harm, you'll have to fight everyone. Not worth it—trust me."

With that, he punched a code into the keypad and opened the door, gesturing for her to go first. Stepping inside, she took in his apartment. It was more spacious than she'd thought it would be, with masculine furnishings and tasteful landscapes on the walls.

There was a kitchen that was open to the living

room and a hallway beyond, which she assumed led to the bedroom. The curtains were pulled back, letting in the sunshine and revealing the gorgeous forest not far away.

"Like the rest of this place, this isn't what I expected," she said.

He shrugged. "It's home. Has been for six years."

"That's when you joined the Alpha Pack?" She faced him, curious in spite of herself. Having information was not a bad thing.

"Yes. I've been here since the Pack was formed and we opened the compound." Leading her over to the sofa, he took a seat and gestured for her to do the same.

Taking a spot next to him, she asked carefully, "So my father helped to build this place?"

"Actually, no. Our first commander was a man named Terry Noble. You met Dr. Mallory—she was his mate. He and some of our other Pack members were killed in an ambush last year, and Nick took over."

The sorrow on his face touched even her jaded heart. She hated her father, but she could relate to Zan because of what she'd been through herself. "I'm so sorry. Losing family is hard."

He nodded. "Thank you. There was one bright spot in recent months—two of our team we thought to be dead were rescued from those lab facilities we were talking about. Micah and Phoenix were found in separate locations, leaving us at least some slim hope that the others are out there somewhere, alive."

"Anything is possible, so don't give up hope."

"You'd do well to take your own advice." The words were gentle, compassionate, not intended to hurt or belittle.

But they struck a nerve all the same. "You know nothing about me or my situation," she snapped. "The only hope I have is to make my father pay for what he did, and beyond that I don't care."

Disappointment edged out his compassion. "I don't believe that."

"I don't give a shit *what* you believe."

"I doubt that's true, either." His eyes pierced to the core of her. "We're mates, and I can already feel your inner pain. Your longing for love and acceptance."

Too close to the bull's-eye. Much too close.

She looked away from that knowing gaze. "Think what you want. It's not like I'm going to hang around after I settle my business with my father."

"You'd just leave without giving our mating a chance?"

That question surprised her, deflating some of her anger for the moment. "I don't know what you expect me to say. Finding a mate wasn't exactly in my plans when I arrived."

He gave a laugh tinged with bitterness. "And

you think it was in mine to discover that my fated Bondmate is a cold, bitter woman who's more comfortable wearing blinders than facing the truth?"

His accusation sent a hot flush of shame surging through her, and she reacted defensively. "Well, since I don't measure up, it shouldn't be too hard for you to let me go so you can find someone else," she said coolly. Inside, her wolf growled in displeasure at the idea, startling her. "Maybe we should just change the subject."

"Fine. What do you want to talk about?"

"I noticed that your voice is . . . different, and you're always looking at the speaker. Are you hearing impaired?"

"Why? Is that another strike against me?"

Now who was being defensive?

"Not at all. I was just asking because I was curious to know more about you."

He gave her a long look, then settled down, apparently deciding the question wasn't meant to be rude or demeaning. "I was injured a few weeks ago during a battle with an Unseelie that came close to killing all of us. His name was Malik, and he was Kalen's and Sariel's father. You haven't met Sariel yet."

She digested that. "Malik is the one Ryon mentioned, who had labs that were experimenting on people."

"Yeah. He was a mean fucking sonofabitch and

almost turned Kalen to his side. His goal was to combine human and shifter DNA to try to create super-soldiers, sort of mass produce them and take over the world. And he damned near succeeded."

"God, that's horrible!" She tried to imagine her clan dealing with such evil, and wondered if they would be prepared to fight it if the situation ever arose.

"What's worse is we now know Malik wasn't the top of the food chain on the rule-the-world deal. Someone in the US government has been behind it all along, and even though Malik is dead and the labs have been destroyed, whoever is pulling the strings has created a huge problem with the rogue vampires."

"I can't imagine anyone being so stupid as to think they could control the rogues," she scoffed. "They no longer possess morals, loyalty, honesty, or any quality that would make them respect another's rule. They want nothing but to feed their lust for blood and sex, and they can acquire those two things without any help."

"Well, someone in Washington didn't get that memo before they royally fucked up. Now we have to find out who that someone is and stop not only him but the latest mess he created."

She shook her head. "I don't envy any of you on that job." Except her father. He deserved that task and all the dangers that came with it.

"It won't be easy. As for me, my fighting days are over unless my hearing improves a lot more." He looked away, out the window. "I almost got Nix killed earlier. That's why I was out for a run when I came across you and Nick. I was trying to decide whether to leave here for good."

For some reason, the idea caused her stomach to twist. "I get the sense that saying good-bye to your team isn't what you want at all."

"It's not." With a start, he looked at her, whiskey-colored eyes wide. "I heard you say that! It sounded faint, as though you were far away, but I still heard!"

"That's great," she said, smiling as she grabbed one of his hands.

"I heard a little when I was talking to Nick, too." He appeared excited about the development.

"I'm happy for you. Do you think it has something to do with our mating?"

"Could be. A strong bond between mates can work wonders, so maybe it can heal as well."

"I hope so." Even if they didn't remain together, she found herself caring whether he could heal.

"What if it doesn't? How will you feel about being saddled with a defective mate?"

"First of all, you're not defective," she said firmly. "You've been injured in battle while fighting evil, and that's something you—and your mate—should always be proud of."

"Thanks," he said hoarsely.

"I think the better question is how we both feel about being mated, period, and whether we want to give this a real shot. I know what I said before about leaving, but I know from my clan that being mated complicates things."

He was silent for a long moment before answering. "Speaking for myself, I've wanted a mate for a long time. Someone special who was meant to be only mine, as I would be only hers. Even before I was turned into a shifter, I didn't date much. And after six years in the compound, life has gotten more than a little lonely." He sighed. "I don't want to be alone anymore, and I'd like to see if we can work it out."

She fell silent for a long moment before answering carefully.

"Among my clan, to find our true Bondmate is a cause for celebration. It's considered one of the greatest events that can befall a born wolf. Not everyone is blessed in that way, and part of me is grateful that it happened, in spite of how I came across before."

"But the other part?"

"I'll be honest, Zan. Even if a miracle should occur and I don't end up killing my father, I'm just not sure I could ever fit in here."

"Fair enough. But would you do us both a favor and keep an open mind?"

She looked away, torn. Finding a mate *was* a gift. But could she put aside revenge for her mate?

"I'll try. That's all I can promise." And that wasn't much.

"Then you'll stay here for a while?"

"Yes. I don't think the commander would let me leave even if I tried, which I won't just yet." Her uncle was going to shit monkeys when he found out. Not about Zander, but about her being around Nick for any length of time.

He smiled, his relief plain. "That's all I can ask. I guess we start by introducing you around."

"I'm sure everyone will welcome me with hugs and kisses," she said sarcastically.

"Yeah, you did try to kill our commander, who's respected and adored by everybody in the compound. So, doing that again is pretty much a deal breaker."

"I'll try to refrain—but only because of you and our mating bond." Her tone made it clear that it wouldn't be easy.

"You won't be sorry."

She wasn't so sure. But for this kind, gentle man she'd mated, she felt compelled to make an effort. She wondered if she really was vindictive or stupid enough to ruin something as cherished as finding her Bondmate in favor of getting revenge.

But she wanted answers. Had to have them or she'd go crazy. She'd been nursing her hatred for so many years, it was damned difficult to let it go.

However, even she could see that things were not what she'd always believed where Nick was concerned.

She'd bide her time. And eventually she'd get what she wanted—her mate *and* the truth.

Five

Uncomfortable talking about her father, Selene changed the subject.

"Do you have two bedrooms?"

"Just one, but I'll take the sofa. No argument," he said when she opened her mouth to protest.

"All right."

"Do you have clothes somewhere?"

"I've been staying at a motel in town. My bags are there."

"We'll go for a drive later and pick them up."

"That's fine. What do we do now?"

"Want to go for a run, let our wolves out for a bit? Mine is ready to let off some tension, and I'm betting yours is going stir crazy from being cooped up in that cell. Besides, we've got a while before dinner and nothing better to do."

She shrugged. "Okay."

In truth, her she-wolf was dying to see him in action again, with his big, sleek form covered in ebony fur. The grace of his limbs and his incredible wolf scent. She recalled how he'd placed himself between her and his Pack, fangs bared, and a shiver of delight traveled unbidden down her spine.

That had been sexy as hell. She could deny a lot of things about this new mating, but one that defied any sort of denial whatsoever was the simple fact that she wanted him.

She wanted his body on top of her. Inside her, taking what only her mate had the right to. And she wanted to be on top of him, too, grinding her hips and ass into him—

"Hey, where'd you go?"

Shaking her head, she looked at him and grinned. "Just thinking about that run. I'm ready when you are."

Following him through the hallways, she made direct eye contact with each person she encountered, not willing to show the slightest weakness. These shifters needed to know that she didn't fear them, or care about their scorn. She didn't crave their acceptance. The only thing she cared about was finding the truth and making her father own up to his part in the destruction of her life.

As she watched her mate's fine ass swaying in his jeans, she was forced to admit perhaps revenge wasn't *all* she was looking forward to. Since it was her right to take it, why not enjoy?

Outside, he led her to the edge of the forest, then a few yards down the path into the undergrowth. There, he began to shed his clothing, and she took another long look at the man who was now hers. He was absolutely gorgeous.

Having no modesty, she got rid of her clothes as well and laid them over a log. Zan studied her in kind, and she couldn't help but feel a surge of pride at the flare of heat in his eyes. He obviously liked what he saw, and her wolf practically whined at the attention.

"How fast is your wolf?"

"Pretty fast," she answered. "Yours?"

"Why don't you find out?" He threw it out as a challenge, a twinkle in his brown eyes, then shifted. In seconds his gorgeous black wolf stood before her, waiting eagerly.

Not about to start out behind, she let the change flow over herself also. It always happened fast, and in moments she was next to him, a white wolf next to his ebony. She thought they must make a striking visual.

Zan took off with a bark, paws churning the earth. She dashed off after him. Stretching her muscles felt damned good after being cooped up in that stupid cell. She was glad he'd suggested this, because her wolf needed it.

She tore across the forest floor, jumping dead trees and dodging rocks, hot on his heels. He was fast; she'd give him that. But she was holding back a bit. He'd challenged a born wolf to a race, and she was determined to win.

But he'd been holding back as well. Just as she started to pass him, he put on a burst of speed that left her eating his dust again. Crap! He pulled several yards ahead, jumped a small creek, then skidded to a halt on the other side and spun, his wolf panting, tongue lolling, his expression looking like a big smile.

Jumping the creek, she barreled into him, taking him to the ground with a playful growl. Together they rolled over and over, nipping and yapping, and it was . . . fun. When was the last time she'd experienced this with one of her clan? Specifically, a lover? Never.

After their play, they lay panting, side by side. Gradually, the high of their tussle began to settle into an awareness of each other she'd never felt with anyone else. The feeling was heat and fire. Arousal.

And not just any arousal, but the kind that took that fire and melted her bones. Pulsed inside with every beat of her heart. Her blood pounded in her veins, and she shifted smoothly to human form, rolling to crouch on her knees. She was aware of him staring at her naked form. Lust shone in his eyes.

"I want you," she said simply.

He shifted too and sat back with one leg straight on the ground, one leg cocked with his knee up, arm resting on it. His cock jutted proudly to the sky, and his smile was feral.

"Then come and get me."

She crawled to him and pounced. Their mouths met with a clash of lips and teeth, and she tasted a bit of blood. This wouldn't be a gentle mating, but a coming together of two primal souls. Two wolf mates, taking what belonged to them.

That was fine by her.

Their tongues dueled, tasted. His fingers found her nipples, plucked and twisted, sending her need through the treetops. Placing a palm in the center of his chest, she shoved him onto his back and straddled his erection.

"Oh, yeah," he groaned. "Fuck me, beautiful."

She lowered herself onto his rod. Already so aroused, she was wet and ready. She slid onto him, loving how he stretched her. Giving in to the moment, she let the wild side of her nature take over—and she did a partial shift.

He gasped as his fingers at her waist buried themselves in soft fur. "You—you're shifted!"

"Half," she corrected him with the throaty voice of her partial form. "Feels good, doesn't it?"

"Yeah. You're beautiful this way."

She knew he was seeing her elongated fangs, the soft white fur. Her claws. "You can do it too, and it'll feel so good to me. Have you had it this way before?"

"No. Is it better for you?"

"Not better, just different. Sort of wild." She grinned. "Did you know your cock will swell even bigger inside me in half form?"

"God! I want to try it."

"It's easy. Just start the change, but let it go only until you have fur and claws, like me."

As she moved on him, fur sprouted under her fingers, soft and silky. Fangs grew to overlap his bottom lip, and his eyes were that of his wolf peeking through. His claws dug into her hips as he thrust. And best of all, his cock grew, filling her almost too much. He was huge inside her.

"Fuck yes!" she cried. "Do me!"

With a snarl, he flipped them. Suddenly, she was scrambling to get on her hands and knees, and he was behind her, poised at her entrance. Then he plunged deep, filling her so full, she thought he'd impale her all the way to her throat.

She screamed her pleasure as he fucked her hard, like a wolf mate should. His hips pistoned into her, his cock stroking her walls with increasing speed, balls slapping against her sex. It was so good, so damned fine.

Then he stiffened and began to come with a shout. His orgasm triggered her own explosion, and she rode out wave after wave of intense pleasure until she collapsed to the ground, limp and sated.

Zan joined her, lying close so that their bodies were touching, but stopping short of pulling her into his arms. It would've been okay with her, but she wasn't going to mention it and sound needy.

"I've never felt anything like that," he said in awe. "Is it always like that in half form? Wait. Don't answer that. My wolf doesn't like the idea of you having done that before."

"I wish I could tell you I haven't," she said, and meant it. "But with born wolves, it's quite natural to give in to our feral nature once in a while. Especially with mates, though you *are* my first in that area. And I'll tell you, nothing that came before came close to being as good as that!"

He puffed up a little. "Yeah? That's because I'm awesome."

She snorted, secretly thinking he was pretty cute. "Come on, Mr. Awesome. Let's splash off in the creek and then see if you can keep up with me this time."

"Hey!"

Shifting back to her wolf, she sprinted, and was gratified to hear his yip sound behind her as he gave chase. They washed off some, then shook their coats on the bank and ran again. They bounded through the forest, letting their wolves play until well after dark. Until her stomach was snarling in anger at having been neglected.

As if sensing her hunger, he turned them toward the compound. Within the hour, they were at the edge of the forest, shifting to collect their clothes and dress again.

"I'm starving," he said, pulling on his T-shirt. "You?"

"I could eat."

"We've missed dinner in the dining room with everyone, but I've got stuff for sandwiches and chips in my quarters."

"Sounds great." Truthfully, she wasn't eager to face his Pack just yet.

Back in his apartment, he fixed them turkey sandwiches on crusty hoagie rolls, with Swiss and spicy brown mustard. She ate like a starving wolf and then yawned, sleepy.

"It's been a big day for you," he said gently. "Why don't you turn in, get some rest?"

"All right. And thank you for tonight. I really needed the run, and the company wasn't so bad, either."

He laughed, as she'd hoped he would. "Same here. Get some sleep."

Padding into his bedroom, she stripped and slid under the sheets with a tired sigh. Again, she thought of their run. And the extremely satisfying sex.

She hadn't felt that alive in a very, very long time.

Selene awoke the next morning, rolled over, and peered at the clock.

Almost noon? She'd slept damn near the whole morning away. Stretching, she tried to get rid of the cobwebs and realized the shower was running. What would Zan look like standing under the spray, stark naked? Even better than he'd looked last night by the stream, she'd bet.

A few minutes later, he emerged from the connecting bathroom, a towel slung around his waist. Glancing toward the bed, he smiled.

"Good morning, Sleeping Beauty."

"Morning," she grumbled. "I guess."

"Well, it's nearly noon, so it's technically morning for a few more minutes. Hungry?"

"Not right now. I just need a shower."

"Help yourself." He pointed to the foot of the bed. "Rowan sent over some more clothes. I figured after you get cleaned up and dressed, we can head to your motel and gather your stuff."

"All right."

It was nice of the other woman to loan her more clothes, but Selene couldn't wait to fetch her own things. She made short work of showering, then toweled off and blew her hair dry with a dryer she found under his sink. Being short, her hair dried fast, and she was soon dressed.

"I'm ready."

He ushered her out. In the hallways, they encountered only a couple of his friends, who clapped Zan on the back and shot her knowing smirks. That pissed her off, and she wanted to rip open their faces. But she refrained. She could be reasonable when she tried. When they reached the garage, her thoughts were diverted by the sight of the vehicle Zan was leading them toward. Unable to help herself, she snickered.

"What?" He shot her a curious look.

"Men are all the same. Their ride has to be an extension of their cock."

She thought he'd get pissed, but unexpectedly, he grinned. "Then I must have a damned big one."

That surprised a laugh out of her, in spite of herself. "I'll be the judge of that."

A sudden realization smacked her in the head as they climbed into the monstrous truck—she was now the only one with the right to know just how big Zan was, all over. And the idea of any other female having that knowledge made her she-wolf growl in anger. It was a strange feeling.

As she pondered this, Zan's voice interrupted her musings. "For the record, Nick didn't do what you're accusing him of. I've known him for almost a year now, and he's as honorable as anyone I've met."

"You're going to tell me there's an explanation, as your friend Ryon suggested?"

"There are good people at the compound. You might want to listen to what they have to say." He glanced at her as he pulled the truck out of the hangar. "You seem like a sharp, intelligent woman who can make her own decisions. All I ask is that you go by what you *observe* for yourself, not by what you've been *told* for years."

His words angered her—probably because he

made sense. Before she'd entered the compound, the issue had been black-and-white. Now her belief was being colored by shades of gray, and she didn't want to change her thinking. It was too painful otherwise. Still . . .

She wasn't one to condemn unjustly. Damn.

He drove them into Cody, and as the vehicle rumbled along, she took the opportunity to sneak glances at the man who was her mate. He seemed to get more handsome the more she studied him, and he had integrity to boot. He was brave. Kind. Most of the males of her clan were extremely stern and unbending, but not so this man.

"What's it like to be a born shifter?" His question might have been plucked from her thoughts.

"I've never known any other way, so I'm not sure how to answer that." She thought for a few moments. "I grew up differently from human kids. We weren't totally sequestered from the outside world, but we were a bit sheltered. We have our own community, schools, and clan law that's enforced by the Alpha's men."

"No humans live there at all?"

"There are some, but most of them don't know what we are. The Alpha is very selective about who's told."

"Your uncle is the Alpha, I assume."

"Yes." He looked like he was chewing on something, but whatever was on his mind, he kept silent.

"Anyway, other than that, there's the immortality thing."

"The what?" He shot her a quick look, briefly taking his eyes off the road.

"It's not common knowledge, even in the paranormal community. Born wolves are immortal. We can be killed by accident or treachery, but other than that, we're around for a long time."

"How old are you?" he asked curiously.

"I'm only thirty, in human years," she told him. "But I won't look much older than I am now for as long as I live."

"That's pretty handy," he joked. "No wrinkles or gray hair."

"There is that."

"What about Nick? How old is he?"

"More than two hundred." *Older than he deserves to be.*

"Holy crap! That's quite a secret to carry around. Just think of all the changes he's seen," Zan mused. "The history. He's been alive since America was a brand-new nation."

"So has my uncle."

"What's your uncle like?"

She considered that. "Stern. A stickler for rules, and he trusts few people. But he's honest and tries to be a fair leader."

Zan said nothing to that. Perhaps he felt Damien hadn't been fair in his dealings with her father.

Not that it mattered what her mate or any of his friends thought. They weren't there.

When they arrived in town, Selene directed him to the cheap motel where she'd been staying. As soon as they pulled in to the parking lot, Zan wrinkled his nose in disgust.

"After seeing this fleabag, I'm glad we're getting you out of here."

"Aww, I was going to invite you to stay here with me instead of the compound."

From her smile, he knew she was kidding. "In a place where the cockroaches are the size of Doberman pinschers? I'll pass, thanks."

Truthfully, she was eager to see this place at her back as well. Inside her stark, musty little room, she gathered her few things, stuffing jeans, T-shirts, and underthings into her duffel bag. A few toiletries and her mini tablet were last, and she was done.

"That's it?" He frowned.

"I travel light."

Before she could protest, he plucked the duffel from the bed and led her out. Then he tossed it into the back seat of the double cab and they were on their way.

"Feel like a drink?"

For some reason, the simple invitation warmed her. "Sure. I found this place called the Cross-eyed Grizzly if you want to go there."

"Oh, we've been there a time or three."

"So I've heard."

God, the man's smile was devastating. She was willing to bet he could get women to do whatever he wanted by flashing them a smile like that. Good thing he didn't seem to be the type to take advantage.

It was still early in the afternoon, and the Grizzly wasn't too busy. Zan parked the big truck at the back of the lot and ushered her inside, his hand lingering at the small of her back in a proprietary manner. That warmed her, too.

They found a booth next to the wall sort of out of the way and slid in, taking seats opposite each other. As luck would have it, Jacee came out from behind the bar to take their orders. The woman shot Selene a wary glance, and she didn't blame her. Though she liked the bartender, Selene had been a bit . . . forceful, last time she was in here.

"What can I get you guys?" Jacee piped up.

"Beer for me," Zan said.

"Make that two."

"You've got it." She moved off, leaving them alone for a few moments.

A sudden attack of conscience hit Selene, and she regarded her new mate steadily across the table. "I feel I have to warn you that Jacee there, she knows about the Alpha Pack."

That shocked him. His eyes widened. "What? How?"

"Jacee is the one who told me you guys hang out here. She keeps her eyes and ears open. And she's not human, herself."

"Shit." He glanced toward the bar, where the woman in question was drawing their beers. "What is she?"

"Coyote."

"Damn, I never scented a thing!"

"That's because she keeps her scent masked. In my world, coyotes are akin to parasites. Not that I feel that way about Jacee, because I don't," she said quickly. "She's nice enough. In fact, I don't believe in putting someone down because of their breed."

"I'm happy to hear you say that, because I feel the same way. Our world has enough prejudice in it without shifters adding to it."

"True."

The object of their discussion returned with their beers and set them down. "Anything else?"

"Nothing for me right now," Selene said.

Zan shook his head. "Maybe later." After the bartender had gone, Zan spoke quietly. "By the way, Jacee used to hook up with my best friend, Jax. So, when you meet Jax and his mate, Kira, you might not want to mention Jacee."

"That could be awkward. Don't worry. Mum's the word."

"Thanks." He took a draw of his brew.

She did the same and then waved a hand at

him. "So, I answered your question about being a born shifter. You were turned, right?"

"Yes, along with almost all the rest of the team I'm with now. We were Navy SEALs in Afghanistan when we were attacked by rogue werewolves."

"That must've been horrible."

"It was. More than half our unit was killed."

"Would you mind telling me the story?" she asked. "I'll understand if you don't want to share something so personal."

"We're going to continue to share a lot more than stories if I have my way," he said with a smile. "So, sure."

She blushed to the roots of her hair, something that hadn't happened in a long time. Not one to embarrass easily, that remark, and the pure sexuality behind it, had caught her off guard.

Then his tale unfolded, taking her back to the awful day when the Alpha Pack came into existence—and life as they knew it was never the same.

Six years earlier . . .

Zan hated Afghanistan.

The days were sweltering, the nights cold as a brass witch's tit. There were no such things as good food, rest, or comfort for the body or mind. He couldn't wait to leave this hellhole. He was marking the days—twenty-eight more days and his six years of service were done.

He was going home, to Atlanta. To his grand-mother's kitchen, where he'd let her smother him in all the motherly love he'd been missing for the past few months. Hell, since his mother had died of cancer years ago. Granny was always there for him. He couldn't wait to give her a big hug.

And hang up his dog tags for good.

"Jesus Christ, I'm rank," Raven bitched, scratching at his crotch. "When I finally get to change this underwear, it'll probably walk off."

Micah grinned. "With assistance from the crabs you caught from that hooker last month."

"Shut up, needledick. She did *not* give me crabs."

Zan snickered. The banter of his teammates was just about the only positive that got him through the long days and nights in the arid terrain of this shitty country.

"Hold up," Jax whispered, coming to a halt. Tensing, he studied the mountain forest around them and frowned.

Zan listened. Somewhere hidden in the brush, a footstep crunched to their left. Another to their right. More from behind. He saw Ryon and Micah exchange a fearful look. He knew this area was supposed to be clear, and they couldn't have reached their target's stronghold already. In that instant, he knew they were toast. Their enemy had them surrounded.

Then the forest went silent. Never, ever a good

thing. Because when the smaller creatures went still, that meant they were hiding from something much bigger and hungrier than themselves.

Thud, thud, thud.

The ground trembled and the leaves shook. Zan thought distantly that he'd seen and heard this very thing in a movie long ago. When a deep-throated roar split the air, Aric jumped, pointing the muzzle of his M-16 into the trees, hands rock steady, a bead of sweat dripping off his nose.

"Fuck," Micah whispered. "What the fuck is that?"

Zan stared in stupefied horror. The thing that broke through the foliage to their left stood erect on two legs and was more than seven feet tall. Covered with a thick mat of grayish brown fur, it had a long torso, two arms, muscular shoulders, and a head sporting two upright ears and a long, snarling snout full of sharp teeth.

It looked like a creature that was half man, half wolf. He and his team stared, mouths open, fingers frozen on their triggers.

The situation might have been salvaged, disaster averted. But their buddy Jones started screaming, pumping bullets into the beast's chest. After that, everything went to shit.

The creature staggered backward and then rallied quickly, rushing Jones. With a swipe of a paw the size of a dinner plate, the big bastard ripped out Jones's throat, tossing him aside like a twig. Then it pounced on Raven, biting into the vee of his neck and shoulder as the man screamed.

They opened fire just as several more of the beasts emerged from the forest. It quickly became apparent that while their bullets could wound, it would take something with far more power to kill them. He saw Aric drop into a crouch and palm a grenade as his friends fell all around him, waging a battle they couldn't win.

The creature who'd killed Jones shook Raven like a rag doll, released him, and ran toward Aric, who let a grenade fly. It hit at the target's feet and exploded, sending the damned thing to hell. But more and more of them took its place.

Micah went down, his knife in hand, slitting one's throat. But another jumped on him, and his struggle was short-lived, his scream terrible. Jax fell next, then their CO, Prescott, Nix, and so many others. All of them, one by one. Dead or dying.

As Aric unsheathed his knife to fight one, a beast rushed Zan. It hit him with the force of a runaway truck, knocking him backward and sending him skidding along the ground. He rolled to avoid the claws that swiped down at him, but they raked his side, splitting him open through his camos. There was no time to acknowledge the fiery pain spreading through his torso. He kept moving, dodging several blows.

Suddenly, he heard a cry in his head.

Help me, somebody! Oh, God—

Nearby, he saw Ryon fighting with a creature of his own and losing. Had the plea come from him? Or was it a figment of Zan's overwrought imagination? The beast plunged its claws into Ryon's stomach, and the man screamed, a horrible sound.

Aric dispatched it, but it might have been too late.

Zan scrambled backward, trying to put enough distance between him and the beast to level his weapon and fire. But he hardly had the barrel lowered before the beast slammed the gun out of his hands. Zan quickly drew his knife and went on the offensive, running into the beast's body rather than away.

With a powerful upward swing, he thrust the blade underneath the bone of the thing's sternum. Drove it at an angle, as deeply as possible. The beast's screech was cut off abruptly, and it went down.

Zan staggered and fell. How long he was sprawled and bleeding in the dirt, he didn't know. He only knew he had to get up. To use his gift on everyone he could save. His conscience wouldn't let him do any less.

He found Aric first. Called forth his healing gift and sent it into his friend. Repaired torn arteries and shredded skin. "Come on, man. Don't die. Stay with me." Painstaking, exhausting work, and when he was done, he wanted to sleep. But there were so many left to go.

He got moving, crawling to Ryon. The man was crumpled on the ground, staring into the sky. His chest was moving, but Zan could see the light fading from his eyes.

"Ryon, hang on," Zan ordered, touching his shoulder. "I'm a Healer, and you're going to be okay."

Disbelief was reflected in that solemn gaze, normally so full of humor and life. No one ever believed at first. And then the few who finally did, like Zan's dad, called him a freak and an abomination. Told him that he was a minion of Satan.

If the bastard were here, he'd know what Satan really looked like.

Sending his warmth into Ryon, he spent long moments healing him as well. And then the next fallen brother and the next. When at last he'd helped everyone he could, his body simply quit.

Burned out, he slumped to the ground, convinced he'd never awaken.

And after what he'd seen today, that was fine by him.

"I'm so sorry," Selene said, her heart breaking for Zan. For all of them.

How had they managed to get past such horror? It must have been the worst thing imaginable. Lives ripped apart, families left in limbo.

"Did you ever go home?"

He nodded. "I did, but by the time I recovered

and got home to Atlanta, I found out my grandmother had died four months earlier. I had no family left, so I sold her house and was trying to decide what to do with my life when General Jarrod Grant and a shifter named Terry Noble showed up at my motel room door. Grant is a contact high in the military who gives Nick our assignments."

"Like, what paranormal beings are wreaking havoc somewhere?"

"Exactly. Who, where, and how dangerous they are. We go out and dispatch the problem. If we feel there's a creature or being who's just confused or scared, we bring it in to try to rehabilitate it to our world. Like Sariel and Chup-Chup, two of our success stories."

"Chup-Chup?"

"Chup is a little gremlin-type creature that we found in a cave on a mission. Nobody knows where he came from. He used to stay in a cell in Block R, chewing on his chain constantly and crying to get out. But he was so mean, nobody could handle him, and we couldn't let him go."

"That's so sad! Where is he now?"

"Jax's mate, Kira, came to live with us, and she has a way with those being rehabbed. She worked with Chup and got him to trust her, and the little guy fell in love with her. He's great now and has the run of the place. When you meet him, just don't stick your hand in his face without letting him sniff you first or you might lose a finger."

"Uh, no worries there." Don't provide a real-life finger snack for the gremlin—check. "What about Sariel? You said he's Kalen's brother, right?"

"Half-brother, but yeah. He's also a Seelie prince," Zan said.

"Seelie, as in Fae?" Her eyes rounded. "I've never met one in real life!"

"Well, you will. His nickname is Blue because his hair and wings are this cool jewel tone of blue. He's really literal, doesn't get a lot of human slang and terms. We have a lot of fun with him, and he's really a great guy. You'll like him and Kalen."

"I'll reserve judgment on the Sorcerer for now," she said dryly. "He popped into my holding cell to basically inform me I was being watched and if I stepped one toe out of line he'd turn me into a slug. I believe salt was mentioned as well."

Zan actually growled, which she thought was funny. "He won't try any such thing, or he'll answer to me."

Reaching across the table, she patted his hand. "He was sort of kidding. I think. Anyway, I'm not going to push my luck around him."

Her touch, and the assurance, seemed to settle him. At the contact, the golden bond between them sang. It was almost a living thing, humming with electricity, firing along her nerve endings to the most primal part of her. The she-wolf inside of her stirred, rumbling in need. They both wanted him again, to feel him as they did before. His cock buried deep inside as they took what was theirs. She could hardly wait to get out of here.

They finished their beers and waved good-bye to Jacee, who smiled as they left. She thought about the coyote having a fling with Zan's best friend and wondered how she'd feel if she ran into someone who'd slept with her mate.

Her wolf snarled, letting her know she'd tear out the bitch's throat.

Guess that answered *that* question.

Back in his truck, she slid into the passenger's side. He didn't start the engine, though, and so she looked at him, waiting. Slowly, he turned to face her. Reached over and traced a finger down her cheek.

"You're very beautiful," he said, the words husky.

Her heart did a strange happy dance in her chest. "As nice as that is to hear, I'm surprised that you'd pay me any sort of compliment."

"Why? Because of your attacking Nick?"

"That's a big enough reason, don't you think?"

"Yes. But there are extenuating circumstances. We both know that, and I'm willing to bet your perspective will change."

"You have a lot of faith."

"Healer. It's an occupational hazard."

With that, he scooted close. Cupped a hand behind her head and pulled her in for a kiss. He smelled so good, warm and spicy, and she inhaled his scent, hungry for more of him.

"Care to take this somewhere else?"

She sucked in a breath. Her body was on a steady burn to taste him, to savor his skin. "Yes."

Desire darkened his brown eyes, and he started the truck. Even though they'd been together last night, she couldn't wait to have him again. In seconds, they were on the road, and she felt a thrill of excitement. She was going to be with her mate, and while they were still getting to know each other, their encounters weren't just fucking among strangers who'd go their separate ways. That pleased her to no end. He was hers.

As she enjoyed the drive, something occurred to her. "Your voice! It's not flat anymore. You can hear, can't you?"

Glancing at her, he nodded and graced her with a big smile. "I can. I wasn't going to say anything yet because I was afraid it might not be permanent, but if you noticed, maybe it's real. I was thinking it might have something to do with you being a born shifter. I think the bond had a good physical effect on me."

"I hope so. I'd like nothing better than if our bond healed you."

"You mean that." It wasn't a question.

"I do."

He drove until they came to a side road leading into the forest, a county road not well traveled from the looks of it. The truck bumped along for a few minutes, and he finally turned off onto a narrow lane that was little more than a dirt path. At the end, the lane became a pretty meadow with a terrific view of the snow-capped peaks of the Rockies and the Shoshone below.

"Gorgeous," she breathed.

"There are lots of parking spots around—not that I've brought women to them often. I mean rarely ever." His cheeks colored.

"Maybe you'd better stop that line of bull while you're ahead. The part about there not being many, that is."

"There haven't!"

"If you say so."

"Have *you* ever been parking?" he countered.

"I plead the Fifth."

"Sure you do. Thought so."

This time, she silenced him by initiating the kiss. His mouth was glorious, just firm enough, made for kissing. He devoured her mouth, slipping his tongue inside, stroking everywhere. Driving her crazy. She could imagine how good that would feel laving her elsewhere.

"Even last night seems like it's been too long," she murmured. "I *need*."

"For me too. Let me taste you?"

"Please."

Lifting her shirt, he reached for the front clasp of her bra. Flicked it open and let her breasts spill free. From that alone, her sex was throbbing. Born shifters were highly sexual creatures, and she was glad Zan was, too. They weren't shy about their bodies, especially not once they found their mates.

They might not know each other well—but that wouldn't stop them from burning up the sheets.

Bending, he took a nipple in his mouth and sucked it to a tight point. Little shocks went through her as he repeated the attention on the other nipple. Then switched again. Just when she thought she'd go mad from want, he turned his focus to getting her jeans unzipped and pulled to her hips. Slipping a hand in front, he palmed the pale, silky curls.

"Mmm. I couldn't tell what you were like here, last night, in your half form. Just the way I like it—a trimmed triangle but bare where it counts."

She loved the way a bare sex heightened pleasure and was glad he found this pleasing. Her legs spread for him, and he delved between them, stroking her clit and diving one finger into her channel.

"So good."

"Let's get these off, baby. I want you to ride me."

Getting off her jeans inside a truck wasn't easy, but at least it was a big cab. In short order, she was naked from the waist down, and he was the same. She stared at his lean, powerful thighs. And the trimmed bush with the cock jutting proudly from the curls like an exclamation point. It was at least eight inches, flushed red and purple, and gorgeous. Heavy balls were nestled underneath, resting on the leather seats.

Reclining his driver's seat, he gestured to his lap. "Climb aboard, sweetheart. Take me for a ride."

"Gladly."

Moving over, she straddled him. Positioned the head of his cock at the entrance between her folds. Gradually, she sank down, adjusting every couple of inches for his width. She'd never felt so stretched, so full. Moments later, he was buried deep inside her, to the hilt. There had never been anything as good as this connection. The thread of their bond glowed, almost in approval.

"Fuck me, baby," he begged hoarsely.

She began to pump on his length. Up and down, spreading her cream on his cock. Loving his moans and her own as she added her sounds of pleasure to his. All too soon, a familiar quickening began in her sex. The throbbing heat became too much, and she shouted her climax, channel spasming around his length.

This triggered his release, and he joined her, his big hands spanned around her waist, helping her ride him, slamming her onto his cock. When he was spent, he kissed her lips and held her on him for a long moment.

He groaned. "I suppose we should get back to reality."

"Why?"

"Good point. But I'm afraid people would miss us, and they'd find us stuck together, expired from multiple orgasms."

Laughing, she climbed from his lap. She was messy and yanked on her clothing quickly to avoid screwing up his nice seats. He did the same, then kissed her once more for good measure.

Selene found herself wishing they could just drive away. Leave her father and the Alpha Pack behind and forget about all of it. But she'd promised to try to give this a chance, and she would.

As she'd said, she was a wolf of her word. And there were worse fates than spending times like this with Zander Cole.

Six

Now the test would begin.

Zan drove them back to the compound, knowing life around there was truly about to change. For himself, at least. He knew the others were going to be wary of his mate at first. Some, like Ryon and Aric, might even be a bit hostile.

But this would work. It had to. As long as his hearing was truly back, he wanted desperately to remain with Alpha Pack, to be a productive member of their team, and for that, his mate had to be part of his world. If she couldn't or wouldn't stay, what the hell would he do? He'd have to follow her. But he wouldn't think about that now.

After he parked, he walked around to her side, helped her down. She looked at him as though no male had ever done that before, and to hear her talk of her clan, he wasn't surprised. He offered his hand and was pleased when she accepted it, clasping her fingers around his.

"Hungry?"

"Starved. But I'm nervous, too, so I'm not sure how the food is going to settle."

"It'll all be fine. Don't worry."

She didn't seem convinced. It wasn't until they got to the dining room that he understood her nerves. No one was rude or outright hostile, but . . . they were normally so open and friendly, whereas today they were reserved and watchful. He and Selene took a seat at one of the family-style dining tables, and nobody sat with them. At first.

They were filling their plates with spaghetti when a shadow fell over the table. Zan almost groaned when he looked up to see Belial standing there expectantly, as though waiting for an invite to sit down.

"Belial," he said in greeting. Not the friendliest, but this one had quite the history with the Pack. He was seductive, manipulative. And if rumor could be believed, he came with a pretty sad story.

"Zan! Can I sit with you guys?"

He looked so hopeful. Zan sighed. "Sure."

The newcomer sat and grabbed a plate. Selene, who'd been observing with interest, said, "Aren't you going to introduce me?"

"Belial, this is my new mate, Selene Westfall. Selene, Belial."

"Nice to meet—wait a second. Westfall? As in our commander, Nick?"

"I'm his daughter," she said, somewhat shortly. "What about you? You're not a wolf."

"Nope. I'm a basilisk shifter." He waggled his dark brows. "Scared now?"

"Should I be?" She seemed unperturbed that one of the rarest, deadliest types of shifters was sitting with them, calmly eating pasta.

Belial considered this. "Probably, around others like me, considering the deadly venom thing. But in my case, I'm rehabbed. Got my rabies shots and everything. Just got sprung from Block R a couple of weeks ago."

"Congrats."

He beamed at her. "Thank you. So, what do you do?"

"Do?" She stared at him, at a loss.

"You know, in your clan."

"Oh! I'm an enforcer, or I was. That was before I left my uncle, our Alpha, without really telling him where I was going and for how long."

"News flash—Alphas don't like when their top people disappear. Especially if they're family."

"Tell me. I've got to call him before long." She made a face that told without saying how she felt about that task.

"What are your plans?" the basilisk asked between bites of spaghetti.

"Stay for a while, try to fit in."

The young shifter blinked. "Fit in among misfits? That's a good one!"

Selene chuckled. "You have a point."

"Well, hello," a familiar, friendly voice said to Selene.

Looking up, she smiled. "You must be Blue—I mean, Prince Sariel."

"I see I'm famous," he said good-naturedly, easing himself down by Belial. The basilisk scooted over, shooting Blue a nervous look. As well he should—for all that Belial was rare and dangerous, Blue, an eleven-thousand-year-old Fae, was even more so.

"Of course you're famous. You're royalty, after all."

Some of Blue's humor faded. "Used to be, but no longer."

"I'm sorry," she told him, sympathy etched on her face.

"It's of no importance. At least I don't have all of those boring council meetings anymore."

They ate in companionable silence for a bit, or rather, everyone ate except Blue. The prince just pushed his spaghetti around, eating an occasional noodle to be polite. Zan knew, because he'd seen the act time and again.

"You don't eat much." Selene studied his plate.

He shrugged. "I don't tolerate the food on this plane very well. But Melina may have finally figured out why."

"Hey, that's good news. Right?" Zan asked when Blue didn't respond.

"Maybe. She says she thinks the problem is psychological. That it stems from me missing my family in the Seelie realm."

"Like grief, or depression?" Zan frowned.

"I suppose so. Who knows?"

"If that's the case, what can she do to help you? Give you medication?"

"Not without knowing how human drugs will affect me. Of course, the best medicine would be to find a way for me to visit my brothers, or for them to come here. Perhaps Kalen and I will be able to figure out how to open a portal like the one I was dumped through in the first place."

That didn't seem likely, though, a fact that was reflected on Blue's sad face. Everyone hated seeing him down, especially Zan. He was a Healer, but he couldn't fix broken hearts.

Another visitor came over. Seemed the group was finally letting curiosity and their natural warmth overcome their reservations.

"Hello, I'm Kira, Jax's mate," the petite blond said, holding out her hand.

Selene took it, and they shook. "I'm Zan's surprise mate, Selene Westfall."

"Oh, we've heard." She smiled. "I just wanted to welcome you and let you know that some of us girls like to get together over a glass of wine occasionally, except for Mac, of course—she's all about juice and milk these days. Anyway, we wondered if you'd like to come to our next gathering."

Selene looked to Zan, and he nodded in encouragement. He realized she'd be hesitant. She didn't know anyone here, so she had to wonder if the offer was sincere. Suddenly, he recalled that they should be able to use mind-speak now that they were mated, and he tried it out.

You can trust these women, Selene. They would never do anything to harm or humiliate you. Her face reflected surprise, and if he wasn't mistaken, pleasure. Whether at the new form of communication or the information itself, he didn't know.

You think so?

Yes, absolutely. If they're inviting you into their circle, accept.

All right. I'll trust your word.

She'd trust *his* word. He liked that, and so did his wolf.

"Thanks, I'd like to join you," she said to Kira. Her smile didn't quite reach her eyes, as she didn't yet want to let down her guard, but she was making an effort.

Zan wondered if part of her had been starved for this sort of companionship with friends. Considering what she'd told him about her birth pack so far, he wouldn't be surprised if folks just weren't all that warm and fuzzy.

Kira returned to her table, and Zan saw her discreetly poke her mate in the ribs. He grunted, frowned, but then rose and made his way over to where they sat. Zan knew that accepting Selene would be harder for the men on the team than the women, because she'd tried to harm Nick. Jax's gesture would go a long way toward swaying the rest of the guys. But it still stung a bit that he'd needed a push from Kira to hold out the olive branch.

"I'm Jaxon Law, Kira's mate," he told her.

"Jax is a Timebender and a PreCog," Belial supplied helpfully. "Isn't that cool? They can all do neat stuff. Aric can set shit on fire and he's a Telekinetic, Ryon's a Channeler who talks to dead people, Hammer is a Tracer, Kalen's a Sorcerer and Necromancer, Micah's a Dreamwalker, and then—"

"Belial," Jax interrupted. He arched a brow, and the basilisk deflated.

"Oh. Sorry."

With a sigh, Jax returned his attention to Selene. "Anyway, despite the rough start, I hope you'll find a place here with Zan. He's my best friend and a great guy, and you could do a lot worse than to be saddled with his ass."

"Thanks, I think." Zan scowled at him.

"You're welcome." With a nod at Selene, he returned to his table.

As Zan hoped, Jax's gesture brought the rest of the guys and their mates around to say hello. Kalen, Mac, Ryon, and Daria she'd already met, but she was greeted by Rowan, Aric, Micah, Hammer, Nix, A.J. and Noah. After they'd gone, Belial continued to happily be a fountain of information.

"That's everyone except Raven DeLuca," he said, flipping his bangs from his face. "He's stuck in wolf form and relegated to Block R, maybe forever."

A light seemed to dawn on her face. "Is he the one who's howling and snarling down there?"

"One and the same. He was a Navy SEAL in Zan's unit. Right, Zan?"

"Yeah. After we were turned in Afghanistan, he shifted in the hospital and never returned to human form, the poor bastard. He's pretty much out of his mind. It's so bad, the doctors might not be able to let him go to the new building that's almost finished for the residents who need special care. They're trying to work it out."

"That's horrible!" she gasped. "Do they know why he's stuck?"

Belial shook his head. "No. And it's not like they haven't tried to heal him. Even Zan's had a shot at it, and nothing doing. That wolf is totally messed up in the head."

Selene sat back in her chair and grew quiet for a few moments. Finally, she said, "Okay. Raven was turned during the fight with the rogue werewolves."

"Yes," Zan affirmed.

"And then he went to the hospital, where he was recovering, at least at first?"

"Correct." She grew silent again. "What?"

"I know I'm just the newbie on the block, but would it be possible for me to see Raven?"

All of Zan's protective instincts surged to the fore, and his reaction was swift. "Absolutely not."

That earned him a dangerous look. "Want to try that again, in a different tone?"

Shit. "What I mean is, Raven is extremely unstable and very dangerous. As in, nobody can get close enough to him to even touch him. Sedatives don't work on him, either. So he's trapped in his misery, and six years of hell have made him mean. So I'd prefer that you stay far away from him."

"But what if I can help?"

He blinked at her. "What light could you shed on his condition that nobody else has ever been able to?"

"Oh, ye of little faith," she quipped. "Don't forget, my clan is different from what you guys are used to."

"So?"

"Did it ever occur to you that I may have seen something like this before?"

His heart sped up, and hope bloomed. "You can really help him?"

"I should clarify I don't know if I can physically *help* him, but I might know what's *wrong* with him. Give me a chance to meet him. If I'm right, the doctors will at least have a new avenue to pursue."

"All right. Let's talk to Mac and Melina, see what we can do." Seriously? He didn't want her anywhere near Raven, the poor lunatic. But if she really could give them a clue what was wrong with their fallen friend, he had to let her try.

Finishing their meal, they headed for Kira's table, since she was in charge of rehab and the soon-to-be-opened building, Sanctuary. Selene quickly gave her the rundown of their conversation about Raven, and Kira got excited.

"Come on," she said, jumping to her feet, meal forgotten. "Let's go talk to Melina about this."

Jax wasn't about to let *his* mate go anywhere near Raven without him, either, so the four of them walked quickly to the infirmary. But the doc wasn't easy to convince.

"No. I can't take a chance with our own Pack getting near him, much less a newcomer."

"Just a few moments?" Selene entreated. "The story Zan told me very much resembles something that happened to one of my own clan members a few years ago. If I'm right, it'll give you a direction to help with his healing."

The tiny doc was skeptical. "We've been studying him for six years and—"

"Without success. So, what will it hurt?"

"He's dangerous."

"Is he restrained?"

"Yes, but—"

"Five minutes. Please?"

"Dammit." When Melina blew out a breath, they knew Selene had won. "Fine. Five minutes, though I don't know what can be accomplished in that time."

Rising, Melina moved from behind her desk and led them out of the infirmary. Down the corridor to Block R, the most barren place in the building. Zan was glad the new Sanctuary would be far more welcoming than this place. A better environment for the residents.

As soon as they went through the solid double doors to the block, the howling assaulted their ears. The mournful racket was soul-wrenching, and Zan hated it every time he came down here to speak to Raven, who never seemed to hear him. They reached the correct cell, and Melina typed a code into the box beside the door. It slid open, and she went in first.

Zan and the others followed her, keeping a respectful distance. The howling stopped, but the large black wolf in front of them began a low, ominous growl that rumbled in his chest like thunder.

"Hey there, beautiful," Selene crooned, crouching. Making herself as nonthreatening as possible as the wolf continued to growl, head down. "Aren't you a big, beautiful boy? Are you lonely in here?

Of course you are. What if I told you that I understand? That we'll do everything in our power to find her?"

At that, for the first time in Zan's memory, Raven stopped growling. Completely. He looked at Selene, right in the eye.

And incredibly, he gave a soft whine.

"Holy shit," Zan whispered. "That's it."

"What? What's going on?" Melina demanded, her gaze bouncing between Zan, Selene, and Raven.

Still crouching, not taking her gaze off Raven, she said, "When a born wolf scents his mate, if he doesn't claim her within a certain amount of time, he'll sicken and die. I'm assuming it's the same for turned shifters?"

"Yes, as far as we've been able to discern," Melina said slowly. "And?"

"I've seen this before, with a member of our clan." She stood, backed away from Raven carefully, and then faced the doctor. "Have you ever wondered what happens when the shifter can't claim his mate but doesn't die?"

Understanding dawned. Zan's stunned expression mirrored everyone else's. "Oh, God."

"Here's what I think happened—in the hospital, Raven scented his mate. Possibly even met her. But he was bedridden, recovering from his attack. As a new shifter, he had no control over his body's reactions. He couldn't claim her, but for whatever reason, he didn't die."

"Why didn't he?"

"I have no idea, but I've seen it happen sometimes."

"And his wolf took over, went crazy," Zan finished in a near whisper.

"Exactly. Until we locate this female, he's going to remain in this state." She looked at Melina. "Does he have any belongings? Clothing he wore before entering the hospital? Something that might have her scent on it?"

"Some of his stuff is still in one of the lockers in the infirmary!" Kira cried. "I'll get the bag." She rushed off.

Zan, Selene, Melina, and Jax stood watching Raven, who was becoming agitated again. Starting to pace, pulling on the strong chain around his neck that allowed him some movement, but kept him from reaching his visitors and ripping them apart. After a few minutes, Kira returned with a plastic bag, the type hospitals use to store a patient's things. Moving as close to the wolf as she dared, Kira upended the bag, spilling out the contents.

Immediately, Raven pounced on the items, rooting through them with his nose. Sniffing, his body vibrating with excitement. A T-shirt, boots, camo pants, dog tags. But it was the plain hospital gown that proved to be the item he was looking for. They watched in amazement as he picked up the gown in his teeth, padded to a corner of the room, dropped the article, and then made his bed on it.

He settled with a sigh, his expression almost sad. Then he closed his eyes and went to sleep.

"Holy fucking shit," Jax breathed. "His mate must've been close to him in the hospital, touched his gown. She might've been a doctor or nurse, or an aid worker."

Zan's throat threatened to close up at the pitiful sight before them. "All this time. All these years, he was going crazy for his mate. All it took was her scent to calm him down."

"Maybe now he'll sleep regularly," Melina said, eyes moist. "If he stays calm, we might be able to reach him, eventually. Selene, I don't know how to thank you for this."

Pink colored her cheeks. "It was nothing. Like I said, I've seen a case like this before. I hope this one turns out to have a happier ending than that one did."

Everyone echoed that sentiment. They slipped out into the corridor and went their separate ways. Zan took his mate's hand as they walked.

"That was a nice piece of work. Maybe Raven will have some peace while they try to locate his mate."

"I don't know. It's obvious he's hurting inside. My wolf was very sensitive to his suffering."

"I can't imagine how horrible that would be, to be stuck like that. Going out of your mind, out of control, and not being able to verbalize what's wrong."

"It's difficult to witness—that's for sure."

"What happened to that wolf you were telling us about, the one who was also stuck?"

Her voice saddened. "His mate was dead, and there was no hope for his recovery. He was euthanized by lethal injection."

"That's awful. Kind of makes you appreciate what you have, doesn't it?"

She slid an arch look at him. "I suppose that was directed at me? It does put things a bit more in perspective."

"So, in spite of how we met, you don't regret mating with me?"

She grinned. "That remains to be seen. Don't get cocky."

He snorted a laugh, his spirits lifting. He led her through the rec room, ignoring Micah and Blue, who called out to him to come play air hockey.

"Idiots," Aric snarked. "The man doesn't want to play air hockey with you bozos when he has a new mate."

Zan just shook his head and kept walking, the whistles and ribald remarks at his back causing him to puff up a little. He had a mate, and a beautiful one at that. Let them tease. The mated guys knew firsthand what an exciting time this was for him and his wolf, and the single ones wished they did. It was his turn.

Outside, his mate looked around. The stars were out, shining bright in the clear sky. The air was a bit crisp, making his wolf want to come out and play. *Later*, he told it.

"Where are we going?"

"I'll show you." He took her to the building that was almost finished, a short distance from the main compound. It was several floors of earth-toned brick and tall glass windows.

"Is this the new rehab center?"

"Yeah. Nice, isn't it?"

"Very. But how does this new construction not attract attention from outsiders?"

"The whole Alpha Pack compound is cloaked with one of Kalen's spells, for extra privacy. No human could see it even if they tried."

"Ah, the spell. Right. That's the reason I wasn't able to get close to the main building when I was watching before. That was Kalen's doing."

He didn't want to have another discussion about why she'd come. Instead, he gestured to the new structure. "Want to see inside?"

"I'd love to."

Everyone had their own security code, so Zan keyed his into the pad by the main doors. They opened with an audible hum and pop, and he pulled the handle, letting them inside. Then he flipped on a light, which illuminated the grand foyer.

"Oh! This is gorgeous," she enthused. Walking

over to the reception desk, she ran her hand over the marble countertop. "This is quite a big place, bigger than I imagined. Is my father going to hire more staff to handle the load?"

"Yes, no question. There will be a receptionist or two, plus at least one more doctor, whom Mac and Melina will be in charge of hiring. Noah will get input on more nurses, and Nick and Mac will hire at least one dedicated counselor. Most of the staff will be paranormal beings."

"How come?"

"Two reasons. One, it will make residents more comfortable to know there are functioning members of society who are paranormal, just like them. It will give them hope and set a good example. The second reason is more practical, which is we want as few humans as possible to know our world exists."

"I see. That makes sense."

"Let me show you the rest."

He took her through the lower floor first, showing her the various exam rooms, counseling rooms, recreation areas, kitchen, and dining room. "The residents will be able to eat here and learn social interaction before being released to society," he explained. "They'll get a sense of normality, and that will build self-esteem."

"This is so impressive. What a great thing they'll be doing here."

"Let's go up." They stepped into the elevator,

and he punched the button for the top floor. "See the O on the panel? That stands for Observation. The resident rooms are still under construction, but the lounge is done, and it has a fantastic view of the mountains."

The elevator doors opened right into the lounge area. Zan flipped on a lamp on the table so the whole room wouldn't be lit too brightly. Beside him, Selene gasped.

"Wow. This is amazing. I can just see the residents relaxing up here and enjoying this place."

Unable to stand her closeness any longer, he pulled her in to his body, facing him. Wrapping his arms around her, he nibbled her neck and jaw. Spread his legs and cradled her there, letting her know just how much he was affected by holding her.

"Zan," she murmured. "I want you again."

"You drive me crazy, baby. Will you trust me?"

"I . . . yes."

He hadn't known her long, but he already knew that trust wasn't something she did easily. "I'm going to make this so good for us."

"Please, yes."

He bent over her, nuzzled her short, silky platinum hair. Kissed the shell of her ear, nibbled. Breathed her warm scent.

He slid a hand underneath the T-shirt, splaying it across her flat belly. He loved the way she fit against his body, like she was made just for him.

His fingers traveled upward, found the taut pebbles of her nipples. He took one, rolling the peak between his thumb and forefinger. She moaned, arching her back, skin heating to his touch. More kisses at the curve of her neck and shoulder. Tasting, playing with her breasts.

"Mmm, I almost wish I were a vampire, so I could bite right here."

"Oh, Zan." She gazed at him. Huge blue eyes were glazed with arousal. Needing, wanting him.

"You know what I'm going to do? I'm going eat you. Then I'm going to fuck you right there against the observation window, with the curtains open."

"Where anyone can see?" She gasped.

"Yes." His lips turned up. "Though the window faces away from the compound, toward the mountains, so it's unlikely we'll be spotted."

"But still! God, that's so kinky."

"The excitement in your voice tells me you love that."

"I—yes!"

He worked her jeans and panties down her legs, tossing them to the floor. The T-shirt followed. Then he pushed her against the glass, face out to the night sky and anyone who'd care to watch him take her this way. Only watch and never touch. All *his*. The heated desire of just thinking of the act rocked him to his toes.

"Spread your legs." She did, making room for him. He knelt between her thighs from behind, trailing kisses from the back of one knee to her sex. "So lovely. So pretty and pink. Already wet for me. I could come, just by looking at you."

She whimpered, raising her hips a bit. With a low chuckle, he obliged, his fingers parting her. His tongue flicked her folds, dipped inside. He lingered, taking his time. Licking slowly, like a man enjoying ice cream.

Selene rocked back into his face, urging him. "Please!"

He fastened his mouth to her sex, suckling the sensitive bud. She came undone, bucking beneath him. Lost in decadent pleasure. The sight of her writhing nearly made him lose control.

Holding back his release shredded Zan as she found hers, wild against his mouth. Her honey bathing his tongue. *Oh, God, so sweet.*

When the last of her shudders stilled, he moved to her side. Bent, turned her head and kissed her lovely mouth. He loved the sight of his mate ready to give herself to him this way, pale hair an angel's halo around her face. Knees spread, the lips of her sex pouting and slick from his attentions, ready to welcome him inside.

He ran his fingers along her slit, spreading her. Jesus, he wasn't going to last. Grasping her lush hips, he guided the tip of his penis to her and thrust home. Buried his cock to the hilt. Her heat surrounded the throbbing length of him, squeezing, driving him mad. *Not yet. Not yet . . .*

"Look at you against the glass," he rasped. "Pinned there. Beautiful. Mine."

She began to move back and forth, stroking him. "Yes, yours. Zan, please, *fuck me hard*."

"God, yes."

He surrendered control. Gave himself over to the beast raging to do her. Hard, wild, nasty. He pounded into her with long strokes. Thrusting harder, faster. Joyous, feminine cries reached his ears, erasing any lingering doubt he might've had about urging her to try his kink. She trusted him completely and loved what they'd done.

Neither the man nor the wolf stood a chance against such heady stuff. With a hoarse shout, he impaled her one last time. Held her body close, buried so deep he actually felt them become one heart, one mind. His release rocked him to the core. Branded his soul as hers, for always. Her climax milked him on and on.

Covering Selene like a blanket, he remained inside her for a moment, sweating and shaking. He'd never come harder or been drained more thoroughly in his life. Had never before shared a shattering awakening, a fusing of hearts, with the only woman he'd ever desire from this day forward. He'd never known this sweet ache, ever.

He just hoped one day she'd feel the same.

Seven

Selene awoke in Zan's room, but this time she knew she was alone.

There were no sounds of her mate showering, or dressing. No puttering in the kitchen, no humming, or any one of a dozen noises she'd come to think of as comforting.

She was alone, and it bugged her that he hadn't awakened her to say where he was going. So what if that made her seem domestic? She didn't care.

Hunger panged in her belly, but she ignored it. First she'd find her mate, and then she'd eat. In that order. Slipping out of bed, she made quick work of showering and dressing. Then she ventured out into the compound alone for the first time since her arrival.

She wasn't sure that was smart on their part, letting her run loose. Then again, they had all sorts of abilities—and a Sorcerer on the team. That made her shudder a little in spite of herself. As badass as she thought she was, there was always someone who could kick her butt and take names. Sorcerers scared her.

The hallways were a maze, but somehow she found her way to the dining room. Several people were there, eating pancakes, and the sweet aroma tempted her. But the pull to find her mate was stronger, so she walked over to Kira.

"Have you seen Zan?"

Kira swallowed a forkful of her breakfast and then shook her head. "Not specifically. But Jax said they were training in the gym this morning, so you might check there."

"Thanks." She turned to go, but the other woman's voice stopped her.

"One word of advice—don't interrupt them unless it's important."

She gave Kira a hard look. "I'm not an idiot. My job requires me to train, too, you know."

Kira's face flushed. "My apologies. I didn't mean to imply you were."

Instantly, Selene felt like a total bitch. "No, I'm sorry. I'm just on edge, but that's no reason to take it out on you. Forgiven?"

"Of course." The other woman smiled, gave her directions to the gym, and Selene felt somewhat better.

"Thanks. Catch you later."

After a series of turns, she found herself facing a set of double doors with a bar on them, exactly like one would see at a school gym. From the shouts, grunts, and groans inside, she figured she had the right place.

As she pushed inside, she almost swallowed her tongue. The whole team was in there, paired off, practicing their fighting skills on mats. They were bare-chested to the last man, wearing only thin athletic shorts and tennis shoes. The Pack made hand-to-hand combat look sexy, even though she knew the reasons behind such strenuous practice were serious. That didn't mean she couldn't look to her heart's content.

Her gaze strayed to Zan, who was facing off with Jax. His black hair tumbled over his eyes but didn't distract him one bit as the men circled each other. His lean muscles shone with sweat, thighs flexing as he faked left and right, countering blows his sparring partner delivered with speed. They made an awesome sight, these warriors, and she felt a spurt of pride that Zan was her mate.

He was brave. Worthy. A mate she could be proud to introduce to her uncle, should the situation ever become possible.

"Impressive, aren't they?"

And just like that, her enjoyment of the morning was shattered. Turning her head, she assessed her father. "Yes. They've been well trained."

"That wasn't my doing. I've been here only just shy of a year."

"And where were you before that?"

"The FBI."

She found herself getting angry, and she hadn't wanted her day spoiled. "How nice for you."

"Not really," he said quietly. "I would much rather have had my family back. And you, most of all."

"Is that so?" She gave a bitter laugh. "Life's a bitch, isn't it, *Commander*? You reap what you sow and all of that."

"You don't know anything about the way things were."

"Suppose you enlighten me, then?" Silence. "No? Why am I not surprised?"

"Someday you'll understand. I promise I will tell you, when the time is right."

"What is that? Some type of Seer bullshit?"

His mouth tightened. "You know what I am and that it's real."

Her anger boiled over. Needed an outlet—now. "Spar with me."

"What?"

"You heard me." She waved a hand at the mats. "Come on. Spar with me."

"No, Selene."

"Afraid to show me what you're made of? Is that it?" she sneered.

After a slight hesitation, he nodded. "All right. We'll go a round."

"What do I get if I win?"

He gave her a half smile. "Satisfaction."

"Bring it."

Walking over to a set of empty mats, she was aware that some of the guys, including her mate, had stopped what they were doing to watch. She couldn't care less. She had a point to make, and it would be made nicely with her father smeared on the mat at her feet.

Bouncing in place, she warmed up, glad she'd worn her camos and a tank top. They'd be easy to fight in and wouldn't get in her way. A few more seconds and she turned to face the man she wanted to put on the floor.

They started out circling each other, knees bent, hands out to the sides. Each ready for the opponent to spring. He was patient, his gaze challenging, and that infuriated her more. Finally, she couldn't stand it anymore and launched herself at him. But he was expecting this.

He easily dodged her attack, stepping to the side with fluid grace. She moved in close to his body, got in a few good blows, but he always countered them without really hurting her. Even though she knew what he was doing, she refused to quit. Her rage was a living thing, poisonous, and she gave in to it.

He was using simple evasive maneuvers, using

her anger against her as a weapon, waiting until she was worn-out. At last he ended the match by swiping a foot behind her heel and flipping her onto the mat hard, on her back. She glared up at him, panting, wishing him dead on the spot.

"Anger will get you killed in the field," he told her, expression unreadable. "You have to learn to block it out and focus solely on reading your opponent, anticipating the next move. Emotion can all too easily defeat you."

"Maybe that's your problem," she spat, pushing shakily to her feet. "You have no emotions, so you can't win the fight that matters the most. Maybe you never could."

Giving him a hard shove in the chest, she stalked out.

Distantly, she thought she heard Zan call out, but she was in no mood to deal with him. She just wanted to put space between herself and Nick—and his men—as fast as possible.

She pushed out of the gym, out into the morning sun. Found a spot under a tree near an open field and stayed there for a long while.

Zan called out after his mate, started to follow her. But Jax laid a hand on his shoulder.

"Let her go, my friend. She's pissed right now, and I doubt she'd hear anything you have to say."

"She needs me," he said in frustration.

"I know she does, but let her cool off. Okay?"

He looked at his friend and gave in. "Yeah."

"Nick too. I can tell he hated having to do that."

Zan glanced at their boss, who was toweling off his face on the sidelines. His body was still tense. And his face as he stared after his daughter? Crushed.

"He needed to put her on her ass," Jax said seriously. "You understand that, right? He never would have stood a chance of earning her respect otherwise."

"You think so?"

"I do. Wolves are proud, and they respond to power. And those two are off the chain when it comes to their own power struggle right now. Your mate just learned she can't push him around, either physically or verbally. He's still her father, and he can walk the walk."

"And she's not going to be happy about it, either." Zan sighed.

"Right, which is why she needs her space." He threw a towel at Zan. "Want to get some breakfast? She'll show when she's ready."

"Sure."

But his heart wasn't in his meal. He couldn't help but worry about his stubborn, hurting mate.

She was going to be the death of him.

There wasn't a much more impressive sight than a Fae prince strolling across the lawn toward you.

Unless it was the broad smile transforming his face from gorgeous to stunning.

"Beautiful day, isn't it?" he mused.

"I hadn't noticed."

"Hmm. May I sit?"

"It's a free country, man."

He frowned. "I'm not really a man. Or not a *human* man, in any case. I'm a Fae male and—"

"Relax, birdman, it was just an expression."

"I'm not a bird, either. I—oh. That was an *expression*, too?"

She smiled. This guy was completely without guile, just as she'd been told. "Yep. How did such a naive male get to be a prince?"

He scoffed. "I'm not naive where I'm from, trust me. There are simply too many strange phrases in this realm for me to possibly keep up."

She studied him for a moment, admiring his unusual golden eyes. The way his wings settled around him like a cloak and rustled in the gentle breeze. "Do you miss home?"

"Not the place so much, but my brothers," he said wistfully. "I know they'd come here if they could. I just hope nothing is wrong. That they're all right."

"Me too, Blue."

"Thank you." He gave her a piercing look. "You're grieving for family as well, and look at me, being all sad and ruining your peace."

"Shut up—you are not," she said, finding a smile for him. Something about Blue was just special. In some ways he was such an innocent. "I believe you'll see them again one day."

"I hope so. From your lips to the ears of the gods."

"How did you wind up here, again?"

He sighed. "The Unseelie Council exiled me. Aric says they voted me off the island, but our home was not an island. Anyway, they learned the Unseelie king, Malik, was my sire and were afraid I carried his evil gene. Whether I did or not, they knew he'd come for me one day, and they didn't want to be anywhere near me when he did."

"That's terrible," she said with feeling.

"To be forced from one's home, made to leave family and friends behind under penalty of death, is just about the loneliest thing that can happen," Blue said, looking her straight in the eye. "I wouldn't wish that feeling on my worst enemy."

A sense of vertigo gripped her. "Are we talking about someone other than you right now?"

"No. But it's worth thinking about—don't you agree?"

"Yeah. And I'm sorry it happened to you." He wasn't talking just about himself before. She was sure of it, but didn't press.

"I'll see them again one day." Blue rose, brushing the grass off his pants with his wings. "I'm going to see if there's any breakfast left. Join me?"

"I'd like that."

Taking his extended hand, she let him lead her back inside.

And she pondered his words for a long while.

Zan was sitting with Jax at the breakfast table when Blue walked in with his mate. The pair was having a conversation, and though his wolf wasn't happy to see her accompanying another male, he immediately knew Blue was no threat. His wolf stood down.

Seeing Zan and Jax, they walked over and took seats, Selene next to Zan. He liked the way she scooted close, pressing her side into his.

"You all right now?" he asked in a low voice.

"I think so." She stared at the plate of pancakes in front of her. "I guess I made a fool of myself, huh?"

"No. You had a point to make with your father. You wanted him to know you're no pushover."

"And instead he handed me my ass."

He grinned, trying to lighten the mood. "And then some."

She rolled her eyes. "Thanks."

"Eat something, baby. I know you must be hungry." She was staring at him strangely. "What?"

"You called me baby. I sort of like that," she murmured.

"Good. Then I'll be sure to call you that often." With a wink, he tore into his pancakes, gratified when she did the same.

They were talking with Jax and Blue, finishing their breakfast, when Nick came into the dining room. Selene went tense beside him, stiffening even more when the commander strode to their table.

"I need an extra pair of hands," he said without preamble. "Most of the others are still working out."

"What's up?" Jax asked, crunching on his last piece of bacon.

"I need to go down to Block T and question that rogue vamp from the ranch again, see if he'll budge this time."

"You know he's not going to give up shit," Zan said with a grimace. "Those bastards are as stubborn as they are stupid."

"Be that as it may, I have to give it one more try. If there's any chance he'll slip and tell us something, I need to learn what he knows."

"I don't like it, boss," Jax said with a frown. "He nearly got you last time, and that was with several of us in the cell."

"What?" Selene's gaze bounced between Jax and her father. "What do you mean?"

"The vamp nearly killed him. That was right after we captured him and brought him here, before you came. Don't worry. We'll be more careful."

Zan tossed down his napkin, surreptitiously watching his mate from the corner of his eye. She was worried for her father. Well, wouldn't you know? His mate wasn't nearly as against Nick as she appeared.

"We'll go," Zan said, and Jax nodded. To Selene, Zan said, "I think you should stay here and keep Blue company."

"No! I'm going with you, and that's final."

Leaving their plates, they walked with Nick to the elevator, then rode it down to the basement. As he'd predicted, the questions started.

"How do you terminate the creatures who stay down here?"

"In the most humane way possible, depending on what type of creature it is," Nick answered, glancing at her. "In this vampire's case, a quick stab to the heart will kill him. Beheading him will make sure he stays that way."

"I've heard they can rise if you don't take their head." She appeared none too happy about that.

"True."

The elevator doors opened to an industrial-type area, the starkest place in the entire building. Zan came down here very rarely, and in truth, hated doing so. There wasn't much that was more depressing than interrogating creatures who were doomed to die—even if the creatures deserved it.

"What did this rogue do?" Selene asked, as though reading his thoughts.

"Murdered a young ranch hand. Drained him and savaged the body. It was a real mess."

"God!"

They fell silent as Nick led them to the last cell. They stopped and studied the pitiful-looking vampire through the bars. His clothes were stained with dried blood and God knew what else. They were filthy, and the creature stank so bad, it was like a rabid skunk had sprayed the entire basement.

"Come to gawk at the poor prisoner," it hissed, raising yellowed eyes to study them in return. Behind him, chains rattled, securing his wrists, though they couldn't be seen.

Beside him, Selene sucked in a breath.

"There's nothing poor about you. You simply made your choices," Nick told it.

"Choice? What do you know about hunger? An aching belly that's never filled?"

"More than you think. There's never a reason to harm someone when you feed. Prince Tarron has a hard-and-fast rule about no killing of blood donors. If you had—"

"Fuck you, mangy wolf!"

"Tell me who's behind these rogue attacks. There are far too many to be a natural occurrence. Who's responsible? Why?"

"Do you still think I'm going to tell you shit?" it screeched. Then it began to cackle, an eerie noise of insanity that made Zan's blood run cold. "That'll never happen."

Jax shook his head. "Boss, he's not going to talk. Let's just get this done."

"Dammit! All right. I'm tired of listening to his

ass, and it's not like we can put him back on the street."

Nick punched in a code beside the door and it slid open. He walked in, Zan and Jax behind him. Then the vampire stood, and Zan realized their mistake.

The rogue was no longer chained. He'd done something he shouldn't have been able to do—he'd broken them in half.

"Hit the button and close the door!" Zan shouted to Selene. He was vaguely aware of the bars clanging shut again and felt momentary relief. Whatever happened, Selene was safe on the other side.

He caught a glimpse of her standing with her hand over her mouth, eyes wide, and then the rogue was on top of Nick, slashing, trying to lay open his throat with claws and fangs. They slammed against the bars, and the commander did a partial shift, utilizing claws of his own to drive them into the rogue's side.

It howled, and Zan hauled it backward. Jax helped him tackle the thing to the concrete floor, and the two of them made quick work of it. Zan stabbed his claws under the sternum and up, skewering its heart. Jax slit its throat, then hacked until the head went rolling away, the rogue's eyes surprised. It was a macabre sight.

"Great," Jax bitched. "I got stinky rogue blood all over my new jeans."

"Hey, he's hurt!"

At Selene's cry, they spun to see Nick stagger and sit down, hard. They rushed to him, and Zan whistled.

"Nasty bite wound. He *did* get you. Stay still while we call for a stretcher."

"No, I can walk," Nick said stubbornly.

"You sure?"

He eyed his boss. The man wasn't going to be budged, so he and Jax gave in. "Fine, but we're helping you. Baby, can you punch in the code to let us out?"

He called it out to her, and in seconds the door was open. He and Jax hauled Nick off the floor, getting him between them and slinging one of his arms over each shoulder. The position wasn't unlike the many times they'd assisted a SEAL buddy wounded in combat. They walked him out to the elevator.

Zan didn't miss the sheer horror on Selene's face as she studied her father's wound.

"You could have been killed," she scolded him.

"Sorry to disappoint you," he rasped.

His mate looked like she'd been slapped. Zan thought it truly hit her then, the ramifications of her anger. Whether it had been unjust all this time. The self-doubt and the first glimmerings of remorse. All of her emotions were there and gone in a flash.

His mate would need him, later.

They hauled Nick all the way to the infirmary,

and Melina met them in the lobby with Noah. They took the commander off his and Jax's hands, which was quite a relief.

"Goddamn, he's heavy." Jax groaned, rotating his shoulder.

"He's going to be okay, isn't he?"

Zan took his mate's hand. "He'll be fine. A bite wound like that is just a scratch compared to some of the injuries we've had."

"Somehow I'm not sure that makes me feel any better."

"Sorry. But he's going to be good as new by to-morrow. Trust me. He's got that shifter healing going for him."

She blinked at him then. "Why didn't *you* heal him?"

"Because it wasn't a life-threatening wound, baby, or I would have. I have to conserve my energy for the really, really bad stuff. Okay?"

"Sure. I understand."

She was truly rattled by her father's injury. This had been a day of revelations for her all around, and he needed to see to his mate. He tried to get her to leave, but she wouldn't be budged until they heard something.

Finally, Melina came out, Nick on her heels. He was a bit pale and had a fresh bandage at the curve of his neck and shoulder.

"Our patient will live," she said, then smiled kindly at Selene. "I'll check the wound again tomorrow, but by then it should be fine. No after-effects from a vampire bite wound but some pain."

Selene almost sagged against him. Then she found her voice and met her father's gaze. "I'm glad you're okay."

His eyes softened. "Thanks. Why don't you let your mate take you to rest now? I think I'll do the same."

Zan knew that was just for her benefit. The stubborn wolf would head straight to his office to work.

"I think I will," she said.

"Come on, baby. Let's go lie down for a while."

After one last look at her father, she let Zan take her hand and lead her back to their quarters. Theirs. He was liking the sound of that.

Once inside, he gently removed her clothes and then his. He scooted her into the bathroom and started the shower, making it hot enough to soothe their muscles and relax them. Then he pulled her inside with him.

He washed the blood from himself, scrubbing from head to foot. Then he got her good and wet, soaping her from top to bottom as well. He made sure to get every cranny, taking care of his mate as nobody else would ever do. It made him proud to care for her, see to her needs.

And right now, what his mate needed wasn't sexual.

She needed her mate to hold her, to let her

know he was there. Would always be there to cherish her. Come what may, she was his.

She'd suffered quite a blow to her *Get Nick* campaign, and her world paradigm was shifting. Without her anger to use as a shield against the world, she was lost.

She was simply a woman who needed her man to hold her bruised heart.

So that's what he did. All through the afternoon and the night. He tucked her close to his heart and let her know, without words, that she could trust him. That she was his.

Sometimes, words weren't necessary at all.

Eight

The next day, Selene walked around in sort of a daze.

She didn't see much of her father, but Zan was there, hovering all the time. She thought it was sweet, but really he needed to train, to do whatever he and his Pack did when they weren't fussing over and fucking their mates.

Not that the fucking part wasn't fun. She and Zan had done plenty of that when they'd woken up this morning, eager to explore each other's bodies. Again. They'd been so enthusiastic, they'd chipped the wall because the headboard had been banging against it so hard. The memory made her smile.

She spent the rest of the day fending off her mate's roaming hands. Horny wolf.

That night, however, was the party with the other women. Selene couldn't contain her nerves.

She'd never had a gaggle of girlfriends, hadn't been invited to many birthdays or slumber parties. After her mother's murder and her father's subsequent abandonment, she'd become even more unreachable emotionally, and eventually the invitations had ceased altogether.

The emotional distance she put between herself and others that made her perfect for a job as one of her uncle's enforcers also made her a social misfit in every other respect.

As she peered at herself in the bathroom mirror, a pair of manly hands clasped her shoulders. "Relax. You're going to be fine."

"Easy for you to say. You're not the wolf from the wrong side of the tracks being scrutinized by the PTA committee."

He laughed. "I promise they're not as bad as a bunch of soccer moms. Not even close. Go with an open mind and you might even be surprised."

"I'll be surprised if I'm surprised. Does that even make sense?"

"Yes." He spun her around and gave her a smoldering kiss. "Now, go and have a good time. Don't threaten to kill anyone and you'll be gold."

She scowled at him. "That's not funny."

"Then you need to work on your sense of humor. Go."

Rolling her eyes, she swept past him and through their quarters, out the door. In the hallway, she huffed, realizing she'd just thought of his apartment as *theirs*. That was an interesting mental tell. Was she accepting her mating to the gorgeous black wolf? It seemed so.

And I do too have a sense of humor!

His gentle laugh sounded in her mind, and she couldn't help but smile. Zan had a way of making people feel *good*. Anyone could see that, and she was slowly coming to realize how lucky she was that the man was hers.

She pondered that on the way to Kira and Jax's quarters a few doors down. But with a shield over her thoughts. Wouldn't do for her mate to get too big of a head.

At Kira's door, she knocked and waited to be let in, and was surprised by the friendly greeting she received. Kira, Mac, Rowan, Melina, and Daria were sitting around sipping red and white wine—except for Mac, who held a glass of milk. Mac was sitting on the comfy-looking sofa, round belly sticking out so that it appeared she'd swallowed a basketball. With her free hand, she scratched the mound and then rested her palm on top of it.

"Damn," Mac muttered, then panted a few breaths. Everyone paused.

Rowan started to rise. "What's wrong?"

But Mac waved her down. "Nothing. Just been having a few contractions today. I'm fine."

"If you're sure . . ." But the other woman didn't seem convinced.

"Jeez, stop worrying! You guys are all like a bunch of mother hens."

"Can I get you something?" Kira asked, returning her attention to Selene.

"White, please?" She didn't drink a lot of wine, but she didn't see beer in evidence. When in Rome and all that.

In seconds she had a glass in her hand and was perched on a chair, part of the circle of friends. Sort of.

Daria must've sensed her discomfort, because she leaned over and spoke quietly in her ear. "I was the newest one before you, not too long ago. So I know how you feel." She patted Selene's knee. "But really, it'll be all right. These are good people, but it's a strange world, for sure."

"I come from a stranger one; trust me."

"Really? Would you mind telling me about your pack?"

Pleased that the other woman took an interest, she described her clan as she had to her mate. Daria and a couple of the other women were listening, nodding and asking intelligent questions about how their society was run. That made her feel good, too. Like she wasn't such an outsider.

"At least you were already a wolf," Daria said. "Try being human and getting thrust into the paranormal world. Talk about culture shock!"

Kira agreed. "Same for me. I had no clue shifters, vampires, and a whole list of other paranormal creatures were real until I was thrown into the middle of a dangerous situation and my very own wolf came to my rescue."

"I didn't know about all that stuff, either," Rowan put in. "I was looking for my brother, Micah, and found this place. When I saw a bunch of wolves surround me and then turn into naked men, I literally fainted!"

Everyone laughed at that, and Selene found herself truly relaxing for the first time. She was fascinated by each woman's tale as she told the story of how she met the Pack and her mate and the dangers they battled. But what didn't escape her notice was that in each of the stories, her father played a prominent role as a strong hero.

She didn't think they were pumping Nick up on purpose. Everything they said sounded sincere. The battles her father had faced, the dangers, the way he'd protected his men time and again . . . The man sounded larger than life.

Brave. Caring. Too good to be true.

What was the truth? Who was the real Nick Westfall?

"Oh!" Mac's startled exclamation put everyone on alert.

Melina touched her arm. "What is it?"

"I don't—oh!" This time she wrapped an arm around her abdomen and grimaced in apparent pain. "I think my water just broke!"

Indeed her maternity pants and the sofa underneath had a spreading stain. Melina rose, calmly giving orders.

"Someone call Noah, tell him to bring a wheelchair."

"I'll do it," Rowan volunteered, then yanked out her cell phone.

"And someone call Kalen," Melina continued. "He and most of the men are in the rec room playing poker tonight."

"On it." Kira took the phone Melina handed her and called Kalen while Melina grilled the other woman, making note of all of her symptoms.

The doctor nodded, her face transforming with a wide smile. "Sounds like we're having a baby soon!" This drew excited exclamations from around the room, along with congratulations and encouraging words about how she and the baby were going to be fine.

Selene sure hoped so. She was starting to like these women, and Mac was so sweet. Kalen seemed like the perfect mate for her, and Selene had no doubt their baby would be as beautiful as the couple.

In less than five minutes, there was a knock at the door. Noah hurried in with the wheelchair, and they quickly got her situated. Then he wheeled her out, moving briskly but not too fast. The other women were chattering, trailing behind, and Selene accompanied them, caught up in the magic of an impending birth. From what she understood, this would be the compound's first child. Sounded like the baby would be spoiled, too.

Kalen rounded a corner, followed by his friends, wide-eyed and looking frantic. "Sweetheart! Are you all right?"

"I'm fine," she panted. But her voice was small, a little afraid. "I can't believe it's actually happening."

"I'm here, okay?" Taking her hand, he walked beside her chair, murmuring soothing words to his mate.

In the infirmary, Mac and Kalen were whisked back to a room while everyone else had to remain in the waiting area. Zan found Selene and gave her a smile and then a kiss in front of everyone, which pleased her enormously. It further cemented that she was becoming part of something here. It was hard not to like these people.

"Did you have a good time with the ladies?" he asked.

"I did. They made me feel really welcome."

"I told you." He looked pleased about this.

"Yes, and you were right. It's not that I doubted you, but . . ." She shrugged. "If the situation were reversed and a hostile female barged into clan territory gunning for my uncle, she wouldn't survive the first five minutes. Much less be invited for cocktails."

"Ah, but they're sneaky. Did you check to be

sure your drink wasn't laced with something nasty? Kidding," he said with a laugh when she made a face at him.

She liked that he could joke with her. It made her feel good inside, at peace in a way she hadn't been in a long, long time.

That feeling lasted until Nick arrived and stood with them to wait on word. As the other team members began to arrive, she took the opportunity to study him.

The first thing she noted was that when he interacted with people, he was nothing like her uncle Damien. Nick was very much their commander, but they were comfortable around him. He was one of them, and they respected him. Damien, however, would've been standing on the fringes of the group, holding himself aloof with that stern expression of his.

Nick talked to his men, and they listened. And he listened to them as well. His face showed that he was genuinely interested in what they had to say. His eyes were warm.

And even her uncle always said the eyes never lied.

She was beyond confused as to what to believe. Yesterday, that rogue in the cell had been going after her father, and she knew in her heart he would have died to protect Zan and Jax. At every turn, it seemed she'd been wrong about him.

As luck would have it, he turned his head and

made eye contact with her. She tried a smile. It felt strange on her face, to show him any sort of tolerance. He appeared surprised and made his way over to her and Zan.

"How is your bite wound?" she asked.

"Already healed, thanks."

"I'm glad."

He appeared as surprised by that as she did, and he cleared his throat. "Exciting news about the baby, isn't it?" he said a bit awkwardly.

Seeing him look so unexpectedly vulnerable caught at her heart. "Yes, it sure is. I was there when she went into labor."

"I've never seen Kalen move so fast," said Ryon. "He dropped all his cards and upended the poker table when he got the call."

"And I was winning for a change too," Zan said, making a good-natured face. "Damn."

Selene chuckled. "That's what you get for gambling."

"Hey, we were only playing for quarters. I save the real gambling for Vegas."

"You go there often?" she asked.

Ryon laughed. "Only to pick up women." That immediately earned him a smack on the back of the head from his mate as his friends laughed. "Ow!"

"*Used* to pick up women!"

"Of course, baby! Used to." He leaned in and kissed her thoroughly.

Selene gave Zan a pointed look, and he raised his hands. "Don't look at me. My carousing days were over before I met you."

Aric coughed loudly, and it sounded a lot like *bullshit*. Zan sent him a sour look that promised retribution, but the redhead just smirked.

Spirits remained high, especially when Kalen came out to update them. "Looks like it's going to be soon! I just wanted you guys to know."

That drew some smiles as he rushed back inside. People took seats in the chairs, or simply sat cross-legged on the floor. When Melina at last emerged from the back, dressed in scrubs, she was wearing a wide smile.

"Mom and baby Kai are doing just great." A cheer met this announcement, and she waited for the celebrating to die down before she continued. "Mac is worn-out, and she and Kalen need time to bond with their son. So, no visitors until tomorrow, but Kalen said he'd text everyone pictures."

This seemed to satisfy the group, and one by one, people began to say good-bye and drift away. Nick lingered, and Selene struggled with what to say. Finally, she settled for looking him in the eye and keeping it simple.

"Good night." *Daddy*. She always used to call him *Daddy*, but her throat closed on the word. She couldn't do it yet. Perhaps never again.

Nick cleared his throat. "Good night." As she

left, she could have sworn she heard him whisper, *baby girl*.

Back in their quarters, Zan held her in his arms as they snuggled in bed. Long into the night, she remained awake, thinking about the events of the evening.

Despite herself, she had started to form a very real bond with the good people at the compound. It felt . . . right. And she found herself wanting to hold on to what she'd found. To let nothing ruin this fledgling peace and warmth.

She drifted to sleep, thinking joyous thoughts of friends, babies, and mates.

And fathers who really loved their children and would never dream of leaving them.

Nick sat behind his desk the next morning, elbows on the top, hands buried in his hair. He glared at the computer screen and read the message again, a slight variation on the first one.

> I'm coming for you. I'm going to make you suffer because I want to and because I'll enjoy it. You will pay for interfering with me, and you'll wish you were dead.

Not very original, but certainly attention-grabbing. Especially since it appeared the asshole wasn't going anywhere anytime soon. He'd dug in and was making it plain he had an agenda—killing Nick. *Fantastic. You'll have to stand in line, fucker.*

Behind his own daughter, no less. Though she didn't seem quite as quick to go off on him as she had when she'd first arrived. Didn't mean she wouldn't kill him given half a chance, but . . .

Last night, she'd seemed different. A bit softer, though she'd hate being called that. There had been something in her eyes when she'd looked at him besides blind hate, and it gave him hope. Without hope, he had nothing. Because he wouldn't be able to stand having his daughter returned to his life and then have her snatched away again.

His daughter wasn't his only problem, either. He'd been on the phone all morning, dealing with the proverbial shit that hit the fan, and he had to call a meeting with the Pack, pronto.

Getting on the intercom, he paged the team to the conference room and then sent a group text just to be sure they'd all get the message. Then he walked down there to gather his thoughts and wait for their arrival. They started filing in right away, and within fifteen minutes, they were all assembled, even Kalen.

He addressed the Sorcerer. "You don't have to be here. In fact, we have to go wheels up, but you're on leave with your mate and new baby. That's an order."

"Understood, sir. But I do want to hear the briefing so I'll know what's going on, if that's okay."

"That's fine." As the group quieted, he got right to the point. "You're all here for two reasons. The first item of business is we've had another rogue attack. This one is bad, so be prepared for what you'll see when we arrive. It happened last night at a private residence outside of Branson, Missouri. There was some sort of family reunion going on, and the rogues killed more than twenty innocent people."

"Jesus Christ," Zan said, appalled. "No survivors?"

"I'm told there was a young man of nineteen who survived by crawling under the porch steps to hide after he was attacked. The Feds suspect he saw everything because he's in shock. Hasn't spoken a word since. As if there isn't enough bad news, the boy was turned vampire."

He let the team's exclamations over that die down before he went on.

"So, we're going there to see what, if anything, we can find at the scene. Then we're taking the young man to the coven of Prince Tarron Romanoff, where we're scheduled to have a meeting with him and his top soldiers about the rogues and how to stop them. Any questions?"

"When do we leave?" Jax asked.

He looked at his watch. "One hour. We'll take the Hueys since I'm told there's a place to land near the house. I'd like to wrap up at the murder scene and be en route to the prince's stronghold in the Smoky Mountains by early this afternoon."

"Will we be able to land the copters at the stronghold?" Aric asked. He was one of the pilots and needed to know.

"No, it's too rocky. We'll put down a few miles out, and then the prince will have an escort drive us the rest of the way. Any more questions?"

Nobody voiced any, so Nick let them go to take care of any last-minute business. No doubt a few of them would use that hour to spend with their mates, then return rumpled and happy.

What he wouldn't give to have someone to fill that void in his soul. To care whether he came home or not.

But then again, fate had blessed him with Tonia, and he'd killed her. He'd blown his one chance at happiness. The image of the mystery woman from his vision flitted through his head. But there was nothing solid to grasp on to there. He would have to focus on what he did have.

It was the only way to get through tomorrow. And all the days after.

"Oh my God! Isn't Kai cute?" Kira gushed, holding up her cell phone. Immediately, cell phones were whipped out and more *ooh*s and *ahh*s followed.

Selene was sitting with Kira at breakfast in the dining room, where she'd been since Zan dropped her off on his way to the team meeting. Something was up, and she was afraid it meant he'd be sent into danger. She had to deal with that reality sooner or later, but she'd rather it be later.

Thankfully, fawning over pictures of the new baby had everyone suitably distracted. At least until her mate and several others came in to find their women. She knew her fears were confirmed when Zan and Jax headed straight toward them, expressions grim.

"What's wrong?" Kira asked, putting down her cell phone. Her mate gave her a kiss.

"We have to leave in an hour. There's been another rogue attack, this one outside Branson, Missouri."

Zan sighed, then bent to give Selene a hug. "They slaughtered an entire family at a reunion, and there was only one survivor. A nineteen-year-old boy, and he was turned vampire during the attack."

"That's awful," Kira said, shuddering.

Zan sat beside his mate, but made no move to grab breakfast. "More than awful. This is getting really bad. Nick has set up a meeting with Romanoff, the vampire prince of North America, so we'll head there as soon as we're done at the crime scene."

"What will become of the boy?" Selene asked in concern.

Zan answered. "We're taking him to the prince. He'll help the kid adjust to his new life, with any luck."

"That's something, at least," Selene said.

Zan looked at his mate, a small smile curving his lips. "On a lighter note, we have an hour before we leave. I'm thinking it would be a terrible thing to send your mate off all stressed and everything."

"Same here." Jax gave Kira a brilliant smile. "Got stress. Lots and lots of stress."

"Good grief." She rolled her eyes, but stood and took his hand. "Come on, big guy. Let's go do something about your blood pressure."

The couple headed out together, and Zan gave her a cute pout. "What about me?"

"I think I can help you out there, mate," she murmured, leaning in to kiss his sexy lips.

"Did I mention that you're the best mate in the world?"

"Glad you think so, since I'm the only one you're getting."

"You're the only one I want or need."

The heavy-lidded desire in his eyes was her undoing. One important thing she'd discovered was that besides him being a good man, he was a skilled lover. He never failed to fulfill her every pleasure. She couldn't wait to make love with him again.

He pulled her to her feet. "I believe we have a date, baby."

When they returned to their apartment, Zan paused only long enough to close and lock the door, then hurried through the living room, pulling her along behind him.

In his bedroom, he urged her gently onto his king-sized bed, then straightened. Quickly, he took off his shirt and slid off his jeans, kicking them aside. Selene drank in the sight of his naked body like a flower dying of thirst. Clothed, he was the sexiest man she'd ever seen. Wearing nothing except a grin, the man was perfection.

She studied the soft brown eyes set in his handsome, angular face. Thick hair the color of the night sky framing his wonderful face, brushing his neck. She let her gaze drift leisurely to his broad shoulders and strong arms and the wolf tattoo on his chest.

He wasn't ripped, but perfectly formed of lean muscle and raw bone. Graceful as a jungle cat. A very light sprinkling of hair covered his chest, trailing downward past flat, hard male nipples. Finally, she allowed her attention to roam to his impressive erection, savoring the sight. Heat flamed low in her belly, between her legs. His engorged penis jutted proudly from a nest of dark curls, arching toward his washboard stomach.

"Like what you see?" His smile told her he knew the answer.

"I always do. I want to touch you."

His eyes went dark, feral. "Please."

Hands shaking with desire, Selene shed her clothes.

He climbed onto the bed to sit next to her. "God, you're beautiful."

"Thank you." Selene's face heated. She couldn't help it, despite the fact that wolves weren't typically shy about their bodies. Selene reached out to touch the broad head of his penis, swirling it with one finger as a drop of pre-cum beaded the tip. Encouraged by his moan of pleasure, she wrapped her hand around his cock and began to stroke.

"*Yes.*" He leaned back and closed his eyes, spread his long legs.

She pumped him slowly, enjoying the texture of silky, baby-soft skin over his rod. Next, she moved her hand to cradle his balls, enjoying the feel of his heavy sex. Marveling that such a powerful man could be reduced to jelly with a caress.

"Baby," he gasped, removing her hand. "I'm not going to last. But I promise I'll make it up to you next time."

Zan lowered her onto the pillows and stretched his big body over hers, settling between her legs. His erection pulsed against her belly as he captured her lips in a sizzling kiss, tongue licking into the seam of her mouth. Teasing, tasting.

He broke the kiss, moved lower, repeating his attentions on her breasts. "You're so perfect."

His teeth grazed one nipple, tongue doing wonderful things to the hardened little pebble. Sending delightful shocks to every nerve ending. When he suckled the other nipple, she came undone, pulling at his shoulders.

"My mate, I need you inside me."

Moving up to cover Selene, his gaze locked with hers. The raw, male heat, the *possessiveness*, on his face made her quiver in anticipation.

He slid a hand between her thighs, fingers brushing the pale curls there. Pushing one finger inside, he stroked in and out, spreading the dewy wetness to prepare her. Lengthening the strokes, he rubbed her clit, setting her on fire.

"Zan, please!"

He pushed in by inches, letting her adjust to him. He was always so gentle, and it brought a rush of tears to her eyes. The slight discomfort became a flame burning brighter. Pleasure unfurled, a joy she'd never known with anyone but her mate. She wrapped her arms around him, skimming her hands over the muscles in his back as he seated himself as deeply as possible.

"Feel me?" he whispered into her hair.

"Yes."

He began to move, slow, tantalizing strokes. "You're *mine*."

"Oh, Zan, yes!"

He held her against his chest, made sweet, beautiful love to her. Sheltered in the safety of his arms, his body covering her like a warm blanket, she'd come home. This wasn't just sex with a handsome man.

This was so much more. She wanted to put a name to it, but didn't dare.

His tempo quickened, his thrusts filling her

harder. Deeper. Faster. But even as he drove into her, taking them to the edge, he was careful not to hurt her, while entering her with powerful strokes. Hurtling them higher, higher—

His release erupted, his big body shaking. She followed, the orgasm shattering her control, the waves pounding her senses. He shuddered again and again, until he lowered his forehead to hers, spent and breathing hard.

She lay unmoving, loving his weight on top of her, his musky, male scent teasing her nose. Loving . . . *him*.

Did she love him?

Selene wanted to say the words freely and longed to hear them returned. But she couldn't. Not yet. Their mating was new, and she had to be sure. She didn't know how to express what she was feeling, much less process it.

You're mine.

Those words had come from the depths of his soul, and she cherished them.

For now, it was enough.

Nine

Zan *hated* leaving his mate.

The pang of separation was much more difficult than he'd imagined it would be. He noted that the other mated Pack brothers weren't faring much better as they said good-bye in the huge hangar, holding on to their better halves.

It might have been petty of him, but he took heart that Selene didn't seem any happier at his leaving than he was to go. That had to mean she was attached to him, liked him at least a little. He longed to tell her how he felt about her—that he was falling hard, and it had nothing to do with wolf biology.

He admired her strength and courage. Her conviction. And her fairness. He admired her ability to put aside her vendetta against Nick and take a second look. That meant she was interested in justice, not vengeance.

And she had a soft spot for babies and for wanting to be accepted by her peers. She loved to make love and held nothing back.

Whether she believed it or not, there was a hell of a lot to love about Selene.

But he wouldn't tell her. Not yet, when it might scare her away.

"Be careful," she said, her voice shaking a bit. "Come back safe."

"I'll do my best." He tucked a finger under her chin and gave her a slow kiss, with tongue. And kept right on kissing until someone cleared his throat nearby, signaling for him to wrap it up.

"Newly mated guys," Aric drawled. "Sheesh."

"Like you can talk," Zan retorted. "Besides, your mate is on the team, so she gets to go with you. How unfair is that?"

"Very. She can kick anyone's ass from here to the East Coast, including mine."

The man had a point. Zan hurried along his good-byes, and then he was forced to let her go and walk away. They loaded onto three copters and then waited while the top of the building slid open to let them lift off.

Aric powered up their Huey, with hired pilots taking the others, as usual. The redhead could fly anything with wings, and he flatly refused to let anyone else pilot his craft. Nick took the front with him.

Zan rode with Jax, Micah, and Nix in the back.

The big copter was a flying tank, really loud, but the ride was uneventful as they streaked toward Missouri.

For Zan, lost in his thoughts, the trip seemed to pass quickly, and soon they were landing in a field not far from the house where the murders occurred. From there they were escorted to the scene by federal agents, and Zan recognized some of them from the ranch killing. This time, they received no lip from the Feds, though they got plenty of sour looks.

Horror couldn't begin to describe the scene at the house. The carnage was unlike anything Zan had ever laid eyes on in his life, and that was saying a lot. Part of the horror factor was the cheerful backdrop of the family gathering that had been interrupted.

There were checkered tables laden with food. Burgers, dogs, brisket, potato salad, chips and dips, beer. All going bad in the morning sun, providing a macabre accompaniment to the main course.

Bodies were literally everywhere. Young and old and in between. Lying by the picnic tables, under the festive canopy among folding chairs. One older man was sprawled across the threshold of the front door, another on the porch.

"There's more inside," an agent said, looking like he might lose his coffee any second. "This beats fuck-all I've ever seen."

"I've seen something similar, back in oh-four," another one put in. "Seven people all murdered in their beds, all drained of blood like these folks."

"Where was that?" Nick asked, looking at him sharply.

"Let me think. Tulsa, Oklahoma, that's where it was. Never caught those bastards, either. Could be the same ones, though ten years is a long spread of time."

Not to a vampire, Zan thought. But he wisely kept that tidbit to himself.

The team spread out and catalogued the bodies, making note of every detail, no matter how insignificant it appeared. The most telling evidence of a rogue attack was the raggedness of the teeth marks on each neck. Rogues were vicious and messy when they fed. They were simply hungry, all the time, and showed none of the neatness and precision of a typical vampire feed.

Another sign was that none of the bodies showed evidence of sexual activity, unlike a regular vampire feed. These killings were swift and all business. Almost like a mission.

"This would have taken a large force of rogues to carry out," Zan mused aloud. Only Nick and a few of their team were nearby, so it was okay to speak freely.

"Is it just me, or does this have the hallmarks of a well-executed op?" Nick asked.

Zan nodded. "That's what I was just thinking."

They finished the search and were just about to give up on finding anything really useful when Zan spotted a crimson drag mark on the back porch. Dried rust-colored blood trailed across the boards, down the set of wooden steps. He followed the trail across the lawn, and the more distance that was put between him and the house, the thinner and sparser the blood was. It was just enough to keep him going, though, and he was determined to locate the source.

He followed a slope down to a creek and across it. Then he looked up to see the trail had led him to an old wood pile that might have been a storage shed at one time. He skirted the pile.

And it was there that the rogue was waiting, beside a human body. Zan barely had time to register his presence before the thing sprang at him, yellowish fangs bared and ready to kill. There was no time to call forth his wolf, so he morphed his hands into claws and launched a counterattack.

They met in a clash of bodies, Zan gaining a slight advantage when he knocked the creature to the ground. He jumped onto the rogue, made a stab at its black heart and missed, sending his claws between the ribs and into a lung. The thing screeched, and he cursed, hoping the Feds at the house hadn't heard.

The rogue did some slashing too, catching Zan across a thigh. It stung like a bitch but wasn't life-threatening, and he raked his claws across the creature's throat, severing its windpipe. While it was busy frantically grabbing at its throat, Zan delivered the killing blow to the heart, stilling his enemy instantly. It died, eyes going blank, and he plunged in his claws and tore out the shriveled heart, then sagged in relief.

"What the fuck *are* you guys?" a voice blurted from behind him. "What was *that* thing?"

Fuck! Turning, he allowed his hands to shift back to normal, but not soon enough. This Fed, the one who'd mentioned the bodies in Tulsa a decade ago, was staring at him in complete shock. Nervously, he shifted his gaze from Zan to the vampire's body, to the vampire's kill, and back to Zan.

Zan sighed, wiped his hands in the grass, and stood. "I'm the guy who exterminates creeps like this one. Just think of me as the Orkin man."

The Fed failed to see the humor. Imagine that.

"You—you tore out his heart."

"Only way to keep them from rising again."

"Rising again?"

His face was white.

"That was a rogue vampire," Zan informed him. The horse was out of the barn anyway. "Some vamps are good, and some have gone bad. That one was bad. And there are a lot more of them where he came from, FYI."

"What are you?"

Zan let his muzzle elongate, showed his fangs.

The claws on his hands. Let them stay just long enough to convince the man he wasn't having a nightmare.

"Holy shit!"

"I'm a wolf shifter, and my team is like me. This is what we do—we rid the world of paranormal bad guys before the general populace has any clue stuff like this really exists. But secrecy is getting harder to maintain, as you can attest."

"What do we do now?" The man was regaining some of his composure, the agent in him returning to the fore to give him some stability.

"I go about my business with my team. You keep your mouth shut about your newfound reality. If you can do this, we might have an alliance at some point that's mutually beneficial to both of our employers."

Now he had the guy. He was all agent again, thinking on his feet. Assessing. "That could work. Okay. I'll keep my mouth shut. May need to call on you guys sometime. My name is Kyle Garrett." Fishing in his wallet, he gave Zan his card. "That's got my cell phone on it."

"I'm Zander Cole. I don't have a card, but here's my cell number." He recited that while Garrett punched the contact into his phone.

As they finished up, Nick and Jax waded through the creek and came jogging over to them. As soon as Nick took in what was going on, he cursed.

"This is Agent Kyle Garrett, boss. He's in the know."

"Goddammit." He pinned Garrett with a steely look. "You breathe a word about this to anyone—"

"I won't. You have my word."

"Good. Let's get this shit cleaned up." His gaze rested on the poor human's body, and he cursed again.

The cleanup took longer than expected, so it was well after noon before they were ready to go. As the Feds prepared to take them back to the copters, Zan posed a question to Nick.

"Why did that rogue stay behind? What was his goal?"

"You're assuming he had one. But yeah, that was odd."

"Was he left behind to watch us from back there? And he was just stupid enough to leave the blood trail?"

Nick blew out a breath. "I don't know. Seems more likely he wanted to lure someone else back there. Maybe he was working on his own, maybe not."

There was nothing else to be gleaned from the scene. At the copters, another car arrived bearing a young man. He was dressed in jeans and a hoodie pulled up over his head, sunglasses on his face. To protect his skin and eyes from the sun, now that he was a new vampire. Poor kid.

The boy ended up riding with Zan and his

group. Zan tried to engage him some, but between the noise and the young man's trauma, it was a lost cause. He hoped the vampires would be able to help the kid start over.

What would it be like to be nineteen for eternity? What a strange thought.

The boy settled in and dozed, so Zan did the same. His thigh throbbed from time to time, but other than making a mess on the leg of his jeans, it looked worse than it really was. He could have it tended to at Prince Tarron's stronghold.

He awoke fully when he felt the descent. They came in for a landing, putting down in a decent flat area close to the mountains. The sun was starting to dip in the sky, and the scenery was stunning. It wasn't unlike where the Pack lived, but the prince and his coven lived *in* the mountains, not at the base of them, from what he understood.

The copters powered down and everyone got out, stretching. Zan was already tired and hoped they'd hold off on the meeting until tomorrow, but vamps were night creatures, so he didn't count on it.

Within minutes, two stretch limousines appeared around the bend and drove up, rolling to a stop.

Aric whistled. "Now, that's what *I'm* fuckin' talkin' about! Why can't we have limos instead of SUVs?"

"Um, because we don't *want* to attract attention wherever we go?" Nick said, lips quirking.

"Oh. There is that."

Their banter was interrupted when a tall, impressive figure emerged from the first limo. If Zan had been expecting a dark cape, he would've been disappointed. The man he assumed could only be Prince Tarron Romanoff was dressed in a stylish dark suit and light blue shirt with a tie. His dark brown hair was touching his collar, all one length and tucked behind one ear. He had a youthful but handsome face and vivid eyes Zan could only describe as purple.

The guy looked like a movie star or a model. He was also wearing a wide smile, and his expression reflected genuine welcome. He strode forward to shake Nick's hand.

"Nick Westfall? Tarron Romanoff. It's a pleasure to meet you in person."

"Likewise." Nick smiled. "I've heard lots of good things about you from our mutual friend."

Zan figured the *mutual friend* was Jarrod Grant.

"Thank you. He speaks highly of you as well. Shall we get going? I know you all must be tired and hungry. We'll eat and then let your men rest tonight. There's time enough for the meeting tomorrow."

"That sounds just fine, thank you."

Thank God!

The team split up, and both limos were more

than enough to accommodate them all. Nick and the prince rode in the first limo, along with the newly turned young vampire, Aric, Rowan, and Hammer. Zan rode in the second car with Ryon, Jax, Nix, and Micah. Each car also carried several of the prince's soldiers, who were not dressed in a military style at all, but in black jeans and long-sleeved shirts and wearing cool shades. Zan thought they looked like bouncers at a club, but refrained from saying so.

The interior of the limo was plush, the ride smooth, even on these roads. Soft music played through the speakers, making Zan sleepy all over again. He was about worn-out for the day, and he was getting a slight headache to match the pain in his thigh.

He was sitting with his head resting against the glass, eyes half-closed, when he saw something that had him sitting upright, suddenly wide-awake. He squinted, trying to see better—

And spotted the fading sunlight reflect off a long, green barrel that was poking through the underbrush. Shit!

"Stop the cars!" he shouted, scaring everyone awake. "Ambush ahead! Stop—"

A stream of smoke erupted from the brush, and there was a loud boom that shook the car they were riding in. *Rocket launcher!* From the side window, Zan watched in horror as the lead car skidded, flipped sideways, and rolled over into a gulley. His own limo skidded to a halt, and the team poured out the doors.

Straight into an assault by at least thirty rogues. Maybe more.

The fight was on, and there was no time to check on his Pack brothers in the first car. He could only hope they were all right as he engaged the first rogue, sliced its throat and stabbed it in the heart, and then fought the next one. And the next.

Exhaustion crept in, but he couldn't stop. Finally, he spotted Nick and the others from the first car joining the fray. That was a relief, though he couldn't spot the boy. Then Nick went down and didn't get up. That moment of distraction almost cost Zan his head. But at the last moment, he whirled and deflected the killing blow and dispatched the attacker.

His arms were tiring, his head throbbing. But he couldn't quit. At one point he was amazed to see that the young man had acquired a long blade from somewhere and was cutting a swath through the rogues like he'd been doing it all his life. Zan figured the kid owed the bastards for killing his family. Maybe he had found a new calling.

Slash, stab, yank out the heart. He shut out fatigue and emotion. Kept going until he and his teammates, and the boy, along with the prince's soldiers, were standing alone on the blood-soaked battlefield, amid their defeated enemy.

Defeated for now.

Jesus, he hurt all over. He was tired and ravenous. Whatever the prince was serving, he was going to eat until he exploded.

Suddenly, a shout chased away thoughts of dinner. He looked around and spotted Rowan crouched over a prone body—Nick! Running, leaping over bodies, Zan made his way to his boss's side and dropped to his knees.

"He and the prince are hurt," Rowan told him. She met Zan's gaze, the knowledge there painful. "I know Melina and Mac told you not to use your healing again, but Tarron's wound is bad."

"I'm not letting either one of them die," Zan said grimly, "so don't try to stop me."

Nobody could argue with that, no matter how badly they didn't want Zan hurt by using his gift. And nobody tried to talk him out of it, though he knew they wanted to. As Zan assessed the two men, he noted that the boy was watching intently. Taking it all in. He supposed the period of shock had given way to a survival instinct. That would hold the boy in good stead for a long time.

"What's your name?" he asked as he placed his hands on Tarron's chest.

"Daegan."

"Watch and learn, Daegan. They're our leaders, and that's exactly why that limo was targeted. Even if the battle is won, if the leader falls, the war can be lost. It's the soldier's job to protect him, no matter the personal price."

"Yes, sir."

Centering himself, he tried not to think about what might happen to his brain. About the doctors' warnings coming true. This was his calling, what he was born to do.

"Stab wound to the gut," he told the group. "Got a bunch of the intestines. Fatal without intervention because he's losing blood faster than his vampire healing can handle. Here I go."

The wound was a raging bitch to repair. Slowly, he knitted together the ripped tissue, reconnected thousands of tiny veins. Pumped up the blood supply to the prince's organs. Halfway through, his head began to ache. Throb. Three quarters of the way, he was struggling not to pass out from the pain as the tiny eruptions began to take place deep in his brain.

"Almost there," he whispered. "Just a little more."

Then he was done. He was almost blind from the pain as he pushed from Tarron's healing body to Nick's nearby. The commander was sitting up, protesting any help.

"No," he told Zan. "I can see you're in a lot of pain. I'll be fine."

Ignoring him, Zan laid a hand on his chest. Assessed. "Femoral artery tear. If you weren't a shifter, you'd be dead by now. Let me work."

He started again, struggling with every second, with every cell he coaxed back together, even though the job wasn't as tedious as Tarron's healing. When he was finished, he swayed on his knees, then collapsed.

Something warm gushed from his nose. He tried to wipe it, but couldn't move his arm. Jax's face appeared over his, worried. Zan couldn't make out what he was saying.

Then the world gradually vanished and the pain with it.

Selene was playing a game on the Wii with Blue when the call came in.

She wasn't the one who answered. Suddenly Melina was striding into the room, and when Selene glanced at her, she immediately knew something was wrong.

"What's happened?" She pushed to her feet, leaving the game. Blue joined her.

"We have to leave right away for Prince Tarron's stronghold."

"Why?" she asked in growing alarm. "What's going on?"

"The team was ambushed tonight by a large group of rogue vampires. They were traveling to the stronghold with the prince and his men in two cars when the attack happened. Zan had to heal your father or he was going to die. The prince as well."

Selene felt the blood drain from her face. "Is Zan okay? Of course he's not, or you wouldn't be here."

"I'm going to be honest. His brain is rupturing from the stress of healing again too soon, and the prince's doctor can't get him stabilized. They think your being there will help him, considering your bond."

"What are we waiting for?" she cried. "Let's go!"

"Good. We can send for some things later."

"How are we getting there? Will we take a helicopter, too?"

"No time, and there's an easier way." Just then, Noah joined her, followed by Kalen, Mac, and the new baby. "We're all going, including Kalen. And Mac and the baby aren't going to be left here virtually all alone in this big place."

She was about to repeat her question about how they were getting there when three males in black jeans and black long-sleeved shirts suddenly appeared in the game room out of thin air. Selene jumped with fright and scrambled back.

"It's all right," Melina reassured her. "These vampires are some of the prince's soldiers. Vampires can teleport, so they're going to take us directly to the stronghold."

"Okay." She hoped she didn't get sick. Teleporting sounded scary as hell, though she'd never done it.

There wasn't much time to worry. The three vampires spread out, instructing them to link arms. Told them to close their eyes.

And in a flash, she felt as though she were hurtling through space. Rushing along like she was seated in a fighter jet—with the top down.

As quickly as she made that comparison, the trip was over. They were on stable ground again. Or rather, a floor. Opening her eyes, she gaped at her surroundings. They were standing in a huge foyer fashioned out of the mouth of a cave. The space was every bit as richly appointed as a palace, and that's in fact what it was. A massive stone fortress carved right into the side of a mountain. She couldn't imagine any enemy strong enough to penetrate it.

"The prince will see you momentarily," one of the soldiers informed her. "Wait here."

Then they were gone. But in the next instant, she spotted her father and a tall, stunning man hurrying toward them. Her father's face was drawn, worried, and the other man's was too.

"I'm Tarron Romanoff," the prince said, confirming his identity. "Your mate saved our lives, your father's and my own. He's a very brave and honorable man."

She resisted the urge to demand he take her to see Zan right the hell now. "Thank you. I think the same of him." She hung on to her composure. "Please, how is he?"

"Not well, I'm afraid. His brain has been pushed to the limits of his endurance, and the bleeding continues. He's unconscious."

"How can I help? I'll do anything." She meant that.

"Our doctor and our team of nurses believe strongly in the power of the mate bond. Especially in cases where one mate is straddling the line between life and death. The mate bond can sway the other partner toward life and healing."

Tears filled her eyes. "I'll do whatever it takes to get him well. May I see him now?"

"Of course. Come along and we'll get you settled with him." To the others, he said, "I'll have rooms prepared for all of you. I'd like to extend an invitation to your medical staff to work in our infirmary while the Alpha Pack remains our guests and we battle this rogue problem. We know so little about shifter medicine; your presence would be a great help."

"Nurse Brooks and I accept, thank you," Melina said. "Dr. Grant is on maternity leave."

The prince graced the baby with a warm smile. "I see that. I'll make sure the baby and his parents have the best accommodations available."

He spun and walked away. The group followed, entering a whole new world.

But all Selene could focus on was making sure her brave Healer was healed himself.

Ten

Selene followed the prince through the maze of tunnels, thinking that if an enemy did somehow manage to enter this place, he'd need a map and a tour guide to find his way out.

When they finally reached the infirmary, she was gratified to see Zan's friends all gathered, waiting on word. She knew they were scared, but not as scared as she was. This was her mate in danger.

Spotting a doctor coming through some double doors toward her, she hurried to him.

"Please, I'm here to see Zander Cole. How is he?" she asked in a tremulous voice. The handsome doctor swung his steady gaze around and scrutinized her, his face softening in sympathy. Selene felt her heart lurch as he came to stand before her.

"Are you Selene Westfall?"

"Zan's mate, yes," she said. A shuffle of feet came from behind her, and she knew his team was listening. They wanted news just as badly. When the doctor spoke, he addressed her kindly, unruffled by the horde of shifters pressing close to listen.

"I'm Dr. Archer. Let's take a seat, and we'll start with the good news. Please," he instructed gently, and waited for her to comply.

She did, afraid her trembling legs wouldn't support her. It hadn't escaped her notice how Dr. Archer had avoided her question, taking calm control like a man accustomed to dealing with the worst scenarios. Given that he had an entire coven of vampires to doctor, she was sure that was the case. The doctor positioned himself on one side of her, and Jax sat on the other. Nick hovered close by, his face set in hard lines.

"I'm pleased to report that tests reveal no massive internal bleeding or damage to his major organs. Of course, we will continue to monitor the slow internal bleeding in his brain."

Hope surged within her, but the doctor's reserve kept it in check. "What can I do to help him?"

"Remain by his side as much as you can, at least until he turns the corner. I'm sure our prince told you how highly we value the power of the mate bond in healing."

"He did, yes. It makes sense."

"There's more you should know. Brain trauma is our most immediate concern. When he arrived here, he was in shock and suffering from seizures. To be honest, he gave us quite a scare. We ran a CT scan and took X-rays. The bleeds are here." He touched a finger to a spot behind his right ear, toward the back of his head, and then at his temple. "There's some swelling putting a bit of pressure on his brain, but he's breathing on his own and is showing signs of normal brain activity. We'll know more once he regains consciousness."

"God." She pressed a shaking hand to her mouth. *Zan could have died.* She'd known that, but now it was more real. Her entire body felt frozen. "How long until we know something? Until he shows improvement?"

"There's no way to be sure. He's holding his own, but I want him under close observation. Once he wakes up and shows no further complications, I can have him moved to a regular room. Try not to worry, Selene. He's strong and fit, so we have every reason to expect a full recovery—with your help."

"When can I see him?"

"He's being moved to intensive care. I'll have the head nurse come get you when he's settled, and I'll check back later."

Zan was back there somewhere, hurting. Fighting for his life. Her lungs and throat burned with the effort to stifle her tears, but she was determined to stay strong for Zan. If nothing else, she could do this for him.

His Pack brothers milled around, unwilling to leave without further word. Time stretched out, and the wait for more news scraped her nerves raw. "Zan," she said through their bond, trying to reach him. There was no answer. People drifted in and out. What could be taking so long? Hundreds of possibilities loomed, all of them frightening.

Her father sat next to her and took her hand. She stared at his big hand on hers, realizing how much she'd missed her father's comfort.

"Tarron's healing was crucial, but I didn't want Zan to make this sacrifice for me. I wish he'd let me go. Then you wouldn't have to go through this."

She gasped, glaring at her father. "Don't you dare cheapen his gift to you by saying that! He almost gave his life for you, and that meant something to him. Don't say that again."

"I'm sorry," he said, taken aback. "I didn't look at it that way. Nothing like that will cross my lips again."

"Thank you. And I'm sorry for snapping; I'm just scared."

"Me too."

"I find it hard to believe you're afraid of anything," she said quietly. She marveled at how he was always there for his men, always so strong. "You really care for your Pack. You could have died tonight, and your first thought is for them."

"That's part of my job."

"I think it's more to you than that. They keep you going."

He hesitated, then sighed. "Those guys saved my life, and they don't even know it."

Her heart lurched. "How so?"

"I'd been in the FBI for almost twenty years, and it was time for me to move on before my human colleagues figured out I wasn't aging. I was at loose ends and feeling down, like I couldn't stand to start my life over one more time. And then Jarrod Grant contacted me about commanding the Pack."

"And joining them saved your life—literally?"

"Yes." He looked deeply into her eyes. "Selene, you haven't lived long enough to know what it's like to spend almost two centuries in the agonizing grip of loneliness, hoping to find your true mate, then to find him and have him taken away. I pray you never do. I've survived in hell ever since, struggling to find meaning in my existence."

"Have you?"

"I've tried. But there comes a time when the loneliness becomes too much to bear," he said softly. "When the guilt of one's mistakes just won't be assuaged, when the past just won't die. When the body is too tired to house a dead soul. This is why humans are fortunate to be mortal, because forever is just too long."

His words scared her terribly. Was he ready to

cross over? She didn't want to lose him, especially before they got things settled between them.

He was silent for a time, and she gave in to the temptation to press him. "What was your role in my mother's death? Did you kill her?"

"Now isn't the time," he said gently.

"You're just trying to get out of answering me!"

"No. I promise you I'm not. I mean it when I say you're not ready to hear the truth yet. I'll know when you are."

"Do you miss her?"

"Every day of my life," he croaked. "Just as I've missed you. When I lost you, I didn't want to live."

Her gaze snapped to his. "You didn't *lose* me like a set of car keys. You *left* me."

"No, I—look, this isn't the time to discuss—"

Just then the middle-aged head nurse finally came through the doors, her grim expression doing nothing to calm Selene's fears.

"You can see him now," she said.

Selene wasn't prepared for the sight of her mate lying in the bed, so pale and vulnerable. He was normally so full of life. Kind and funny and sweet. His expressive brown eyes were closed, lashes resting against his cheeks. There were tubes and wires all over his body. An IV in his hand.

Taking a chair next to his bed, she sat and held the hand without the IV. For a time, she watched the slow drip, drip, drip of clear medication through the line until that made her a little stir-crazy, and she went back to watching him instead.

Come on, baby. You can beat this. I know you can. The doctor says the mate bond will help you get well, and I believe that. Please, do this for me.

There was no answer.

At some point she grew weary and slept. A nurse came in later and set out a cot for her, and she gratefully stretched out beside him. Before she fell back asleep, she mentally tested their mate bond, finding it strong. It had taken some blows, but it was intact. She imagined Zan at the other end of the thread stretched between them, like he was a fish she had to reel in. Slowly, she tugged at him in her mind.

She could be wrong, but it felt like he was moving closer. Tying off her end of the thread, she at last gave in to the sandman.

Zan surfaced by gradual degrees.

At first he couldn't place where he was at all. Sometimes he thought he heard Melina and Noah talking, but other times he heard an unfamiliar male voice. He seemed to be a doctor, and someone called him Victor . . . something. He couldn't grasp it at the moment and didn't care.

He drifted for a while. Tried to figure out what had happened to land him here. Wherever here was. Cracking his lids to a tiny slit, he saw stone walls. Like natural cave stone, not man-made. What the hell?

Then he turned his head, and all was suddenly okay with his world, no matter where they were. Selene was sitting in a chair beside him, fast asleep. He drank in the sight of her pale blond hair framing her face, her tall body slumped with her legs sticking out in front of her. She probably would want him to wake her, but he was tempted to let her sleep.

"Selene?" His voice sounded like he'd been gargling glass, with whiskey chasers. *Baby*, he sent mentally.

That seemed to do the trick. Yawning, she sat up and looked at him—then her electric-blue eyes widened. "Zan! You're awake!"

"Hey, baby," he whispered. "Where are we?"

Leaning forward, she touched his arm. "We're in the prince's stronghold. Your entourage was attacked on the way here."

"How are *you* here? Why?"

"You were really bad off." She swallowed hard, as though remembering. "They thought you might die. They sent some of the prince's men after me, Melina, Noah, as well as Mac and Kalen. We're all staying on as the prince's guests until this rogue situation is resolved. The Pack is working with his men."

"I knew we'd work with them, but we're living here? I wasn't expecting that."

"That last attack changed everyone's perspective. They're targeting Nick and Tarron, and now you all have to find out why." Leaning over, she kissed his lips gently. "Enough about that right now. How are you feeling?"

He thought about that. "Head aches some. Tired."

"My poor mate. I don't want you to think about anything but getting well, all right?"

His eyes got heavy, and he slid back into sleep.

When he awoke again, he was feeling better. The ache in his head wasn't as bad, and he wasn't as tired. But where was his mate? *Selene?*

Coming, honey. Are you all right?

Better. I just wanted to see your beautiful face.

Just then she walked into his room, her smile only for him. He smiled back, but he was sure his expression looked as drugged as he felt.

"I leave to eat lunch, and there you are." She sat next to him and took his hand, kissed his lips. "Been awake long?"

"No, just a minute. Where is everyone?"

"The team is around the stronghold somewhere. Some have been in to see you, but you weren't awake. My father's been here a lot, and so has Jax. Everyone has been really worried."

"I'm all right. Especially now that I'm with you again."

She looked pleased by that. "Our mate bond helped you turn the corner and get well."

"If anybody could help me do that, it's you."

Her happiness dimmed. "You almost died, though. I know Melina is coming to talk with us soon."

He had a feeling he knew what she was going to say. And he would be able to heed her words pretty much like he had before—not at all.

"I'll listen to her, but—"

"I know, honey. You don't have to explain to me. I've got my father and a grateful vampire prince who owe you their lives. I know why you do what you do and that you wouldn't change it."

"You really do understand."

"Yes. Doesn't always make it easier to accept or not to worry, but I get it."

Noah came bustling in, checked his vitals. After the nurse left, he figured it wouldn't be long before the doc followed, and he was right. Melina came in, her elfin face wearing a carefully composed frown. He wondered if she practiced that look in the mirror to intimidate her patients and instantly felt bad for the uncharitable thought. The doc was dedicated to her work, and she was good at it.

"Zander, we need to talk," she began.

"Do we? I already know what you're going to say."

"I have to say it anyway—Zan, you *cannot* heal anyone again for at least six months if you want to stay alive. That's the short version."

"And the long version?"

"Your brain has been taxed to the limits of its endurance. On the way here, you stopped breathing. Then you had seizures and a slow bleed that came tenuously close to becoming an all-out hemorrhaging. Your brain is done. It can't take anymore, or you'll be done, too."

"Melina," he said softly. "I've known you for years. You're an awesome doctor, and you want what's best for your patients. I know you have to give it to me straight. So here's where I have to do the same."

She waited while he rested, gathered his thoughts. He was getting tired again.

"The thing is, being a Healer is who I am, just as being a doctor is who you are. I can't separate that from myself any more than I could cut out my wolf. I discovered I could heal when I was just a child and a neighbor's cat broke its leg. I picked it up and just . . . fixed it."

"I didn't know that." She gave him a fond smile.

"I never told anyone about what I did. But from then on, I used it whenever I could. In my mind, there was no need for others to suffer if I had the power to stop it. You see? I have to give my soul to see others well. That's what I know."

"I understand."

"I know you do. I just had to tell you that I'm not being reckless, or using my gift lightly. I know exactly what's at stake, but when it comes to the lives of my Pack brothers and my mate, there's no question I'll risk everything to make sure they're okay."

"And if you die?"

"Then I die," he said with a small smile. "Most creatures do, sooner or later."

"You're a rare man, Healer." She stood and looked between him and Selene. "I hope you both realize how lucky you are."

With that, she left them alone. Zan stared at the door she'd just gone through. "She's lonely. I wish she could find a mate who completes her the way you complete me."

Warmth shone in his mate's eyes. "I wish she could, too. Did you know her deceased mate very well?"

He cocked his head. "You know, it's funny you should say that. The team and I worked under Terry for five and a half years. But in all that time, I never felt I knew him as well or was as close to him as I've become with Nick in the months since he took over."

"What about the rest of the team? They feel the same way?"

"I'm pretty sure they do. Especially Jax. He never cared for Terry that much."

"That's sort of strange."

"Yeah. A part of me wonders whether Terry had anything to do with the ambush that killed half our team. Then I feel like a complete shit for even thinking ill of the dead."

"It's a legitimate concern. When someone holds himself aloof and then something bad happens, you find yourself questioning what you thought you know." She suddenly got a strange look on her face.

"What is it?"

"That's exactly how I feel about my uncle right now," she said quietly. "He's always held himself so aloof, up on his moral high ground that nobody else can possibly reach. And now I find myself questioning why he's always been so against me finding my father."

"Have you asked Nick lately about the past?"

"Yes. He said I wasn't ready to accept the truth, and maybe he's right. It scares me."

"You don't want to find out something you believed was really a lie."

"Yes, same as with your team and this Terry."

"Sometimes the truth isn't meant to come to light," he said. "I wonder at times if that's not best all around."

"I don't agree, at least not where my uncle and my father are concerned. Despite our differences, I'm really worried about Nick. He's depressed, Zan, and I mean that seriously. Something has to give, and one of them is going to tell me the truth if I have to beat it out of him!"

He smiled. "I don't doubt you would."

"Believe it."

He did. Selene was fast reaching the end of her patience with both men.

For now, all Zan could do was be a comfort and source of support to his mate.

Nick was about to crawl out of his skin.

He was starting to feel like a fucking bat, and he had to get out of this big rock and into the sunshine before he went crazy. How the hell did the vampires stand living inside a mountain?

Walking the corridors and searching without success, he finally found a vampire who directed him to the nearest exit. One that had a pathway leading from it into the forest below the mountain.

When he arrived at the exit, he discovered a large vampire soldier guarding a heavy metal door, presumably to the outside. The vamp stood straighter, eyeing Nick suspiciously as he approached.

"I was told this way out leads to a good place to go for a run. I'm assuming that's not a problem?" His light, friendly tone had no effect whatsoever on the vampire.

"You assume wrong. Prince Tarron doesn't like anyone leaving the stronghold in daylight."

"Well, I'm guessing he meant vampires, members of his coven who shouldn't go out because they'll get burned. I'm neither—I'm a wolf and I'm a visitor."

"Same rules apply." The soldier was as immovable as the rock they were standing on.

Shit. "Listen, man. My wolf needs to run or he

goes a little nuts. If he goes nuts, there might be trouble when he gets mean. And then it would get back to the prince, and he'd demand to know why I wasn't allowed the simple courtesy of—"

"Fine," the soldier growled. "But if something happens to you, it's your ass."

"Thanks."

The soldier muscled open the heavy door and let it swing wide. Fresh mountain air, tinged with just the right amount of cold, hit him in the face, and he sighed in appreciation. As he stepped through and made his way down the steep path, the sights and scents of the wooded area below had his wolf straining to be freed.

The woods met the path some one hundred yards down, and he found a good place to stash his clothes. Quickly, he stripped and let the change flow over him. Muscle stretched and bone popped, his body reshaping into his wolf—a form he didn't get to enjoy nearly enough just for the sheer pleasure of it.

And there was so little enjoyment in his life.

His wolf darted into the forest, and he thought of Selene. She hadn't spoken to him in the two days since Zan had begun his recovery. His daughter wanted him to open up and he'd claimed she wasn't ready. He didn't want to face that he was the one who wasn't ready to open wounds best left closed.

Except those wounds were festering, and would

be until they were dealt with once and for all. In the aftermath, he could very well lose his baby for good.

Heart heavy, he ran. His wolf gradually took the forefront of his mind, and it was a relief of sorts from the troubles that had been crowding his mind and giving him no peace. He reveled in the leaves and dirt under his paws, the fresh air. His wolf body, unencumbered by his human limitations, soared over rocks and fallen trees.

He'd been running for maybe half an hour when he slowed to a trot and heard . . . singing. Halting, he cocked his head, unsure at first. But yes, there it was. The sweetest female voice, softly singing a popular tune about love lost and found again. The voice was captivating, the melody like a bird's trill among the branches. For a moment, he thought maybe he was hallucinating and it would turn out to be a bird after all.

But as he approached a break in the trees, the breath left him. If he weren't in wolf form, his knees would've buckled and he might have uttered a quiet exclamation.

The woman was beautiful. The most stunning piece of living artwork he'd ever seen. She was of average height, about five feet, five inches tall, and a dark cloak hugged what he figured was a slim frame. Her face was exquisite, her skin pale and creamy, with high cheekbones and a thin nose. Her long-lashed eyes were huge, dominating her face, perfect pencil brows arched over them. He couldn't tell their color from where he stood, but that hardly mattered.

Gorgeous, straight, shining chestnut hair tumbled around that striking face and to her waist in a silken fall. She was sitting on a rock by a babbling stream and thankfully wasn't aware of him watching. He shouldn't spy, but he wanted to observe this beautiful creature unimpeded for as long as he was able.

She kept singing. And he kept watching and listening, the sound reaching somewhere deep inside him to soothe the hurts that had been raw and bleeding for too long. He tried to catch her scent, but the breeze was blowing in a different direction.

Though he couldn't be sure, he assumed she was one of Tarron's coven. They were so far into the mountains, and there were no houses around these parts. If she *was* a vampire, how could she be out in the sun? He'd heard only ancient vampires, and now rogues, could do that.

The urge to reveal himself was strong. In fact, the pull became so irresistible that he took a few steps forward—but a loud voice shattered the tranquil atmosphere.

"Calla! Calla! Dammit, where are you?"

Tarron. That was the prince's voice, and he sounded both annoyed and worried. The vampire he now knew was Calla snapped her head up, startled, looking around. Moving quickly, she slipped from her rock, uttered a curse—

And vanished.

Nick couldn't understand the sudden despair that washed over him as he stared at the empty space where she'd been. He'd observed her for only a brief time, so his reaction didn't make sense.

In the next instant, Tarron appeared close to the spot where the mysterious Calla had been. Muttering, he looked around and shoved a hand through his hair. Nick kept his cover for some reason, instead of going to his new friend. Who was Calla to Tarron? Friend? Family?

Lover?

A low growl rumbled in his chest, but thankfully Tarron didn't hear the noise. The vampire vanished, translocating to who knew where. Teleportation was one ability that sort of freaked Nick out. Hammer, his friend and right-hand man, could do it, but he was the only Pack member who could.

Deciding to head back, he took off at a trot. All the way back to the stronghold, he found himself recalling every minute of his observation of the beautiful vampire. Calla. He wondered if he'd see her again, perhaps meet in person sometime. He very much hoped so.

He located his clothes and got dressed, then made his way back to the metal door and knocked.

The same guard let him in, appearing no happier than he had before.

He thanked the soldier anyway, started to take his leave, then stopped and faced the man again. "By the way, do you know a vampire named Calla? About five-five, beautiful, long chestnut hair, sings like a bird—"

"That would be Princess Calla Shaw," the guard said, eyes narrowing. "Prince Tarron's sister."

Well, fuck a duck. "Maybe we're talking about different females? Tarron's last name is Romanoff, not Shaw."

"The princess is the only Calla in this coven, and she is a widow. She is much adored and fiercely protected by her brother, and I suggest any leanings you have in her direction you allow to pass." His tone was curt.

Aw, hell. "Thanks for the warning."

Heaving a sigh, he walked to Tarron's office, cursing his luck, which never seemed to change. Then he booted up his laptop. He'd check his e-mail, see if anything of interest had come in today.

Immediately, he was sorry he looked.

All thoughts of beautiful vampires vanished at the knowledge of the choice he now faced.

Two days later, Zan was declared fit to leave the infirmary, as long as he promised to take it easy. Which he did, with his fingers crossed under the sheets. He was a wolf. They didn't do sedentary very well.

He wouldn't be taking it easy in other areas, either. Today, his rampaging dick simply would not stand down. All of this nearness, cooped up in the infirmary, smelling his mate's sweet scent night and day, was making him bug nuts, so to speak.

He wanted to have wild monkey sex in the infirmary bed. But that's where his mate drew the line, messing around in such close proximity to people who weren't well and where the doctors and nurses could appear any minute. Kink in the dark of night was one thing, this something else entirely.

Zan got his walking papers, and he was never so glad to get out of confinement.

One of the prince's household staff led him and Selene to their room. The vampire stopped in front of a door, opened it, and stepped in, gesturing to the expansive suite.

"This is yours while you are here," she said; then, to his surprise, she stepped boldly forward, as if his mate weren't standing *right there*, and rubbed the front of her body against him. And, unfortunately, his rampant erection. "If there's anything I can do to improve your stay, let me know."

Two things happened simultaneously. He jumped back, putting distance between himself and the vamp as though he'd been electrocuted, and his mate partially shifted, shoving the vampire to the floor and snarling at her with canines the size of butcher knives.

"Get the fuck off my mate! And don't ever touch him again unless you want to end up as my evening meal!"

White-faced, the vampire stammered an apology and practically ran from the room. Selene stood there seething with rage. Hating to see her upset, he stepped forward and caressed her face.

"Come on, baby. Deep breaths. I'm not interested in her. You know that, right?"

She nodded. "You're mine!"

"I know. Yours." Inside, his wolf howled in joy at her possessiveness. Her claim.

"Why would the stupid bitch do such a thing? Does she have a death wish?"

"Vampires are very sexually free, my mate. To her, that offer was probably as natural as breathing."

"Well, if she wants to *keep* breathing, she'll keep her fucking body to herself!"

Gradually, she shifted back to her human form. But her possessiveness remained. He knew what she wanted without question when she palmed his erection through his jeans and rubbed.

"God, that feels good! It's been too long," he murmured.

"I want to suck you."

"Reestablish who I belong to?"

"That's right!"

"Fine by me." Grinning, he unzipped his jeans and shoved them down, exposing his hard cock to her hungry gaze.

The veins stood out, purple against the reddened skin. He was so fucking horny. The slit oozed pre-cum, and she swirled some with her finger, then brought it to her tongue to taste.

"So good," she moaned.

"Have as much as you like. It's all for you."

She sank to her knees on the carpet in front of him. But if he thought she was going for his shaft right away, he was wrong. Between his legs, she brought her face to his balls and nuzzled. Nipping and licking him, she rubbed all over his sac, marking him with her scent. No female within a hundred miles—no sane one anyway—would come near her man with him carrying her scent.

He groaned, spreading wider for her. He liked this side of her, aggressive, taking what was hers. Her questing tongue laved every inch of his balls, even bathing his perineum, and he almost shot right then. But he managed to hold off, because this was just too damned good.

Finally, she licked his cock, making sure it was well loved also. There wasn't a single erogenous zone left unexplored, one spot left untouched. Then she took his rod deep into her throat, slowly and with lots of good suction, and he thought he must have died and gone to heaven after all.

There wasn't much that was better than having his cock sucked. He defied any man to say differently. That guy would be a liar.

Making satisfied noises, she sucked him until he was cross-eyed. Until he was pumping down her throat in regular rhythm, deeper and faster, loving that she wanted it like this. Wanted him.

He felt his balls draw up. "Baby, gonna come!"

She held on fast, grabbing a double handful of his ass and squeezing. That was all he could take. With a shout, he emptied his seed down her throat, spasming on and on. She swallowed every drop, easing him down, her tongue massaging the underside of his cock, producing a bunch of little aftershocks.

Eventually, he reached down and helped her up, then carried her to the big bed that awaited them. They slept for a while in each other's arms, but he woke up hungry for her again sometime in the night.

He kissed down her back, loving that she was stirring awake with pleased little sounds. She liked what he was doing. Encouraged, he trailed his tongue down her spine, to her butt. Then spread her legs and flicked her sex with his tongue.

Making an incoherent noise, she spread wider.

So he licked her slit, laving her as though eating ice cream. He enjoyed returning the favor, getting her all sloppy wet, making her writhe on his face, lost in pure pleasure.

"Oh! God, yes!"

She was a vocal lover, and he liked that. He wanted to hear her get loud, so he latched on to her little clit and suckled like a starving man. She came undone under his attentions, bucking and screaming the mountain down. On and on, he sucked and lapped her cream, until she was boneless on the bed. Replete.

After wiping his face on the sheet, he held her and they fell asleep, content.

Sometime later, he awoke to find her studying him. Then she smiled and kissed his chest. "Good morning."

"Is it morning? It's hard to tell what time of day it is when you're holed up in a mountain."

"According to the clock, it is. Hungry?"

"Yes. But I need a shower first. You game?"

"Always."

The shower was fun, and he felt like a new man when they finally emerged—long after the hot water had run out. Then they dressed and at last went in search of food.

They found most of the Pack and a bunch of vampires in a dining area not unlike the one at the compound. Zan was a little surprised to see vampires eating normal food, but he knew they had to have blood as well to survive.

He and Selene tucked into eggs, bacon, and toast, with a healthy dose of coffee to go with it. "Wonder where Nick is," he said, looking around.

"I don't know. He's scarce lately."

"You're still worried about him."

"More than ever. He's not eating much, as far as I can tell."

They were chatting with a group of vampires about their coven when one of the soldiers came into the room and approached.

"Selene?" She nodded. "Your father would like to see you in Prince Tarron's study. He said to tell you that you're as ready as you'll ever be. He said you would know what that means."

Beside him, she paled. "I do, thank you."

"Baby? Do you want me to go with you?" But he already knew what she'd say.

"No. I have to do this alone. You understand, don't you?"

She suddenly looked so fragile. He wanted to hurt Nick for putting that expression on her face, but that wasn't fair, either.

"Of course I do. I'll wait for you in our room. Come to me as soon as you're done."

"I will."

Rising, she gave him a kiss and then left to have a long-overdue conversation with her father.

Zan said a quick prayer for them both.

He had a feeling they would need all the help they could get.

Eleven

Selene's knees shook as she walked to Prince Tarron's study to speak with her father.

This was it. The moment she'd waited so long for, when she'd learn the truth about her mother's death. And now she found she wasn't ready at all, because she knew the facts would somehow be different from what she'd been told all her life. It would be a dull knife rending open a scab to expose ugliness and pain.

Part of her no longer wanted to know. But she couldn't back out now.

Opening the door to the study, she stepped in and closed it behind her. Nick was alone, sitting in a chair near the large antique desk that dominated the room. For a moment, she thought it would be easier to fall back on the old hatred. To blame him for her past misery and simply walk out, refusing to hear. But the anguish on his face stopped her cold.

"Sit down, please."

Granting his request, she took a seat on the antique chaise longue closest to him and waited for him to continue.

"I can't protect you anymore, though God knows that's all I ever wanted to do," he said, voice catching. "I've put this conversation off for too long, and now I've run out of time."

"Run out of time, how?"

"That's not important right now."

She swallowed hard. "Okay. Protect me from what, then? Tell me, and don't leave anything out."

"From the past. Leaving you was the very last thing I ever wanted, but I had broken clan law and made a mistake too horrible to be rectified. I was banished from the pack forever."

Selene gasped and gripped the arm of the sofa. "What? I was told you ran like a coward after Mom was killed. And you didn't care enough to take me with you."

"No. I made a grave mistake that caused your mother's death, and I deserved to be punished. But I didn't run away, and I didn't leave you voluntarily. Damien rallied the support of the clan and stripped me of my title of Alpha and took over. He forced me to leave—without you."

"I can't believe that!" she exclaimed, voice rising. "Uncle Damien wouldn't lie to me!"

"But he did," Nick said quietly. "Whether or not you believe me, it's the truth. I imagine my brother lied in part because he knew that believing the worst of me would make your life more tolerable. You would be accepted and protected by the clan, and you were. I don't blame him for telling you and the others what he had to in order to make things easier for you."

Her mind whirled in confusion. "Do you hear yourself? You actually expect me to buy all of this?" Desperately, she cast about for another explanation. Her lifelong beliefs about her uncle Damien and what a great man he was, that he and his mate and family were her own, were suddenly crashing around her feet.

"I have a hard time buying that your motives for leaving me behind were so altruistic," she countered. "If you didn't kill my mother, why didn't you just take me with you when you left? You could've gotten us away, and we could've had a good life together!"

Nick hung his head for a long moment, breathing hard. It occurred to her that he was trying hard not to cry, and her heart stuttered.

"I couldn't, baby. When Damien confronted me, he brought a witch with him. He said if I didn't go peacefully, without you, he'd have the witch strip you of your gift. He wasn't bluffing, and my sight had told me that someday you'd need your special ability desperately, so I left."

"Oh my God," she whispered.

"I don't expect you to believe my story over-night, but I'm telling the truth. I didn't leave you out of fear for my own life, or any other selfish reason. I hoped to see you again one day, but if I didn't . . . I did what I had to do to protect you."

Staring at Nick, she struggled to process all he'd told her. Her soul grieved for all the time they'd lost, even as hope sparked anew. Still, there was plenty she didn't understand.

"What gift are you talking about? I don't have any special abilities."

"That's where you're wrong." One corner of his mouth hitched in a half smile. "You have a very special gift that will manifest when you need it most. I can't tell you what it is and risk swaying the future again."

"Again? What do you mean?"

"I want you to remember that I knowingly broke clan law and Damien felt he had no choice but to act. He's not a bad man. He did what he believed he must at the time to discipline me and protect you."

Steeling herself, Selene asked the tough ques-tion. "So, what did you do? And what does it have to do with Mom?"

Here it was at last. Her father looked her right in the eye and gave her the rest.

"I had a vision. It showed me one of our clan members being snatched off the street by a rogue vampire, assaulted and brutally murdered. I used my gift to change the outcome."

"Oh, no . . ." Tampering with the future was a grave offense, and obviously his interference had gone terribly wrong. "What happened?"

"My vision showed that the victim, a mere child, was going to be snatched off the street by a rogue vamp after a dance lesson while waiting for her mother, who would be running late. I made certain the woman knew of my vision, and then I picked the child up myself as a precaution, thwarting fate. Or so I thought."

He cleared his throat, obviously fighting to keep it together. She waited, heart pounding, dreading what he was about to say but knowing she had to hear it.

"The rogue was watching, and he became enraged. In revenge, he turned his attention to the child's mother. Four days later, he caught her alone and killed her."

For a few seconds, she simply stared at her father. Then she whispered, "The child was me."

"Yes."

"You interfered, changed my fate, and he killed my mother instead."

"Yes," he choked. "But I know how much your mother loved you, as I do, and she wouldn't have survived had the vampire gotten his hands on you instead. She wouldn't have changed the outcome even if she could have."

Selene couldn't speak.

"I learned my lesson on tampering with fate," he said hoarsely. "And I learned that sometimes death just won't be cheated, no matter how we try to avoid it. I'm so sorry, baby. Your mother died in your stead, and I wish it had been me. I lost my mate and, despite my efforts, you as well. Sometimes I—" He fell silent, leaving the rest unfinished.

The clock in the study ticked, and Selene grappled with her emotions. "I don't know how to feel. You thought you could control everything, and all you did was get my mother killed! I don't hate you anymore, but honestly . . . I don't know if I can forgive you, either."

As soon as those words left her lips, she regretted them. Raw pain flashed in her father's eyes before being quickly hidden. "I understand. I just wanted you to know the whole story. If you still doubt what I've told you, I don't think Damien would deny the truth now."

Damien. There was another person on her shit list.

She stood. "I'll talk to you later. And thank you . . . for telling me."

Turning, she walked out before she gave way to the sorrow.

Nick sat in Tarron's study long after Selene left.

Shadows closed in on his soul, crushed his

heart. *She's never going to forgive me. I've lost her for good.*

And he knew, then and there, that when death caught him, he was done. He'd die without a fight because he had nothing left.

For the first time since his mate was murdered, since he lost his baby girl, Nick hung his head and cried.

Zan knew something was wrong the second Selene stepped into their room.

Shutting the door behind her, she leaned against it and met his gaze. Tears were streaming down her face, and he jumped up and hurried to her, gathering her into his arms.

"Baby, what's wrong?" He kissed the side of her head. "Tell me."

"I talked to my dad. He finally told me everything."

His blood froze. "What did he say?"

"It was supposed to have been me!" Her voice broke, and she cried harder.

"What?"

"I was the vampire's target, not Mom!" she rasped, sobbing. "He saw what was going to happen and got me away. The rogue killed her instead."

"Oh, no." He squeezed her tighter. "That's why he never interferes with fate."

"Why? Why did this have to happen? I loved my mom and dad. We were happy."

"I know, baby. Shh, please don't cry."

"They were the best parents."

"I'm sure they were."

In stops and starts, Zan managed to get the rest of the story out of her. He led her over to the bed, eased her down, and held her as she cried. He'd known the story would be tragic when it finally came out, but God. His heart broke for all she and her father had lost. And her mother, too.

Gradually, her tears subsided and she turned to him, placing soft kisses on his chest. Arousal stirred, his cock lengthening in his jeans and making the fit uncomfortably tight. "We don't have to do this now, sweetheart."

"Make love to me, my mate," she said breathlessly. "Please."

He knew what she needed—to be loved. To forget for a while.

"With pleasure."

He removed his jeans and underwear first, then helped her off with her shirt, shoes, and jeans. He left her lacy black panties for last, spreading her out for his gaze, wearing those and nothing else.

"You're beautiful."

"So are you—inside and out."

Leaning over her, he took her mouth in a deep kiss, putting all of his feelings for her into it. He stroked her hair, her cheek, shoulder, and finally cupped one full breast. He loved the weight of it in his palm, the warmth. Kneading the mound, he flicked the tight nipple a few times with his thumb, enjoying her gasp and the way she arched into his touch.

His hand moved lower still, fingers slipping beneath her panties and combing through her pale bush to probe at the heated flesh between her thighs. She moaned, opening for him, and he sat up, helping her get rid of the offending garment. Dropping the scrap of material to the floor, he returned his attention to loving his mate.

He positioned himself between her thighs, spreading her legs, baring her to his hungry gaze. His cock throbbed, eager to be buried inside her, claiming her once again as his. Not just yet, though. He wanted a taste.

She loved being eaten, so he obliged, laving her slit. Getting it nice and wet for him while savoring her salty sweetness. Her essence. He lapped her until she pulled on his hair, as eager for him as he was for her.

"Please, I need you inside me!"

Settling himself in place, he guided the head of his cock to her entrance and slid home.

"Fuck, yeah," he groaned.

She clung to his shoulders as he began to move, pumping slowly into her depths. Shocks of pleasure raced along his length, tightening his balls long before he was ready to shoot. He wanted this to last. Slowing down didn't help him hold back. In fact, it only heightened the ecstasy that set him on fire and made him lose control altogether.

Especially when his fangs lengthened and he sank them into the soft curve of her neck and shoulder, reasserting his claim.

White-hot lightning raced down his spine and wrapped around his cock and balls. There was no stopping the intense orgasm that rocked his core, sending his seed spurting into her again and again. Her legs wrapped around his waist and she cried out, finding her own release, and they rode the rest of the waves together. At last they floated gently down, holding to each other tightly, and basked in their love.

He loved his mate. There was no doubt.

"I love you," he said, kissing her hair. "You don't have to say it back. I just wanted you to know."

"Thank you." Her arms tightened around his neck. "You have no idea how much it means to me to know how you feel. Give me more time?"

"Always."

He couldn't help but be disappointed that she couldn't yet say the words. She'd been through too much in her life, so much heartbreak. He didn't blame her for waiting until the time was right. She did love him. He believed that. Every look, every smile, her support of him, every small thing she'd done since their surprise mating showed him how her feelings had grown. And weren't actions more important than words anyway?

That would be more than enough.

For now.

Zan left his exhausted mate sleeping and slipped from the bed, pulling on his jeans and a shirt as quietly as possible. She'd been through too much today and needed the rest. Besides, he had a visit to pay to Nick, and he preferred to do it while Selene was sleeping.

Tugging on his boots, he gave Selene one last glance and eased from the room, shutting the door with a soft snick. He strode down the lit corridor, glad he was finally learning his way around Tarron's immense stronghold. The entire team had gotten lost at one point or another, and he still half-expected a friendly vamp to leap from the shadows and try to jump his bones like the one who'd shown him and Selene to their room.

He chuckled as he recalled how fast his mate had put the vamp in her place.

His amusement was short-lived as he arrived at Tarron's study. A peek inside revealed that his commander was still in there, seated behind the desk. His head was bent over his laptop, and he wore a troubled frown as he stared at the screen. Zan knocked quietly.

Nick looked up and sat back in the chair. "I've been expecting you."

"Had to see to my mate. She was pretty upset when she came to our room." He kept the accusation from his tone, but it was difficult. He reminded himself that Nick was just as much a victim of tragedy as Selene. "She's sleeping now."

Regret and sadness were etched on the man's face as he answered. "My daughter has been through so much. The last thing I wanted was to bring her more pain. But she deserved the truth."

"I know." Moving into the study, Zan took a seat with a sigh. "And she'll be all right, eventually. I just wanted to say I'm here for both of you. Whatever you need."

"Thank you. That means a lot to me."

"Why did you tell her now, though? I thought she wasn't ready."

"Maybe it was me who wasn't ready," he said ruefully. "In any case, I had run out of time." His gaze slid to his laptop screen again, and Zan didn't miss the tension in his posture and expression.

"What's going on?"

"I got another threat. This is the main reason why I couldn't hold off on telling Selene the truth any longer." Turning the laptop around slightly, he gestured for Zan to read what was on the screen. "I showed this to Jax and Micah a bit ago. First one I've received since we've been here."

It was an e-mail. Another threat from Nick's unknown tormentor.

Do you know me yet? Do you feel my breath down
your neck, my fangs scrape your skin? Next time
you won't get away. Very soon I'll tear you apart,
just as I did your mate when I ripped out her throat
so long ago. Just as I will your precious daughter.
She won't escape me a second time.

His blood ran cold. "Fuck! Where the hell are
these e-mails coming from?"

"Micah's hopeful he can trace this one."

"You think this really is the bastard who killed
your mate and destroyed your family?"

Rage and agony waged war on the commander's face. "And he's going to attempt to finish
what he started."

"We'll stop him. That son of a bitch isn't getting
his hands on my mate," he growled. His wolf bristled, ready to do battle. All he needed was the enemy.

"Zan—"

"No. I know that tone, and don't even *think*
about telling me to stay on the sidelines," he said
in a low voice. "I can hear now, and I can fight. It's
not gonna happen."

Before the commander could protest further,
Jax came into the study, followed by Micah, who
was toting his own laptop. Both men looked excited, especially Micah. Zan hoped like hell the
gleam in the younger man's eyes was a natural
high, and instantly, he felt bad for even thinking

it. The Dreamwalker was working hard to regain his place on the team.

"We've finally got that bastard. He fucked up!" Micah proclaimed loudly, hurrying over to plunk the computer onto the desktop. "Wait till you see this."

Nick scooted his equipment over to make room, and Micah opened the lid on his laptop to wake it up, then typed in his password. The desktop screen came to life and displayed a photo.

"What's this?" Nick's brows drew together as he studied the picture.

Then a car drove by in the background, and Zan realized they weren't looking at a still photo—it was a video.

"It's a live feed of a Motel 6 about twenty miles from here. And guess who's inside?" Micah was practically bouncing in place.

"Elvis?" Zan joked to lighten the somber mood.

The Dreamwalker snorted. "Close! Only these guys really *are* undead. There's a whole nest of rogue vamps enjoying the fine comforts of the place where they 'leave the light on for ya.'"

Jax broke in, absently stroking his goatee. "Despite those amenities, why would they pick this particular venue as their base?"

"Hide in plain sight?" Zan guessed.

"Maybe. But it requires them to pass themselves off as human, which is an unprecedented level of restraint for such a large group of rogues."

"They have a leader," Nick said. "Someone strong. Cunning. Any hits on who that might be?"

Micah nodded, gesturing to the commander's laptop. "That's how we found the rogue we think is the head honcho—through the e-mails you've been getting from the asshole. I traced the IP address and tracked it to the motel, and—"

"Wait a second," Nick interrupted, pushing to his feet. "You're saying you think the bastard who's been harassing me is leading all of the rogues?"

"Yeah, boss. That's what I'm telling you. After we honed in on the location, Tarron's men did some recon and got us the footage. I've got some still pics, too."

Bending, Micah clicked on a file and opened a series of black-and-white shots taken outside the motel. Then he clicked through the pics. Most of them showed a group of males surrounding a figure who walked slightly ahead of the rest, like they were his entourage.

"See this guy?" Micah tapped the screen. "He's the one running the show. The others are there to protect him."

"How can you be sure this vampire is the same one sending me the e-mails?" Nick pressed.

"See this?" Micah pointed to an object in the vamp's hand. "He's the only one who's brought a laptop case in and out. It's an educated hunch, based on the notes themselves and how the others defer to the vamp in the pictures."

Zan studied the photo, or more accurately, the leader in it. He was tall, a bit broad through the shoulders. He carried himself like a powerful male, head up, acknowledging no one around him. His light hair, perhaps dark blond or sandy brown, was pulled into a ponytail at his nape.

"He's wearing a suit," Zan murmured to himself.

"Huh?" Micah looked at him in confusion. Jax and Nick waited, curious.

"The leader is wearing a damned suit, and so are the members of his posse. The rogues who've been attacking unsuspecting citizens in outlying areas haven't been dressed this nicely. In fact, the others were wearing holey jeans and torn shirts at best."

"So why the nice threads?" Jax mused, following his line of thought. "What makes these fuckers so special?"

"Exactly. The groups we've dealt with were starving, sloppy, their bodies unkempt and unwashed." Zan flicked a hand at the screen. "Somebody's taking real good care of this group, but who?"

"Wouldn't the leader be doing that?" Micah frowned. "Maybe he's got a tighter rein on the ones in his immediate circle."

Nick paced the study. "Yeah, but how? That brings us back to them being too well organized, too controlled to be regular rogues. They almost resemble a mafia."

"Could be that's exactly what they are, in a sense," Zan speculated. "And in that case, *this* guy answers to somebody higher up, because there's always another asshole above you in the food chain."

Nick looked at Jax. "Can you get a read on the leader from the stills or the video? His name, at least?"

"I may be able to answer that last question." Tarron's form materialized from nothingness, and he stepped forward.

"Jesus, that creeps me out," Micah complained with a shiver. "Do you have to sneak around like that, walking through walls and shit?"

Tarron's mouth quirked. "This *is* my home, pup. Get used to it." Ignoring the younger man's discomfort, he walked to the laptop and peered at the screen. Immediately, his humor vanished and he blew out a breath. "I had to be sure, but there's no doubt. Their leader's name is Carter Darrow. He used to be a member of my coven, long ago. He eventually went rogue, and to make a long story short, he's been my enemy ever since. I've hunted him for a couple of decades, only to have him turn up within arm's reach now. That in itself is quite troubling."

"He's not here just to get at me," Nick said, staring hard at Darrow's image. "This is much bigger."

Jax shifted on his feet. "I can try for a reading,

but I can't do it from a video or a photograph of him. It has to be an object he owned, or something he touched. It doesn't have to be of particular monetary value, either. I just need his essence, if you will."

Everyone was quiet for a moment, and then Tarron got a strange look on his face. Quickly, he strode to his bookcase. "I may have something."

After searching through a few shelves of old books, the prince withdrew one carefully and studied the cover. Turning to face the group, he held it out to Jax.

"A vintage copy of *The Count of Monte Cristo*," Jax said, running a hand over the lettering in appreciation. "A man is wronged, is tossed into a cell, and bides his time for years to bring down his enemy and exact vengeance. One of my favorite stories ever."

"Mine too," the prince agreed. There was something wistful in his expression. A bit sad. "The book was a birthday gift from Darrow more than twenty years ago, when he was still among my coven. I always wondered if the gift was symbolic on his part."

"Maybe." Jax opened the cover. "He inscribed it to you. His writing will definitely help with a reading."

"Is there anything special you need to accomplish it?" Tarron asked him.

"No. Just a few minutes of quiet."

Moving back, they gave the RetroCog silence and space as he settled on the sofa and placed the book in his lap. As he traced the handwriting with his fingers, his expression became distant. His mind was no longer in the room with them, but in a different time, perhaps a different place. Zan tried to imagine how tough it would be to pull together the threads of the past, form them into a vision or series of snapshots. How disturbing.

He knew sometimes the memories were horrid. That went with the territory; Jax had little reason to handle an object unless the person who'd touched it had either done something terrible, or been subjected to it.

Slowly Jax's eyelids drifted shut. His breathing grew faster, more ragged. His face became drawn and he mouthed the word *no*. A bad one, then. A glance at Nick told Zan that the commander knew it, too, and was dreading what would be revealed.

When Jax slumped back and the book slipped from his grasp, Zan jumped forward and rescued the volume, setting it on Tarron's desk. Then he hurried to sit beside his best friend and placed a palm on his forehead.

"Don't," Jax croaked, grabbing his wrist. "You can't afford to spend any healing energy on me."

"Dammit, Jax—"

"No. I just need some water and some rest; then I'll be fine." His gaze found Nick's, and he paused. "You might want everyone to leave."

The commander shook his head. "They all know anyway. Just tell me if Darrow is the one responsible for murdering my mate."

A heartbeat passed. "Yes."

"There's no doubt?"

"None," Jax said gently. "I saw."

Nick's knees seemed to buckle as he grabbed the corner of his desk. Zan was ready to catch his boss if need be, but it proved unnecessary. Nick straightened his spine, and the devastation in his dark blue eyes was replaced by steel.

"I want Darrow dead. And I want to kill him myself."

Those cold words sent a shudder through Zan. He'd heard the commander talk about taking out their enemies before. Hell, they all said stuff like that. But this was the first time he'd heard Nick speak personally about killing. It brought home how dangerous their world was, how tenuous.

"We're going to get him, I assure you," the prince vowed. He looked to Jax. "The vision you got . . . does this mean Darrow had already committed that atrocity when he gave me the book?"

"Unfortunately, yes. That's how my visions work—I can't see an event if it hasn't happened when the object was handled. I'm sorry."

The weight of knowing for certain that he'd had a rogue living under his rule, right under his nose, was hard for Tarron to bear. The news that Darrow had killed someone's mate was no doubt even worse. The vampire closed his eyes and clenched his fists, obviously battling his anger and frustration.

"We'll get Darrow, but it won't be easy," Tarron finally said, opening his eyes. "I'll bring as many of my men as I can spare to tip the odds in our favor."

"I appreciate that. Thank you. When's the best time to strike?"

"I would say daylight, but only my oldest soldiers can handle the sun's rays. The younger ones will suffer nasty burns if exposed too long."

"A nighttime offensive, then. Tomorrow night?"

"The timing should work. The question is, how the hell are we going to attack a coven of rogue vampires at a Motel 6 without alerting every human in the area?"

Micah grinned at the prince. "That's why it rocks that we come equipped with our very own Sorcerer. Wait until you see him in action."

Tarron's smile transformed his face. "I've seen him performing his magic for the members of my coven. He's quite good."

"Good? A few parlor tricks are nothing compared to what Kalen can do." Micah laughed. "You should see him turn a horde of rogues into dried-up raisins. He's seriously badass."

"Excellent. We're going to need every advantage we can muster."

The prince was right—and that's what worried Zan.

Something about the upcoming fight didn't sit well with him. He had a feeling they were missing something important.

"You're going to *what*? No!" Selene blurted.

"I can fight, baby," Zan said evenly. He tried not to take her reaction personally. After all, she was his mate and she had a right to be worried. "Like I told your father, I have my hearing back and I'm fine. I'm not going to put the team in danger."

"I'm not worried about the team!" she hissed, cupping his face. "You're the one I care about. Can't you just stay behind this once? Nobody would blame you."

"*I* would," he said gently, pushing a pale strand of hair off her brow. "I wouldn't be worthy of the Pack if I allowed my brothers to face danger without me when I'm perfectly capable."

"Being able to hold your own is not the same as being one hundred percent. Plus, if someone gets injured, you're going to use your healing ability on them when that's the very last thing you should do."

He shook his head, seeking to reassure her. "I won't do that unless it's a matter of life and death."

"But then *you'll* be the one at risk, don't you see? I'm not going to stand by and say nothing while you kill yourself to save someone else!"

His heart sank. It seemed they were at a stalemate on the issue, and he didn't know how to ease her fear, short of going against his own beliefs. "Baby, please. I can't stand by and condemn someone to death if it's in my power to prevent it. If I could, I wouldn't be a man you could respect at all." Much less love. And he hoped one day she would, though he didn't voice it.

Thankfully, her face softened and she released a long breath. "I know. God, this is so hard. I don't want you anywhere near the fighting, but that's who you are—a tough Navy SEAL turned wolf shifter and Healer. Something tells me the waiting and worrying doesn't get any easier."

"Probably not. This is where you have to trust me. I know what I'm doing."

She was silent for a long moment, and finally she nodded. "Okay. I'm afraid, but I *do* trust you. I want to prove that to you."

"Sweetheart, it's not about proving anything to me." Unable to help himself, he kissed her slowly. Then he drew back and curved his lips in a smile. "Whatever comes, we take it on together. All right?"

She made an attempt to relax. "Yeah."

That night, when they made love, it was beautiful. Intense. Zan poured his soul into loving her, and afterward whispered the words that meant so much to him. She still didn't say them back, and he tried not to be disappointed. He knew she cared for him. That much was obvious from how scared she was for him.

I don't need the words.

But it sure would be nice to hear them. Just once in my life.

He told himself to be patient. They had time. There wasn't any need to rush something so good, so right.

If only he'd remembered the lesson he learned in Afghanistan—that life is brief and time waits for no man or beast.

The next evening, he gathered with his team and a few of the prince's best men near the front entrance to the stronghold. They agreed to take several SUVs since not everyone could teleport and they preferred to remain together.

"Remember, this is a seek-and-destroy mission," Nick called loudly, making sure all the men could hear him. "Recon first, assess the situation, and then take them down."

Tarron broke in. "We want Darrow alive." This was met with widespread disapproval. "We need to question him about what he knows, and after we're satisfied, he will be put to death for his crimes. You have our word."

Grimly, Nick gave a nod. "Let's go!"

Zan hugged Selene to him tightly, then set her back. "Be back as soon as I can, baby."

"I'm holding you to that."

She smiled, trying to be brave, but her eyes were moist. He hated leaving her, but they'd talked about this. He saw in her face that she understood, but she wasn't happy.

With a last kiss, he got into the SUV that Ryon was driving, in the middle seat next to Phoenix. Jax got into the front. He didn't see where the other members of both teams chose to ride—his mind was too occupied with how they were going to get this mission done quickly, with a minimum of bloodshed.

Right.

"Selene didn't look too thrilled with you leaving," Nix remarked, breaking into his thoughts.

"About as happy as Noah looked just a minute ago."

"Shit, that's the truth."

"Trouble in paradise already?"

"Not as far as my being in the field, but . . ." He shrugged, his normally bright, cocky smile noticeably absent. "It's not easy, you know?"

"What's not?" But he had a good idea. So did the occupants in the front of the vehicle, if their exchanged glances were any indication.

"I always thought my mate would be a woman," he said quietly.

Oh, boy. So the man wasn't quite as nonchalant about that fact as he appeared. "How does Noah feel about having a wolf shifter for a mate?"

Nix snorted. "Are you kidding? He's ready to order a rainbow wedding cake and line up bridesmaids." That drew some snickers from the front. "Shut up, assholes. You guys got the ladies of your dreams."

"So, what?" Zan pressed. "You feel cheated?"

That word seemed to startle their friend, and he practically bristled. "No, that's not what I meant. It's just different than I expected. Noah has a good soul, and he's one of the best people I know."

There. That was more like a mate defending what was his.

"I know that. I was just wondering if *you* did."

After that, they let the subject drop. They rode in near silence, the tension growing as it always did the closer they got to a dangerous target.

All too soon, the vehicle stopped, and Ryon turned off the ignition.

Time to bag a rogue. His mate was waiting for him to return to her arms.

Twelve

The Pack's first move was to bring Kalen forward to do his thing.

All eyes, including Zan's, were on the Sorcerer as he summoned his staff and closed his eyes, his body going very still. Then he uttered a few words in Latin, the sound of his voice almost musical. Zan thought it was so cool how the guy did that and found himself a little envious of the man's gift.

"That is fuckin' awesome," Micah whispered from beside him.

"No shit," one of the vampire soldiers replied, eyes wide. "Even *I* wouldn't fuck with that dude."

Another vamp arched a brow. "Right?"

Yeah, a Goth guy all in black, right down to the ankle-length leather duster, who could actually turn you into a toad tended to impress people.

In moments Kalen was done, and he turned to the group at large. "I placed a cloak of invisibility around us as far as the humans are concerned, and the good news is there aren't many. I'm thinking they were probably compelled to leave. The bad news is the cloaking spell won't work on the rogues." He appeared troubled. "They'll see us the second we move in, if they haven't already."

Nick swore. "Then we need to move in fast to press whatever advantage we've got before it's gone. Get into position."

"One more thing," Kalen told them. "I unlocked the side and back entrances as well as all the interior doors to the rooms so we can go in quietly."

"Good job," Nick said.

Tarron motioned for his men to go, and they all spread out to surround the motel. Zan headed for the back of the complex, along with Micah, Nick, Hammer, Jax, and Phoenix. Last-minute intelligence gathered from one of Tarron's men showed that the rogues were concentrated at this end of the building, on the lower floor. Thank God for small favors. Their job would be hard enough without the creeps filling the whole motel.

There was scant cover, so they hurried to the outer wall and flattened themselves against it, near the back entrance. The door normally required a card key, but Nick pulled on the handle and the door opened, just as Kalen had claimed it would. He slipped inside first, Zan and the rest after him.

The first thing that struck his notice was that the inside was like a tomb—and in more ways than just the dead silence. The interior was dark. Lightbulbs were out, either naturally or unscrewed, in a few of the hallway sconces. He figured the rogues were trying to even the odds, make it harder for their enemies to see what was coming. There was also a bad smell permeating the air. Like stale garbage and rotten eggs. And old blood.

His stomach turned, and his wolf let out a low growl of disgust. He didn't know how any vampire could choose this life, one of death and stink. Killing and hiding, rinse and repeat. It didn't make sense to him how any creature derived pleasure from causing suffering and death.

Moving fast, they split up and started a room-to-room search. Once again Kalen had come through, as none of the doors were locked. Zan simply twisted the handle and went inside the first room—only to find it empty.

Puzzled, he went through the small space in a matter of seconds, checking the bathroom as well. Nothing. Conscious of the possibility of an ambush from above, he even checked the ceiling, but found nothing unusual. There was nobody here.

He repeated the process along with Nick and the others, their search turning up no trace of rogues as they progressed. Other than the stench indicating they'd once been there, that is.

"Someone must've warned them we were coming," Nick said, obviously pissed. "Goddammit!"

"Who?" Zan wondered aloud. "Nobody knew the plan but us!"

"Except Grant." The words caused their whole group to freeze.

Zan shoved a hand through his hair. "You don't really think he's involved, do you?"

"No. But someone close to him is, which supports what Daria's uncle told us—someone in our own government is fucking us over."

"No, *really*?" Micah retorted sarcastically. "And that would be different from any other day, how?"

Nick rolled his eyes. "Come on. Let's get this finished so we can get out of here and figure out what to do next."

Resuming the search, they checked the rest of the guest rooms on their wing and then eventually ran into the teams coming from the opposite direction. Tarron reported the same results, that they'd found no one. The whole scenario didn't sit well with the group.

The last areas to check were the office, the conference room, the laundry room and workout room. As Zan and his team finished the office, one of the vampires jogged up to them and gestured excitedly down one corridor.

"We found something weird in the laundry area. The prince wants you guys to take a look."

Following him, Zan exchanged a curious glance

with Nick. In his experience, "something weird" left in an abandoned building could not be a good thing. He was right.

As they entered the laundry room, Zan looked around at several industrial sized washers and dryers. Big rolling carts were sitting along one wall, waiting to transport towels and linens, and there were large cartons of detergent stacked nearby as well. But what dominated the space were the two big, round metal drums sitting in the middle of the concrete floor.

"Bleach?" Micah frowned, pointing at the block lettering on the drum. "Why would two huge containers of bleach be sitting in the middle of the floor like this?"

Nick held up a hand. "Everybody stop talking and moving around. Listen."

The room went quiet, and at first, Zan heard nothing. But gradually, a soft *tick, tick, tick* reached his ears. It was the one time he regretted that his hearing had returned.

Edging forward with Hammer, the commander carefully lifted a lid on one of the drums. Zan joined him as he set it aside, and they all peered down. A tangle of wires and a black box with a red digital readout met their shocked gazes. The numbers were counting down.

14 . . . 13 . . . 12 . . .

"Shit!" Nick shouted. "Clear the fucking building! Go! Go!"

He and Zan stepped back and let the others out first. It was a sacrifice that would cost them dearly.

They ran. Zan's heart thundered in his chest as he sprinted for the outer doors, knowing he wouldn't be fast enough. He could see the exit, so close. Saw the rest of his Pack and a group of vampires burst outside. He had a split second to feel relief that they'd made it—

And then the force of the detonation hit him from behind, hurling him into the air. He slammed into something hard, slid to the ground, the pain in his torso and skull hardly registering through the noise. The building came down all around him, pinning his body to the floor. All he could do was cover his head with his arms. Pray this wasn't the end.

He wanted to see his mate again. *Selene.*

The word whispered through his mind, and he felt it connect with hers. He hadn't meant to actually reach out. He didn't want her to be afraid, didn't want her to be in his head if he died. She was tough, but that would be too much.

Zan? What's wrong? What's happening?

It was a trap, he sent to her. *There was a bomb and it went off. Baby, we need help.*

Oh my God! Are you all right?

He paused, struggling to breathe through the dust and debris.

Zan? Her voice in his mind was starting to panic.

I will be. I love you, baby.

Were you caught in the explosion?
I'm trapped. But I'll keep until help comes.
You hang on. Do you hear me?
Yeah. Love you.

A buzzing started in his head, and his brain swam. As hard as he tried, he couldn't hold on to consciousness. With his mate's cry of alarm fading, he went totally under.

Love you, Zan said. He sounded tired, hoarse.

She started to reply, but felt him fade. "No!"

But the connection had been severed. Her heart leaped into her throat as panic threatened to take over. She started to run from the room she shared with Zan, but realized she was naked under one of her mate's T-shirts. She had wanted to be ready to seduce him when he returned. Now she just prayed he'd come back safe.

Quickly she dressed in jeans and one of her own T-shirts, and pulled on running shoes. Then she dashed into the corridor, shouting for help. One of Tarron's soldiers rounded the corner, obviously seeking the source of concern.

"Get as many of your men together as you can," she gasped, grabbing the man's shoulders. "They walked into a trap, and there was a bomb! Hurry!"

The soldier eyed her skeptically. "How do you know—"

"My mate is with them, and he contacted me through our link. Please, we have to go!"

"On it." The vampire bolted in the opposite direction.

Heading for the wing that housed the infirmary, she poured on the preternatural speed. In a matter of seconds, she reached the hospital, yelling at the top of her lungs. "Noah! Melina!" As she shouted again, the two of them jogged from somewhere in the back, followed by Victor Archer and a female nurse. The vampire doctor looked just as alarmed as his own nurse and temporary staff.

"What is it?" Melina demanded, grabbing Selene's arm.

"The men were led into a trap," she informed them, pulse tripping. "There was a bomb in the motel, and it detonated. They need help."

Noah's face turned white. "Nix."

Melina snapped, "If you're going to be of any assistance to your mate and the others, you'll have to keep it together. Can you do that?"

He nodded, making a visible effort to keep control. "I can."

"Good."

"We'll take two ambulances and meet you all out front," Victor said. "We need to hurry."

Selene would have preferred to ride with them, but she needed to make sure the vampires were mobilizing and let them know the medical staff was coming as well. She found them out front, assembling and loading themselves and weapons into three vehicles.

Spotting the soldier she'd spoken to in the corridor just minutes ago, she marched up to him. "Dr. Archer is coming around with their transports. I'm riding with you."

He opened his mouth to possibly refuse, then reconsidered. "Fine. Just stay out of the way when we get there."

Like that would happen. But she wasn't about to say that and risk being left behind.

The twenty-mile ride was the longest she'd ever endured. Every minute was fraught with fear because that was another minute her mate was trapped in the rubble of the motel. Unless the others had managed to dig him out. *Please, let him be safe!*

But he hadn't contacted her again, and that filled her with terror. Wouldn't he have let her know he'd been rescued? She knew the answer. As they pulled into the parking lot and she got her first glimpse of the devastation, cold sickness gripped her stomach. The building was in shambles, little more than the outer walls still standing. Vampires and Pack team members were everywhere, tending to the injured.

She spotted Tarron and Jax first, standing at the edge of the debris field, bent over, tossing aside bricks and Sheetrock. It struck her hard that they were looking for more victims, and her breath caught. They looked up as she rushed to them.

"Where's Zan? Is he all right?"

Jax's face was pinched. "Selene, you should

have stayed at the stronghold. There's nothing you can do here."

Instantly, her internal alarm went off, and she reacted, shoving the wolf in the chest. "Fuck you, Jax! Where is he?"

"Easy," he said, his tone gentle. "We haven't found him yet."

"What? But he contacted me! You should have found him by now!"

"We're doing everything we can. But . . ."

"But what? Don't hold anything back from me," she warned.

His voice was tortured. "He and Nick were bringing up the rear. They didn't make it out before the bomb went off. And now they're both missing."

She stared at Zan's best friend, trying to process the last part of what he'd just said. "Missing? They have to be here somewhere. I spoke to Zan through our mind link. He said he was trapped."

"I don't doubt he was at one time. But we've been over almost every square inch of the grounds and we haven't seen any sign of them yet."

Shaking her head, she looked out over the rubble. Cast her senses along their bond and tried to feel him. *Zan? Honey, I'm here, and they're looking for you and my dad. Are you still there?*

No answer. *Zan?* The lack of response was more frightening than her mate saying he was trapped. Feeling helpless, she glanced around and saw

Noah wrapped tightly in Nix's arms. She couldn't help the bolt of envy that shot through her at seeing the men reunited and immediately felt shitty about it. Truly, she was glad the others were safe to return to their loved ones. But she wanted hers safe, too.

She was about to lend a hand and start digging in the debris herself when a vampire trotted over to Tarron. She listened intently.

"Your Highness, one of our wounded, Trace, has just come around and says he saw something important. He's on a stretcher over there." The soldier pointed.

Selene accompanied the whole group to the fallen vampire's side, eager to hear his news. The young soldier's face was covered in blood and his breath wheezed in his chest. He gazed up at his prince, eyes wide.

"The rogues . . . have to stop them." A cough rattled his body.

Tarron spoke kindly as he crouched next to the young vampire. "Tell me what you saw, Trace."

"They took the two shifters. Plucked them right from under our noses. Picked them up and . . . vanished."

"Oh, God," she moaned. Suddenly her legs went weak and her mind whirled. Kidnapped. Her mate and her father, taken by those bastards. This couldn't be happening. "Where would they take them? How do we find out?"

"I don't know." Tarron's jaw clenched in barely concealed anger. "But we'll find them and make them pay. Especially Darrow."

"Cut off the head of the snake," Jax put in, clearly seething as well. "I'm going to enjoy watching Darrow writhe on the ground."

She gave a humorless laugh. "Not if I get to him first."

Icy-cold purpose flowed through Selene's veins. She was going to find her mate and her dad, and then she was going to gut Darrow like a trout.

You hear me, my mate? I'm coming.

Still no answer. But she wouldn't fall apart yet. She'd know if either of them were dead; she was convinced of that.

She held on to that knowledge. Because if she didn't, she'd go insane.

Zan awoke to the strange sensation that his arms and legs weighed a ton. He could barely move them, and when he did, he heard a metallic rattling sound. Opening his eyes, he blinked and then squinted, letting his eyes adjust to the gloom. When he did, he knew he was fucked.

He was in a large chamber, chained to a wall. He'd been left sitting, and he supposed he should be thankful considering that across the dim space, Nick had been left hanging by his wrists, toes just barely grazing the floor.

"Nick?" he called, voice rasping. "Nick, wake up."

His heart lurched when a figure stepped from the shadows and crossed to him with preternatural speed, striking him on the side of his face. His head snapped back against the wall, making his vision swim. "I was just making sure he's alive, asshole," he growled.

"Shut up."

Another blow landed on his face, and his jaw began to throb. This time he held silent, but he glared daggers at the rogue, who was enjoying their torment.

"A feisty one, huh? The boss loves the ones who fight." He smirked. "He'll have a lot of fun breaking you, for sure. But that will have to wait until he's dealt with Westfall. Long time comin', that one. A little revenge served with his evening wine."

Zan tried to think of the rogue as a caricature. A bad joke that would be gone any second, soon forgotten. But the cackle the creature let out was hair-raising, making goose bumps prickle on his skin. It was the sound of a mind three-quarters gone, reminding him of a hamster trying to run on a broken wheel.

Just then Nick groaned, saving him from forming a response that likely would've gotten him hit again. He didn't want their attention shifted to Nick either, but any hope of putting it off was dashed when Carter Darrow entered the chamber.

Zan's first thought was that the vampire looked sophisticated. As though he had just finished dinner at the country club with a few wealthy friends. His suit was expensive and well tailored, his shoes no doubt an equally pricy brand. The vampire's face was chiseled, good-looking for anyone who went for that sort of *I'm-too-good-for-you* attitude, he supposed—and the rotten fucker had attitude in spades.

That much was apparent by how he walked and carried himself. Just like on the video feed, he had his head back, so that he appeared to be looking down his nose at you from under his lashes. His ash-blond hair was pulled back into a ponytail, revealing a fresh scratch on his cheek, which ran to his neck.

Zan studied the scar and a plan began to germinate. He just hoped he was able to put it into action.

"I see I have *two* of you availing yourselves of my hospitality," he said, his voice oozing with cultured, urbane charm. "A bonus."

The male had been rogue for more than twenty years. How had he managed to forestall the level of insanity exhibited by his underlings? Or did he simply mask it better? Probably the latter.

"Not by choice," Zan informed him. "Personally, I'm not happy to be missing another episode of *Ghost Hunters*."

Darrow laughed, revealing straight, white teeth. "I think I like you, wolf."

"Funny. The sentiment isn't returned at all. No hard feelings."

"Hmm." The vampire studied him, crossing his arms casually over his chest. "I think what—or who—you're really missing is your mate. Nick's daughter, the prey that should've been mine."

Horror seized his throat and his head began to pound. In that instant, he knew why he'd been kidnapped along with Nick. "How did you know what she is to me?"

"Same way I know everything. I have sources."

"Who?"

"That's what I'd like to know," Nick put in, voice groggy.

"Ah, you're awake!" Darrow looked pleased about that. "And answers you shall have. It's the least I can do for you before you die. What would you like to know?"

Nick shot him an incredulous look. "Seriously? Why did you go after my daughter back then? She was just a little girl."

Darrow shrugged. "She was so pretty, she caught my notice. And I was hungry. I made a bit of a game out of stalking her. It was pure sport."

Anger and disgust suffused Nick's expression. "Sport? Hunting *children*?"

"What's the big deal? Hunters shoot doves and

deer all the time, fix them for the dinner table, and no one blinks. Yes, *sport*."

"That's nowhere near the same thing. That's monstrous," the commander spat.

"I didn't succeed anyhow, but your mate was a nice consolation prize." He smiled as though in fond memory. "Did you know even as rogues, we can choose to make our bite pleasurable? Bet you thought we lost that ability when we crossed the line, but the truth is, we just don't bother to use seduction very often."

"And you're telling me this because?"

"I made your mate orgasm several times . . . before I killed her."

If the chains had been any metal but silver, Zan had no doubt Nick would have ripped out of them as though they were made of paper. As it was, he lunged against his bonds and snarled his rage, his wolf so close to the surface it was painful to witness.

While the vamps continued to laugh and taunt Nick, Zan took stock of his own injuries. His back was sore from the blast, and he had a few cuts and scrapes. The most worrying thing was the pressure in his head, building steadily into an awful headache. The stabbing kind where it felt like a knife was twisting in his brain. This was going to be a bad one, like nothing he'd ever experienced, and he knew what it meant.

The blast and blow to his head had hurt him, inside. He was in real trouble.

Somehow, Nick managed to keep the men talking and learn their secrets.

"Why come for me now, after all this time?" he demanded.

"That's the question, isn't it?" Darrow casually stepped to a table sitting against one wall, close to Nick, and fingered something lying on it. From his sitting position, Zan couldn't see what it was. "Come on, Westfall, *think*. I'm savoring my revenge for your interference in my plans to savor your precious daughter, but do I strike you as the sort who'd go too far out of my way to get it?"

"No," Nick said slowly, eyes narrowed. "Not unless there was something more in it for you. My guess is money, flowing from whoever is keeping you in Armani suits."

The vampire's fangs flashed as he laughed. "There now, was that so hard? Care to further guess who I'm working for, and why they have such a stiffy when it comes to seeing you burn?"

"I'll go out on a limb and say it's probably the same asshole in the government who is privy to our movements and keeps feeding them to you."

"*Ding-ding*, right again!"

God, this fucker was crazy.

"So who is the traitor, Darrow?" Nick pressed. "Who's behind the ambushes on my team? Who needs the Alpha Pack dead and gone? The White House? The president himself?"

"No. The tentacles don't extend quite as far as

the president. But close." The vampire studied his nemesis thoughtfully for a moment. "Your Alpha Pack was set up to be attacked in Afghanistan when they were still Navy SEALs, turned into wolf shifters, then recruited to become the Alpha Pack before you ever knew they existed, and then betrayed time and again. By whom? And why? You may as well have your curiosity satisfied before I kill you."

Zan waited, hardly breathing as Darrow circled the room, obviously deciding where to begin. Finally, after six years of wondering, it seemed they were going to learn the truth about the Alpha Pack and the worst of the challenges they'd been dealing with since.

"As you may have surmised by now, the formation of the Alpha Pack was a planned operation all along. The US government had somehow learned about the rogue werewolves in Afghanistan and placed a team there, purposely in harm's way, to let nature take its course."

"Then what August Bradford told us is true," Nick said.

"Ah, the good scientist. He's quite dead, you know. My boys were called upon to dispatch the man after he escaped your team."

Zan winced at the news, feeling bad for Daria, Ryon's mate. Bradford was her uncle, and the news that he was one of those behind the experimenting on shifters had been hard on her.

"I can't say I'm disappointed by that news," Nick said dryly.

"I imagine not. Anyway, the circle of those in the know about the Alpha Pack project from its inception was quite small. One member of the White House cabinet, one higher-up in the CIA, and one general."

"Jarrod Grant?"

If Jarrod, Nick's best friend, had been involved in the attack in Afghanistan, it would kill Nick. Plain and simple.

"No. He was brought in afterward as the handler of the team and told only what he needed to know."

"You mean lied to."

"Of course. Now, things went all right in the first couple of years," Darrow said. "The Alpha Pack emerged exactly as the little government group had hoped—top-secret military fighters who were shifters with special Psy abilities, battling the paranormal bad guys. Truth, justice, and the American way, blah, blah. Makes me want to sing the fucking national anthem."

Nick ignored the caustic remark. "So what went wrong?"

Darrow turned, his smile chilling. "The head of the government circle pulling the strings from the start, our very own secretary of state, Owen Matthews, was approached by a certain Unseelie king named Malik."

Oh fuck. And there's where it all went to shit.

"And the rest, as they say, is history." Darrow picked up the object from the table and unfurled it. A rawhide whip. "Matthews and his circle were bad enough for the nefarious methods they used in forming the Alpha Pack. But they never stood a chance against the persuasion of a dark creature like Malik, and soon scientists were hired, labs built for the purpose of experimenting on shifters and humans. Malik wanted to integrate himself into society, posing as a rich human entrepreneur while creating a race of super-soldier shifters with Psy abilities to be his own personal army. He wanted to rule the world."

"But we stopped him," Nick finished. "Destroyed the labs and came too close to the truth. And now Matthews is trying to sweep all of his shit under the rug—including the Alpha Pack."

"Exactly. He approached me to accomplish just that, and in return he set up a team of scientists in Washington to create special drugs for paranormals. They produce several types that target different areas, most important, to make already aggressive vampires turn rogue and to allow them to walk in the daylight."

"Matthews wanted one last shot at creating a fighting force he could control." Nick laughed grimly. "What an idiot. My Pack consists of good men, heroic men, who'd do anything for their country and fellow man. They'd battle any creature anywhere to save even *you*, Darrow, but Matthews is so short-sighted he'd see them destroyed to save face."

"That's about right."

"What's he paying you? I have contacts that can see the figure doubled if you help us bring him down."

Darrow looked shocked for a moment, then shook his head. "It's not *all* about the money. I have power now."

"Not for long. He'll see you all dead as well to save himself, and you're a fool if you don't realize it."

The vampire's gaze hardened. "And this is where our conversation ends, Westfall. I'm finally a part of something big, and I won't allow you or anyone else to stand in my way. You're done."

"Not yet." Nick gave him a feral grin. "You think I'm going to die here, in your sorry excuse for a home?"

"That's precisely what's going to happen. I'm going to kill you right under Prince Tarron's regal nose, another perk of my revenge. I love sticking it to that pompous bastard whenever I can, and I'm going to enjoy dumping your body on his doorstep."

"Really? You're either ballsy or extremely stupid to make your home base so close to the prince's stronghold."

Nick's gaze flicked briefly to Zan and away

again. Heart racing, Zan listened, hoping the commander could wrangle a bit more information from Darrow.

"I've been here for almost a year, and he never suspected," Darrow bragged. "We would've attracted too much attention if we'd moved into a regular home in some neighborhood. But nobody pays much mind to new tenants in a formerly empty office complex, especially if it's in an area with some traffic."

"Clever," Nick mused without humor. Another glance at Zan sent the message: *Tell Selene. Get us help.*

"I thought so." He gave the whip a loud snap, then nodded to his minion hovering nearby. "Turn him to face the wall and then get out of my way unless you want the same."

As the rogue repositioned Nick in his chains and stripped off his shirt, Zan opened the mind link with his mate.

Baby? To his relief, she was waiting.

Oh, God! Honey, where are you? Tarron and his men, the Pack, everyone is looking for you and Dad!

Sweetheart, listen to me carefully. Darrow is holding us in a building he claims is very near Tarron's stronghold. It sounds like this place is in the nearest town, in an area where there are other businesses, so their comings and goings don't stand out too much.

All right. I'll tell the others. Anything else?

He said they've been here almost a year, so check real estate sales or rentals. If there's nothing under Darrow's name, check under Owen Matthews or any name he might use for his holdings.

There was a pause. *You don't mean Secretary of State Matthews, do you?*

Unfortunately, yes. He's the head of the snake, always was. When he goes down, all of this stops.

Okay. You hang on! We'll find this building and we'll be there soon!

I will. I love y—

A scream shattered his thoughts, and quickly he shut down the connection. There was no way he could subject his mate to what was happening to her father.

He didn't want to watch, but he couldn't look away. Nick's back was bowed, muscles bunched as he gripped the silver chains that had to be burning his palms. His head was turned to the side, dark hair falling over his eyes, and his teeth were gritted against the pain.

Darrow raised his arm, brought down the whip again. The rawhide struck Nick's back with a horrible slap, wrapping around his upper shoulder, crossing down his back diagonally to his hip. A line was scored into his flesh, a deep furrow that immediately began streaming with blood. Crimson streaked down his flesh, into the waistband of his jeans.

Over and over again, the blows rained down. Zan held on to the contents of his stomach, though just barely. That is, until Darrow's devious mind revealed Nick's ultimate torture.

"Smell that?" He inhaled, then shivered with pleasure as he stepped forward. Trailed a finger through the red liquid and brought it to his lips. Tasted. "Delicious blood. Born shifters taste so exquisite, not even the finest red wine can compare to the full-bodied richness."

"Get off me, you freak," Nick hissed, yanking against his bonds.

"Don't be so dramatic. After all, you're going to love the next part."

"What are you talking about?"

"Remember what I said before? Your mate loved what I did to her. . . ." Darrow moved close, into his captive's back. Ran a palm down his shoulder and side, rested his chin at the crook of his prey's neck as a lover might do.

Horror filled Zan to the core, and he fought in earnest not be sick.

"No," Nick whispered. "Don't."

"Oh, yes. I'm going to feed from you, wolf. And you're going to love every moment of it . . . right until you breathe your last."

"You twisted motherfucker—"

Nick's words were cut off as Darrow struck, sliding his fangs into the curve of his captive's neck. Nick cried out, his body tense . . . and then he relaxed, letting out a hoarse moan. It was a sound of defeat. Broken.

With a dark laugh, Darrow pulled their bodies together tightly, Nick's back to his front, and began to feed slowly. With long pulls and the occasional lick, nuzzling his prey's neck, then repeating. His captive sank further under the wicked spell, unable to stop what was happening. Past caring.

Seduced.

"You're mine now," Darrow murmured against his skin. "Say it."

"I'm yours."

"What do you want, wolf?"

"Drink from me. Take it all."

"Patience. I'll do as you wish. After we've enjoyed this fully."

They moved together, vampire and prey, in a dark, ancient ritual that went back in history to the gods themselves. Zan knew, should help come in time to save their lives, even a man as mentally strong as Nick would find it nearly impossible to get past this.

The commander would rather die than be seduced into finding pleasure at the hands of his worst enemy. His murderer.

And with that thought, Zan finally lost the battle and became violently ill.

Thirteen

Selene paced, almost coming out of her skin.

Tarron and Jax were each on their cell phone, calling everywhere they could think of to find out who had leased or purchased buildings in the area in the past year. They were searching for an office structure large enough to hold a coven of rogues, in an area where they'd blend in with normal traffic. How hard could that be?

"All right," the prince said, ending a call. Movement in the conference room halted and everyone gave him their attention. "One of my men has found a paper trail on a building in Grove Park, a midsized city less than a half hour from here. It fits all the criteria, except in the owner's name."

"Let me guess," Aric said. "It's a dummy corporation?"

Tarron nodded. "A fake telecom business. But

at the end of the paper trail, the owner is our illus-
trious secretary of state."

"So, when do we leave?" Selene demanded impatiently. "Time is wasting. And don't even think
I'm staying here, because I'm not."

"Selene, Zan would kill me if anything happened to you," Jax said with a frown.

"No, he wouldn't, because he knows by now
how stubborn I am. Besides, you guys forget I'm a
born wolf. I have teeth and claws just like you,
and I fight dirty."

The men looked at each other, no doubt trying
to figure a way to make her stay. In the end, however, they understood she would follow them if
necessary. They knew she had to get to her mate.

Jax sighed. "All right. But if he takes a chunk
out of my ass, I'm blaming you."

"Fair enough."

In less than fifteen minutes, several SUVs full of
vampires and shifters were ready to roll. Selene
rode with Jax, sitting in the middle with him while
Ryon drove, as usual. Aric was up front beside him.
The mood was tense, the team ready for a fight.

There was little conversation on the way, their
minds too occupied with the takedown. With
finding Zan and her father alive. That last was far
from a sure thing. It terrified her the way her mate
had cut off their contact so abruptly. He was either
hurt or protecting her from something. Or both.
None of those was very comforting.

Arriving a couple of blocks from their destination, they parked on a side street out of view of the building. Then they climbed out and began making their way to the address they sought, surrounding the premises. Flanked by Zander's friends, his brothers, she prepared to rescue the man she loved.

Carter Darrow had fucked with the wrong people.

It would be his very last mistake.

Nick regained consciousness slowly. Wished he hadn't.

He was still hanging in the silver chains that had burned his skin almost to the bone. His body was limp, heavy, his strength almost gone.

Along with his will to live.

Closing his eyes, he struggled not to remember how he'd begged that murderous vampire to drink from him. How good the pull had felt, how his cock had hardened in his jeans . . . and how he'd come in pulsing waves, unable to help himself.

His physical reaction had *nothing* to do with Darrow. He knew that. He wasn't even sexually attracted to males. Vampires were masters of compulsion, and even the vilest of their bunch could hold the strongest will in thrall.

But he hated himself all the same.

Darrow had murdered his mate. Had seduced

her in the same fashion and had wanted to do the same to his beautiful daughter. Nick knew he'd never be able to erase this day from his mind, even if he should survive another two hundred years.

The heavy door opened, and footsteps shuffled in. *Please, let this end. Let them save Zander, but please, let me go.*

Just then, the familiar buzz began in his head, and a picture began to form. He saw this very chamber, bathed in blood. So much of it, coating every surface. Bodies were strewn about. His mind's eye took in the scene—and then stopped on one prone figure.

Selene, his baby girl, was lying on her side in a pool of blood. Eyes open, fighting for her next breath.

Then she lost the fight.

Jolted from the horrifying vision, he sucked in a deep breath. "No. It can't happen like that!"

"What are you babbling about, wolf?" Darrow asked, amused. "Losing what's left of your mind already?" He chuckled, picked up something from the table, and moved to Nick's side. "Wait until you experience some of my fondness for knife play. You, bring our other prisoner out here so he can watch and wait for his turn."

The other rogue did as he was told, unlocking Zan's chains and pulling him into the center of the room. Then he pushed the Healer to his knees.

The silver blade came into Nick's line of vision,

and he knew. This was the weapon that would take his daughter's life. What could he do to change the outcome when death just wouldn't be cheated? Hadn't he learned that lesson well?

"I prefer claws, myself," he managed to retort.

Before Darrow could respond, a commotion reached their ears. A crash, banging noises. An explosion that shook the walls. Cursing, the rogue spun to face the door.

Then it slammed inward, banging into the inside wall. His Pack and the prince's men spilled inside—along with Selene.

"No! Selene, get out!" he shouted.

Or thought he did. He would never be sure. Not appearing to hear him, his daughter rushed straight to Darrow and a vicious fight was on. In a blink, she took the rogue to the floor, shifting her hands into sharp claws and baring her teeth. Just when it seemed she had the upper hand and would finish him, a flash of silver caught his eye.

And Darrow buried the blade in his daughter's side. The whole thing had taken only seconds.

She stilled, eyes wide, gasping for air. "Daddy? Zan?"

With a nasty grin, the rogue pushed her off him and the knife pulled free with a sickening squelch. He laughed as she fell limp and boneless to the floor.

The monster had killed his baby at last. Death had collected his due.

Daddy. Now, after all those lonely years, she'd called him Daddy again. When it mattered most.

Grief-stricken, Nick gratefully surrendered to the darkness.

He could finally let go.

When they burst into the hideous chamber, Selene took in two things: her father chained to the wall, covered in blood, and her mate kneeling on the floor.

Red clouded her mind, and she rushed for the object of her bloodlust. Darrow barely had time to react, taking a step toward her as she leaped at him and took him to the floor. Shifting her hands into claws and letting her fangs drop, she had every intention of ending him right there. She heard shouts, perhaps her dad's voice. And Zan.

Then Darrow punched her in the side, hard. The blow stole her breath and she glanced down . . . to see a knife buried in her side to the hilt.

"Daddy? Zan?" she whispered.

Grinning like a jackal, he yanked out the blade and shoved her to the floor. She was so heavy, couldn't move. Just as her eyes drifted shut, she heard her mate howl. The sounds of renewed battle.

And then nothing.

When the door slammed against the wall and their backup started streaming into the chamber,

Zan barely had time to react. His mate flew at Darrow, took him to the floor. She was about to rip him apart.

In an instant, he'd buried a knife in her side.

Zan's howl of fury rang throughout the chamber, above the din of the fight, as more rogues teleported in to engage his friends. Zan had only one goal, however—to kill Darrow.

Becoming a machine, he shifted a hand into sharp claws and slashed his way through rogues, gutting them. Ripping out their hearts. In the cacophony, they didn't matter. His entire focus was only on the cool blond monster who'd so ruthlessly stabbed his mate.

At last he spotted an opening and threw himself at Darrow. They met in a clash of bodies, the bastard not going down easily this time. He'd been ready for Zan's attack, but he didn't have grief-fueled rage on his side.

Zan's assault was relentless. Grabbing the arm with the knife, he smashed the wrist into the floor, crushing the bone instantly. Screaming, Darrow dropped the knife, and Zan went for his throat. But the vampire rolled, got his legs under himself, and shoved Zan off. It gave his enemy enough leverage to leap at him and try to pin him, but he was at a disadvantage with the broken wrist and didn't get purchase quickly enough. Zan twisted to the side, easily breaking his hold and launching a counterattack.

Landing on top of Darrow, he grabbed a fistful of the vampire's hair, pulled him up. He had to end this, and now. Executing a partial shift, he lunged forward and ripped out his enemy's throat. It was over that fast. Darrow's expression was one of disbelief and shock as the light faded from his gaze.

Zan dropped him and crawled to his mate's side, heart pounding in fear. "Baby?" Gathering her into his arms, he was hardly aware of the sounds of the battle around him coming to an end. His team and the prince's vampires had won the fight. But if he didn't do something fast, his mate would lose hers.

She was still, pale. Hand trembling, he pushed an errant lock of platinum hair from her gorgeous face and gathered his strength. This was it. Selene and Nick needed him, and he would not fail them. No matter the cost—and it would be the highest.

His eyes never leaving her face, he took a deep breath. Summoned his power from deep within and sent the warm fingers of healing into her body, seeking the damage. His light traveled through veins and muscle to the source of the substantial blood loss from the wound in her side. Without his intervention his mate would die, and he wouldn't allow that to happen.

Already, his head was throbbing. But he pushed the pain aside and concentrated on the damage the blade had caused internally. The tip of the knife had pierced a lung, so he sent his energy to that tear first, knitting together the tissues and re-creating air to inflate the organ.

Next came the stab wound, and he painstakingly repaired the flesh, making it as brand-new. Once the gash was closed, he focused on generating the blood she'd lost, not stopping until she was well on the road to recovery.

Done, he slumped over his mate. Held her close for a moment. "I love you. So much. I'll love you forever," he whispered.

Veins in his brain were flexing. Throbbing. Sending out agonizing pains as dire warnings to stop, which he couldn't possibly heed. Because Nick was next.

He studied her face, committed it to memory. Then, throat closing on a burning lump, he handed her into Jax's arms. "Take care of her. Promise me."

His best friend didn't bother to pretend all was fine. His eyes were moist, his expression miserable. "I promise. But you're going to be okay, Alexander."

At that, Zan smiled. Nobody ever called him by his full name, and Jax knew it. He supposed his friend knew their minutes were numbered. Zan had never known how precious time was until it was almost gone.

Giving his mate one last kiss on her lips, he turned away and hurried to Nick. Whipped almost to death and nearly drained, the commander was in even worse shape than Selene had been, and if there had been any doubt this healing session would be Zan's last, there wasn't any longer.

As he placed his palms on Nick's chest and sent the warmth of his energy into him, Zan actually felt the tiny ruptures starting to happen in his brain. Each little pop battered him with dizziness. Then the pops became agony, like a sharp spear being driven into his skull and deep into his gray matter.

He couldn't quit. Nick had seemingly given up on his own life, but Zan wouldn't do the same. The commander had more living to do, a daughter to make amends with and to love. Zan was sad he wouldn't be there to see it, to grow old loving his mate.

Muscle and bone knitted, healed. He saw to that, every single furrow from the whip's lashes, every drop of blood, cleaned. No scars. Gone, like a wisp of smoke. He replaced the man's blood, improved his circulation. All Nick had to do was awaken.

He was done. Sitting on his heels, he tilted his head back. Tried to suck in air. But it was no use. His skull was in a vise, so much pressure crushing his brain. One by one, the rest of the arteries and veins gave way, releasing a flood of pain, and he fell backward, crying out. Warm liquid gushed from his nose, filled his mouth.

He was caught, held by someone on the team. Jax? Shadows hovered over him as voices called out to him. Begged him to hang on. He wanted to tell them it was okay, he was fine. Anything to take away their panic, their sorrow.

For one brief moment, his vision cleared and he saw them all. His whole team, except for Nick. His brothers. He loved them all. He wanted to see Selene one more time, but he knew she was healing. She would be all right, and that was all that mattered. Maybe he'd see her again in heaven one day, if such a place existed.

The last of his breath left him on a puff of air. Then his brothers' beloved faces faded into white.

And Zander Cole died.

The first thing Selene became aware of was the tomblike silence all around her. Then the soft sounds of . . . sobbing? Who was crying?

"Oh, fuck no! Please . . ."

That was Jax's voice. The hair on the back of her neck prickled, and fear shot down her spine. Gingerly, she sat up and rubbed her temples, trying to get her bearings. She'd been going after the rogues. Darrow. Rescuing her father—and Zan!

Glancing to her right, she spotted Darrow on the floor, his throat ripped out. She was glad he was dead, the fight obviously won since the Pack, the prince, and his men were all standing around. But why was everyone so quiet?

"Zan?" she called. Alerted that she was conscious, some of the prince's men met her eyes and then quickly looked away. Most alarming of all was when she focused on the faces of the Pack team; every one of them had tears in his eyes, some streaming down his cheeks. A cold lump formed in her chest.

They moved aside as a unit to reveal Jax sitting on the floor. And in his arms was her mate. His head was tilted back, and he wasn't moving.

"What's going on?" Her voice rose. "Zan?"

On her hands and knees, she scrambled over to kneel beside Jax and looked into her mate's handsome face. His beautiful eyes were half-open, staring into space. His chest wasn't moving. Blood had streamed from his nose and mouth, but was drying now. Seconds ticked by, and she couldn't process what had happened.

"Zander?" Reaching out, she touched his face. Still warm, but cooler than he should be, perhaps. Trying again, she shook him. "Wake up, honey. We won!"

"Selene," Jax said on a sob. "I'm sorry."

"How come he's not waking up? What's going on?" No. It wasn't true. She refused to believe.

Suddenly, Aric crouched next to her, took her hand. The normally cocky wolf was the picture of devastation. "Selene, he's gone," he said gently. "There was nothing we could do."

"No!" Shaking her head frantically, she searched

the others' expressions, seeking affirmation that he was fine. "H-he's going to be all right! He's just in shock, or tired. Needs to rest."

Suddenly, a large hand squeezed her shoulder. Turning, she found herself looking into her father's stricken face. "Daddy! You're all right! Tell them Zan's going to be fine, too, just as soon as he rests. He's—"

"Baby girl, listen to me. Zan did a brave thing tonight. He sacrificed himself for the people he loved most—you and me. He healed us both, but his brain just couldn't take any more. Do you understand?"

The truth crept in, no matter how hard she fought to keep it out. Her throat began to burn, and her eyes blurred as she looked to the man in Jax's arms. "Daddy?"

"Zan's dead, baby," he said hoarsely, hugging her close. "I'm so, so sorry."

Stunned, she momentarily leaned in to her father. Then she pushed away from him and pointed a shaking finger at Jax, voice rising. "You're a Timebender! So reverse time and fix this!"

"I can't," he croaked. "Zan would never forgive me."

"I won't forgive you if you don't!"

"I can't do it, Selene." His eyes begged her to understand. "I won't trade in your life to save his. I can't use my gift that way."

He wouldn't help. Frantic, she looked to Tarron. "You can change him into a vampire, right? Bite him or something?"

"No," he said with real regret. "I can't turn a person who's already departed. You don't know how sorry I am."

No, please. She held out her arms to Jax. "Give him to me."

Relinquishing his burden, Jax placed her mate in her embrace. She held him tight, close to her heart, stroked his beloved face. His silky, ebony hair.

"I waited too long," she whispered, tears streaking down her cheeks. "I wanted to tell you that I love you so. I thought I had time. I'm sorry I waited. I love you. Love you."

She rocked him, a well of grief surging to choke and overwhelm her. Her heart broke, and a keening noise reached her ears, ragged. Raw. She couldn't go on without him. Wouldn't.

"God, this is so wrong," someone said quietly. It sounded like Ryon. "Why?"

There was no reason. No justice in this. She couldn't accept that he was dead.

The anger took her by surprise. The refusal to let him go. That's when she became aware of a strange tugging in the region of her heart. A thread, golden and strong. It began in her chest and stretched to just beyond Zan's body in her arms. *Our bond.*

That's when she knew he hadn't left.

"The bond," she gasped, eyes widening as she looked at her father. "It's still there."

Relief and something like hope stirred on his face. "Then there's still a chance."

Her pulse tripped. "What do you mean?"

"Remember what I told you about your gift? That it would manifest when you need it most?"

She nodded. "Yes. But I don't understand. I don't know what to do!"

"Follow the thread; find his spirit. Lead him back to his body, and then we can help him heal."

"Is that really possible?"

Ryon stepped forward. "Zan and his wolf are still here, and he doesn't want to leave you. He'll hang around as long as he can."

"But—oh, God, what do I do? How?" What if she'd missed her chance?

"You're a Spirit Catcher," Nick explained. "That means you can follow your mating bond and bring his spirit back into his physical body. You can do this."

Several gasps met Nick's revelation about their immortality. But for now, she concentrated on doing as he said. Carefully, she focused on the thread as she'd done when Zan was in the coven's infirmary. But this time she was bringing him all the way back instead of simply anchoring him to this world. She imagined winding the thread around the two of them, drawing him to her. When that worked, she gave him a mental push toward his broken body.

Selene? Baby? What's happening to me?

Her heart leaped. *Let yourself slide back into your body. Don't fight it.*

But it hurts. My brain is fried, and I don't think you can fix it.

Somehow we will. Please, trust me?

A pause. *For you, anything.*

I love you.

She heard the smile in his voice. *I knew, and I love you too.*

He followed her lead without hesitation, hovering over his body and then slipping back down into his shell like smoke, his wolf following. Once he was inside, she heard a rattling intake of air and saw he was trying to breathe.

"Help me," she cried. "What now?"

Suddenly, Tarron was crouching at her side. "I'll give him a bit of my blood to speed the healing. Then you give him some of yours to bind him to you forever. Together we will gift him with immortality, though he likely would've had that anyway as your Bondmate. Now it will be a sure thing."

"All right," she said gratefully. "Let's do it."

The prince went first, slashing his wrist. Without wasting a second, he held the sliced skin over

Zan's blue lips while she pried his mouth open. The first drops fell into his mouth, but there was no movement. And then, without warning, he latched on to Tarron's arm and sucked like a newborn. A murmur rose in the room, growing in excitement.

When he'd taken enough, Tarron gestured to her. "Your turn."

Encouraged, she repeated the process using her own blood, thinking it was strange to be feeding him as one would a vampire. But she was for anything that helped him to heal.

"That's enough," the prince said. "Now we take him back to the stronghold and get him into the infirmary. With any luck, we'll see signs of improvement within a few hours."

"Do you think he'll be well that soon?" She stroked her mate's hair again, unable to stop touching him.

"No. I expect it will be days before we know whether his brain has recovered from the damage it sustained today. But don't lose hope." His smile was gentle.

"I won't." The tears flowed anew, but this time she could handle them.

Her mate would live. She couldn't ask for anything more.

He had thought he was dead, for good.

Still, he hadn't been able to go into the light that

beckoned from beyond the chamber of suffering. To give his soul over to the gorgeous white presence that promised eternal happiness, peace among the angels. That hadn't sounded so bad.

Except Selene wouldn't be there.

He didn't know what to do, and so he'd hovered, watching everyone he loved fall completely apart over his death. Not only his mate, but Jax, Nick, Hammer, Aric, Ryon, Micah, Nix, A.J., and the rest. Even Tarron, who'd known Zan only a short time, seemed full of sorrow.

I wanted to tell you that I love you so. I thought I had time. I'm sorry I waited. I love you. Love you.

Her words had torn at his heart, made it not just difficult, but impossible, for him to go. He had known how she felt, of course, but hearing the words spoken aloud was his dream come true. How could he leave now?

And then a miracle. Thanks to his mate having a very special gift of her own, he was pulled back into his body.

Opening his eyes was too hard, so he contented himself with listening to the sounds of his mate and his Pack brothers' joy that he'd been brought back from beyond. That eventually, he'd be all right. He relished his mate's warm hand holding his as he was lifted and placed on a gurney, the nearness of her sweet scent.

He basked in her repeated declarations of love, given freely where she'd once been wary and unsure. Her feelings bathed him like the warm waters of a whirlpool, all of the sadness and struggle being cleansed and washed away.

The gurney bumped and rolled along, but there was no pain with the movements. Just a bone-deep exhaustion that threatened to drag him to the depths. He sensed he wouldn't die now, but neither did he want to let go and sleep. He wanted to spend every second soaking up his mate's love.

The cool air of the outdoors caressed his skin, and in seconds, the gurney was being loaded into a vehicle. An ambulance, most likely. Selene had to let go of his hand temporarily, but soon clasped him again as she climbed in and they shut the doors.

When the vehicle started rolling, she began humming a song to him. No words, just a soft tune, something low and pretty. Romantic.

I didn't know you could sing.

Hardly singing. He heard the laughter in her voice in his head. *I can't really carry a tune. More like expressing my happiness.*

Keep doing it. I like hearing you.

Okay, but you have to promise to sleep so you can recover. Deal?

Deal.

And so, his mate's unnamed song lulling him, he finally gave in to healing slumber.

Fourteen

When Zan awoke to find his mate at his bedside, he blinked to be sure he wasn't dreaming. "Selene?"

Her head snapped up, the magazine on her lap falling to the floor, forgotten. "There you are! It's about time, too. How are you feeling?"

He considered that. "Good, I think."

"Nothing hurts?" Bruised shadows colored the skin under her tired eyes. She looked worn-out. Anxious.

"Nothing," he assured her. "Have you been getting any sleep, baby?"

She gestured to the other side of the bed. "Tarron had a twin bed brought in for me."

"But it doesn't look like you've been using it much."

She smiled ruefully. "Guilty. But I couldn't sleep

until I knew for sure you were coming back to me."

"Sweetheart, you had to know I would," he said, taking her hand. "You brought me back. No way was I leaving again."

"I know. But the past few days, worrying about you, especially after what happened . . ." She swallowed hard, her eyes filling with tears.

Reaching up, he brushed away a stray drop from her cheek. "Hey, now, none of that. I'm fine, and I'll be out of here before you know it."

Sniffling, she composed herself. "You've been asleep for four days. Melina said after you wake up, you could be out the next day, or the day after. As long as you continue to take it easy and lay off the healing for a while."

"For how long?"

"At least six more months."

"Shit. I don't know if I can promise . . ." But one look at the worry on her beautiful face and he knew he could do it. For them. "All right, yes. Six months. I promise."

Her relief was palpable. "Thank you."

"For us? Anything," he said with a smile. "I won't risk ruining my health or at worst, killing myself. Again."

She cleared her throat, looking uneasy. "Well, that's the thing. I'm not exactly sure you *could* kill yourself now, at least not by overtaxing your body."

He studied her curiously. "Hey, that's great. But I have to ask, why not?"

"You remember that as a born wolf, I'm immortal, right?"

"Yeah. You told me that you and Nick both are, as is most of your clan."

"Right." She looked uneasy. "The point is, I have a gift. I'm a Spirit Catcher. That's how I was able to pull your spirit back into your body so you could be healed."

He nodded. "Even when I was dead, I gleaned that much. That's a wonderful gift to have."

"I think so, too, though I'm not sure it would work on anyone but you. I'd rather not find out."

"I get the feeling there's more?"

"Yes. When I was successful in bringing your spirit back, it was necessary for both Tarron and me to feed you some of our blood. For healing. Only it has a side effect—you're now immortal, just like me."

His mouth fell open, and he gaped at her. "No way."

"Way."

"I'm frigging immortal?" he blurted.

"Are you upset?" Her teeth worried at her bottom lip, and some of her anxiety began to return.

"Sweetheart, no," he rushed to assure her, squeezing her hand. "That means I get to spend an eternity with you, right? Now I won't die and leave you alone in a few decades."

Once again, she breathed a sigh of relief and smiled. "That's right, and I can't tell you how happy that makes me. You might have been immortal anyway, because of our initial mating. Or you might have enjoyed a longer-than-normal human life span because of being a turned shifter. But now it's certain you'll be like me."

"So, will I be able to deflect silver bullets off my chest and shit like that?" he teased.

She snorted. "You're not Superman, buddy. You can still get your ass killed in any number of ways, so be careful."

"Hmm. I'd rather have the red cape."

"Sorry—no can do."

"Guess I'll have to be content, then."

Leaning over, she gave him a gentle kiss on the lips. He wanted to deepen the kiss and show his mate just how much he missed being in her arms.

A knock on the door interrupted their tender moment, and Selene sat back. "Come in."

When it opened, Nick walked in, followed by most of the Pack and Prince Tarron. They were all wearing smiles, but was it his imagination or did the commander's seem forced? Was that sadness lurking behind his eyes? God, he hoped Nick was getting over what Darrow had done to him. It wasn't his fault. Surely he knew that.

"Damn, it's good to see you guys," Zan said, grinning at them.

Each of his brothers came forward to shake his

hand, and some even gave him careful hugs. When it was Jax's turn, his best friend held on a bit tighter than the others.

"Don't *ever* do that to me again, jackass," he said hoarsely.

They both laughed to lighten the moment, and Jax let go to stand with the others. Zan looked to Nick. "So, what's going on? Any news about Owen Matthews? How are we going to bring that bastard down?"

"We won't have to. It's already done."

"Jeez, somebody works fast. How'd that happen so quickly?"

"I placed a call to Grant, seeing as how he's the only one we can trust," Nick began. "He contacted a couple of high-up government officials *he* can trust, and they handled the situation. Seems as though an 'anonymous tipster' sent videos of Secretary of State Matthews, a CIA agent, and a White House staffer soliciting one Carter Darrow to commit the mass murders of innocent American citizens."

Zan whistled through his teeth. "How the hell did they pull off faking a video like that one?"

"Easy. It wasn't fake."

"Holy shit."

"Yeah. Seems like creating super-soldiers and rogue vampires just wasn't enough to keep our little terrorists busy. They were ready to graduate to homeland and eventually global genocide, targeting citizens they felt were undesirable or unmalleable to their rule. Matthews and his followers, including Darrow, had a plan to bring down our government from the inside."

"Insane much?" Aric muttered.

"For real," Micah said, shaking his head.

"Grant's contacts created a story for the media that reported Darrow killed in a standoff with federal agents. Close enough to the truth. So, Matthews and his cohorts are undoubtedly going to prison for life."

"So, it's over?"

"Yep," Nick said, looking satisfied about this, at least. "Except for the pockets of rogues here and there we have left to eliminate, it's really over."

Zan could hardly believe it. The reign of terror that had started with Matthews betraying their team of Navy SEALs and forcing the creation of the Alpha Pack, then soon trickled down to Malik, Orson Chappell, Dr. Gene Bowman, and August Bradford, was finally at an end.

But there would be another threat, another day. There always was.

Just then, Melina pushed into the room—and stopped in her tracks, eyes narrowing on the large group. "What the hell are all of you guys doing in here? My patient needs rest, dammit, not to be worn-out yakking with you knuckleheads!"

"Now, doctor," Tarron said in a smooth tone, eyes raking her petite form appreciatively. "We were just supporting our friend, that's all. By the way, I was wondering if you could take a look at me. I have this uncomfortable stiffness that won't go away."

A couple of the guys snickered. Melina scowled at the prince. "I'll just bet."

"Oh, but I really do. Shall we?" Taking her arm, he steered her toward the door, ignoring her sputtering protests. Just before Tarron walked out, he looked over his shoulder at his new friends and winked.

The guys hooted the second the door closed behind them.

"That'll take the starch out of her panties," Aric declared over their laughter.

Zan just smiled. Maybe their resident doc was due for some happiness of her own. He sure hoped so. She deserved it.

As for himself, he planned to treasure every single minute with his mate.

Several barbecue grills were rocking, vampires and shifters were engaged in a fierce game of football under the floodlights, and the beer was flowing.

And Selene was glowing under the attentions of her mate, who'd declined to join the game. The evening cookout was a success so far, planned after sunset so the Pack's new friends and allies, Prince Tarron and his coven, could join them. They'd traveled a ways to come from the Smoky

Mountains to the Shoshone for a visit—but when your whole group could teleport, it wasn't like travel was a problem.

Besides, as she watched Tarron flirt relentlessly with Melina—and the doc doing her best to avoid his attentions—she had a feeling they'd be seeing a lot more of the vamps around the place in the near future.

"Penny for your thoughts?" a low, sexy voice murmured in her ear.

"You can have them for a kiss."

Turning to her more fully from his seat on their picnic blanket, he cupped her face and planted a sensual kiss on her mouth. Took it like he owned it, and he did. His tongue slipped inside to taste, and she wanted to drown in him.

After the kiss, she drew back and smiled. "Keep that up and we'll ditch the rest of the party."

"Fine by me." A finger traced her lips. "But then you'd miss the arrival of your special guest."

"I'd managed to forget." A sudden round of butterflies assailed her stomach lining.

"No, you hadn't."

"You're right, I hadn't. It's got me so nervous I'm about to be sick."

He kneaded her shoulders. "Try to relax, okay? Everything will be fine. And if he steps out of line, he's gone, and I'll make sure he knows he's not welcome here again."

"Thank you." She sighed. "But I want this to work, so badly."

"I know you do, sweetheart."

Just then, Blue walked up holding baby Kai, Mac and Kalen following behind him. "Ooh, let's say hello to our friends Selene and Zan," the Fae prince cooed, bouncing the boy and making funny faces at him. Then Blue used the feathered tip of his right wing to tickle Kai under the chin. The baby seemed delighted by his antics and gurgled a slobbery laugh. "Yes, you love Uncle Sariel the best, don't you?"

Zan laughed and addressed the couple. "I don't think you guys are ever going to get the kid away from him. Might as well join the party and let him entertain the baby."

"True. He's already got Kai so spoiled he cries if anybody puts him down." Mac rolled her eyes, but her fondness for her mate's half brother was obvious. She grinned at Zan. "Would you like to hold him?"

"Can I?" His eyes lit.

"Of course."

Blue made a face but gave the baby up reluctantly. Bending, he transferred Kai to Zan's arms as though handing over a box of blown glass, instructing his friend on how to support the baby's head. Watching Zan as he marveled over the small bundle, a strange pang of longing pierced Selene in the chest. There wasn't much that was cuter than seeing a strong, handsome man cuddle a baby.

Her mate looked darned good doing it, and she couldn't help but picture how he'd look holding *their* baby.

Just then, the phone at Selene's hip buzzed, and she withdrew it to peer at the readout. Instantly, her gut churned anew. "They're here."

"Visitors?" Kalen asked curiously.

"In a manner of speaking," she said. Fingers trembling, she returned the text, sending the visitors' code for the security gate. "My uncle and one of his enforcers are here."

Kalen's eyes widened. "What the fuck for? And does Nick know?"

Mac smacked her mate on the arm. "Kalen!" To Selene, she said, "What he means is, is there anything we can do? Will you and your father be all right?"

She gave the couple a shaky smile, thankful for her own mate's comforting presence beside her. "Thanks, but we'll be fine. I hope. And no, Dad doesn't know I've invited them. I had to do something, though, to get him out of this funk he's been in."

Kalen rubbed his chin. "Well, I agree Nick needs some intervention, though I'm not sure a heartfelt family reunion with the man who stole his daughter is the way to do it." He ignored Mac's murderous glare. "But if things get ugly and you need

ne, holler. I'll turn him into a pine tree, and we
an all piss on him every time we shift and go for
 run."

The image broke through Selene's nervousness,
nd she laughed along with Zan. "I'll keep that in
nind. Thanks."

"What are friends for?" The wicked gleam in
is eye suggested he'd enjoy doing it. With that,
e reached his arms out to Zan for the baby.

The trio said their good-byes and wandered off
o the party. Selene stood, and Zan joined her,
ulling her into his arms and holding on tight.

"It'll be fine. I'm here for you."

"I know. I love you."

"Love you, too, baby."

Taking his hand, she headed across the lawn
nd around the building toward the end of the
riveway, where the guest parking was located.
Headlights were approaching, signaling that it
vas too late to back out now. Whatever happened,
here would, hopefully, be closure between her fa-
her and Damien.

Zan squeezed her hand in reassurance and then
tepped forward so that the bulk of his body was
lightly in front of hers as the car stopped. She
vould've smiled at the unconscious protective
nove, but she was too nervous.

How would she feel when she met him again,
nowing what he'd done? Something Ryon had
old her a while back whispered in her mind.

Sometimes there are explanations for things we don'
understand at first, things that seem unforgivable. Yo
might want to remember that.

Now she knew the explanation. And she knew
she could forgive.

Under the outdoor lighting, she had no problem making out her uncle and Taggart as they go
out of the car. Closing the doors, the two men approached and then stopped a few feet from her
and Zan, eyeing them with somewhat wary expressions.

"Uncle Damien. Tag." Her greeting was equally
reserved.

Damien's eyes softened. "I'm sorry," he said
quietly. "For everything."

"You should be." Harsh, but true.

"I did what I thought best at the time. I can see
now that I should've handled things differently."

"It's done now. I didn't ask you here to make
you grovel to Dad or me."

"Why *did* you invite us?" Tag asked, studying
Zan with open dislike.

"Healing." She took a deep breath. "I want us
all to be a family."

"That's going to depend on Nick," her uncle
said.

"I'm so glad I get a say in things."

Selene's heart stuttered. She turned to see her father standing just behind her and Zan, his body
tense and still. Eyes shuttered. He watched Damien

ike the lethal predator he was, ready to spring at he slightest provocation. Stepping from Zan's proective presence, she went to Nick and drew him orward.

"I invited them here because there are things hat need saying between you two. You need closure, and unless I'm way off base, you need your brother."

Smoldering anger crept into his face as he glared at Damien. "I needed my brother twenty years ago, when I was grieving for the mate I lost. I needed him when my heart was broken, and he turned his back on me."

Damien took a step closer. "I'm standing right here, Nick. I only did what I thought—"

Not waiting to hear another word, Nick closed the remaining distance and delivered a powerful punch to Damien's jaw that sent the other man reeling backward to land on his ass on the asphalt.

"Fuck what you thought!" Nick roared, every muscle in his neck standing out as he loomed over his brother. "Fuck your uptight rules and the clan! Fuck you for kicking me when I was down. *Fuck you!*"

Oh, God! She hadn't even realized she was moving to get between them until she felt her mate's arms around her, holding her back.

"Let them sort this out," her mate whispered in her ear. "It'll be all right."

"Nick—" Damien began.

"I made a mistake and I *paid* for it." His voice cracked, filled with anguish. "But you had to punish me more. Did it occur to you to reach out to me and Selene, to help us get past our grief as a *family*, to be there for us? Instead, you took my baby! You took her from me and I had nothing left. Nothing."

That last word was spoken as a hoarse whisper, and Nick's rage suddenly deflated. He looked . . . defeated. Older. More silver had crept into his black hair since the ordeal with Darrow, and he appeared haunted all the time. The hopeless expression on his face, his entire demeanor, scared her.

This was why she'd called Damien. Her dad needed help.

Damien must've seen the same thing in him, because he met Selene's gaze briefly. Nodded. Then he pushed himself to his feet, ignoring Tag's outstretched hand, and stepped up to Nick again. Took a chance.

"I can't erase the years I took from you and Selene," he said, his tone laced with sincere regret. "But I can offer a new beginning. I'd like to see us all put the past behind us, start over, and find our way as a family. Would you be willing to try? Can you accept me back into your life?"

Selene held her breath. Long moments ticked by as they waited for another explosion.

But it didn't come. Instead, Nick met Damien's gaze, his eyes moist. "It won't be easy."

"But you'd like to try?" The hope there was almost painful to see.

"Yes."

Just that one word. But it was enough.

Taking a big chance, Damien wrapped his brother in a strong embrace—and slowly, Nick's arms came around him. Tears rolled down Selene's face as she watched him take that first tenuous step to reconciliation. No, it wouldn't be easy for them, but it was a start.

As they drew back, Selene cleared her throat. "Well, since it seems there won't be bloodshed, I'd like to introduce someone. Uncle Damien, Taggart, this is my mate, Zander Cole. Zan, my uncle and my friend Tag."

Zan shook hands with both men and offered them a smile. Tag's answering greeting wasn't quite as enthusiastic, but he appeared to accept Zan's place in Selene's life as he shot her a glance of resignation and then took Zan's hand.

"Good to meet you both," Zan said. "Hey, I smell some burgers cooking. Anybody hungry?"

There was a general consensus that eating sounded good, and Zan skillfully led Damien and Tag toward the party. *Talk to your father*, he encouraged through their bond. *We'll be fine.*

Thank you, love.

He winked and disappeared around the corner. Heart aching with love, she went to Nick. Touched his arm. There were only two things she needed to say, and her father needed to hear them.

"I forgive you, Daddy," she said quietly. "And I love you."

For a few seconds, he hung his head. And then he pulled her into his arms with a choked sob and held on as though he'd never let go. She relished being in her dad's strong embrace, let his love surround and fill her. Until this moment, there had been a piece of her soul missing.

Now it had been returned.

"I love you too, baby girl. So damned much." They clung together for a few more moments, until he kissed her on top of the head and set her back from him, giving her a watery smile.

"Are you going to be all right? Really?"

"I will." He touched her hair. "I've got you and the Pack in the meantime to get me through. I'll be okay."

"And Damien, too. You've got him."

"We'll see."

It was as much as he'd admit for the time being, and that was fine with her. He'd opened the door and that would have to be enough.

"Come on." She took his arm. "Let's go find the party."

"Sounds good."

Zan led Damien and the glowering Tag to the area where the burgers and hot dogs were being served and introduced them around. The intros were met with open curiosity, but he was glad the Pack and their mates were welcoming. He got a plate for himself and assembled a towering burger, trying not to smirk as Tag spoke.

"Selene has been my friend since we were pups. If you hurt her, I'll become your worst nightmare."

Unconcerned, Zan took a huge bite of his burger, chewed and swallowed. Then he said, "I think you wanted to be more than friends. Am I right?"

"That doesn't matter now."

"You're right. It doesn't." He let some steel creep into his tone. "I'll take good care of my mate—don't you worry. You want to remain friends with Selene, and that's fine. But if you cross the line, I'll teach you what the word 'nightmare' really means."

"Fair enough." The big man smiled, and Zan had the feeling he'd somehow won the guy over.

Born shifters were weird.

It was a relief to see his mate rounding the corner with Nick. The pair was arm in arm, and the stress around Nick's mouth seemed less. He looked more at peace than he had in days.

Nick kissed his daughter, then made for the burger station. Spotting Zan, she made a beeline for him, lips curved in a soft smile.

"How's Nick?" he asked when she walked up.

"Better, I hope. I'm so worried about him, though."

"I know you are, baby. Why don't you get some food and let's go back to our blanket."

He waited as she made a plate for herself, and then they walked together back to their spot. He held her plate as she sat, then placed them on the blanket before taking a seat beside her. He tucked her into his side. That felt good. He and his wolf approved.

For a time they simply enjoyed each other's company and finished their food, watching the party in progress. Across the way, Damien approached Nick and made an attempt at conversation, though Zan could tell from here it was tense at best.

"They'll make it," he said to his mate. "Wait and see."

"I hope so. I love them both." She turned to him, vivid blue eyes sparkling. "Almost as much as I love you."

"Oh, my mate wants something," he teased. "What could it be?"

"Hmm, I don't know." She pretended to think. "You, sprawled out naked on our bed?"

His cock stirred to life, suddenly taking an interest in the conversation. "That, my beautiful mate, can be arranged."

"Now?"

"Oh, yes. Right now."

Wasting no time, Zan pulled her to her feet and led her back inside to their quarters. Then he undressed her slowly, kissing and licking, savoring every gorgeous inch of her creamy skin as each part was exposed. Shoulders, breasts, tummy. And lower.

When he had her panting for more, he shed his clothes and made her scenario a reality, spreading himself on the bed, cock resting hard against his thigh. Crawling over his body, she returned the favor, nibbling, laving, and stroking his cock and balls until he thought he'd explode.

Then she straddled his lap and took him inside her slick heat, and he did just that. As she moved on top of him, he couldn't stop the orgasm from erupting, and he emptied his seed deep inside his mate with a cry of completion that rocked his soul.

"I love you," he said as they floated down together.

"And I love you too. So much."

Rolling them, he tucked her back into his front, spoons in a drawer. Just breathed her sweet scent and counted himself a very, very lucky wolf.

He was immortal and mated to the woman of his dreams. Yes, there were challenging times ahead for him, for his mate, and for their Pack. For her father and Damien.

But they would make it, he was certain. They had love.

And he was living proof that sometimes love truly could conquer all.

I forgive you, Daddy. And I love you.

The words Nick had been desperate to hear for so long. Selene was the light of his life, his only source of happiness. She wanted them to be a family—all of them, including Damien. At one time, he would have sold his soul to make that happen. And now?

Would it be enough to save him?

Rounding the corner of the building, he rejoined the party, but kept to the fringes. His men and their mates gave him space, sensing he wanted to be left alone. Under a tree, he leaned one shoulder against the rough bark.

And that's when he saw Calla.

She'd arrived late, apparently, and was greeted by Tarron. Brother and sister were all smiles as he hugged her warmly and began introducing her to Nick's friends and colleagues. Watching her as he'd done that day in the forest, but with much less privacy, his heart began to pound. His palms began to sweat.

Calla was beauty personified, wrapped in an ethereal package of sexy vampire.

Vampire. His heart pounded harder, for a different reason now, and his skin grew cold. Carter Darrow had been a vampire, too. His nightmare, his secret shame.

You're mine now, Darrow had murmured against his skin. *Say it.*

I'm yours.

What do you want, wolf?

Drink from me. Take it all.

Patience. I'll do as you wish. After we've enjoyed this fully.

He had enjoyed it. He'd begged Darrow to do it and had craved more.

God help him, he craved more even now.

Suddenly, Nick realized that Tarron and Calla were headed his way. As they approached, the pair gave him a friendly smile, and it was obvious that introductions were about to take place. Nick pasted on a smile and steeled himself, ready to brave out a few moments for the sake of politeness.

"Nick, I don't believe you two have had the opportunity to meet," Tarron said, gesturing to the vision at his side. "This is my sister, Princess Calla Shaw. Calla, Nick Westfall, commander of the Alpha Pack."

"It's very nice to meet you, Princess," he said.

She smiled, showing the tips of her fangs. "Just Calla, please."

Nick took her hand—and a shock traveled up his arm, taking his breath. Her wonderful, tantalizing scent reached him first. Then the vision hit him so suddenly, there was no time to prepare.

Calla, wearing white. Sobbing on her wedding altar. Alone.

Tears were streaming down her lovely face, and she was devastated. Heart shattered. She'd gambled on love and lost.

He came back to himself and found his guests staring at him in alarm. "It's all right," he said hoarsely. "I'm fine. I'm sorry, but will you both excuse me for a few moments?"

"Wait," Calla called out.

But he kept moving. Strode inside the building and made for the safety of his office, where he could think. Reaching his space, he closed and locked the door and then dropped into the chair behind his desk.

"Oh, God," he groaned, burying his face in his hands. "It can't be."

His body flashed hot and cold. Grew clammy with fear. Lowering his hands, he reached for his desk drawer. Slid it open.

And stared for a long time at the gleaming pistol inside.

His hand shook. After a time, he closed the drawer, leaving the weapon untouched. But it was tempting. It would be too easy to end the pain of submitting to Darrow. The nightmares.

The dreams of what could never be.

Against all odds, fate had given him another chance at love—with a woman he could never touch.

A woman he couldn't allow to touch *him*. To feed from him.

The very idea of another pair of fangs sliding into his skin, lips sucking, pulling at his life's blood, the compulsion making him beg . . . He couldn't do it. And so, fate had screwed him one last time.

Because Princess Calla Shaw, vampire, was his Bondmate.

Read on for an exciting preview of
the first in the Torn Between Two Lovers
e-book trilogy by Jo Davis,

RAW

Available from InterMix.

Anna Claire sipped her dirty martini and observed the restaurant from her soothing darkened corner. From back here, nobody could see her slip off her Pradas under the table and stretch her aching feet.

This place was her domain, her baby. Every stick of furniture, every glass, every fork, knife, and spoon belonged to her. The staff moved as efficiently as a well-oiled machine under her ownership and also the direction of her brilliant head chef, Ethan Collingsworth. They respected her and were quite terrified of Ethan's wrath, an arrangement that suited her just fine.

She didn't need to be bosom buddies with her employees to be a success. Quite the opposite had proven true in her previous business experience.

She merely needed intelligence, persistence, and lots of money.

Anna had plenty of all three.

Which didn't explain why she was sitting alone in a corner booth of her own high-end New York establishment, feeling sort of down, when by all rights she should be basking in the glow of two years of hard work come to fruition, from conception to success.

Soft laughter and a tinkling of glasses drew her attention toward a table on the far side of the main dining room. A group of four was having some sort of celebratory gathering, and they looked happy as they toasted with champagne. At ease and on top of the world. A promotion perhaps or the landing of a big account. An engagement or a pregnancy. Whatever the occasion, Anna couldn't help but feel proud that they'd chosen her restaurant for their celebration. On the way to her own table, Anna had welcomed them and told them so.

But as she watched, a sense of melancholy stole over her. Nobody had ever really celebrated *Anna's* accomplishments. Even her own mother didn't "get" her, didn't understand what drove Anna to succeed, especially in the restaurant business. Margaret Claire was set in her ways and her thinking and never minced words. Like many parents, she had the power to make Anna bleed from hundreds of tiny invisible cuts, even if she didn't realize it.

Her mother stared at her incredulously. "Let me get this straight—you worked hard to make that little café of yours a success, and now you're going to just throw it away . . . spend a ton of money to open a fancy restaurant in New York City." The older woman sighed. "Honey, you were doing well as a manager, and then you went out on a limb with the café and did all right. But this? I don't understand why you need to take a risk this big."

Anna's heart froze. Was she kidding? "This restaurant has been my goal for as long as I can remember! You haven't listened to a word I've said!"

So unbending, her mother. Such a product of her own upbringing as the daughter of a steelworker and a teacher. The Claires were good, salt-of-the-earth people who worked hard and loved harder. But the fact remained that they were also narrow-minded in their view of what equaled success—and that typically involved punching a clock nine to five and earning a retirement after forty years or so of working for someone else.

She tried again. "Mom, did it ever occur to you that employees have to work for somebody? Someone intelligent who knows their business? And that the boss might as well be me?"

Margaret Claire just stared at her daughter as though she'd spoken in tongues and sacrificed a chicken in the front yard.

"Miss Claire?"

Anna snapped to the present and blinked at the

man standing in front of her table. She'd expected to see one of her waiters but instead was greeted by a tall man dressed in kitchen whites. In the dim lighting, it took her a moment to focus on his features.

He was a big man, fit and broad-shouldered, and she could only guess at the muscles hiding under the drab required uniform. His short golden brown hair was mussed in that sexy just-rolled-out-of-bed look that turned her on when a man knew how to pull it off—and this one did. His full lips quirked upward, and she found herself wondering, not for the first time, how he would taste. Brows that were a bit darker than his hair arched over expressive blue eyes, which conveyed a very male interest he couldn't quite hide, or hadn't bothered to, from day one.

The last idea intrigued her in spite of herself—what kind of man would hit on his boss? One who was either very stupid or very confident.

Anna had always found confident men to be extremely sexy.

"Mr. James? What can I do for you?" She made it a point to know the name of every single employee, so his came effortlessly—and the question emerged more flirty than she'd intended.

Grayson James, the new prep chef, was one rung on the ladder above the janitor of this building. At age thirty-three, he was a bit long in the tooth if he hoped to make head chef one day, but he'd come highly recommended from Le Cordon Bleu, one of the most prestigious cooking schools around. That, and his letters of recommendation from the senior partners at his former law firm, had been enough for Anna. She'd hired him on the spot, despite a few reservations Ethan had voiced.

Who was she to hold back someone determined to follow his dream?

"Chef sent me to see if you wanted anything special for your dinner," he said in a smooth, deep voice.

A "radio voice," her mother would say if she were here. Anna toyed with her martini glass, trying to ignore the warmth that pooled in her middle at the sound and traveled south. The man was an employee and she had no business drooling over him, much less playing this flirtatious cat-and-mouse game with him for the past few weeks. But she supposed what he didn't know wouldn't hurt anyone.

She cocked her head, lips curving upward. "I highly doubt Ethan did any such thing."

He made a face. "Busted. But how else was I supposed to get away to talk to the most beautiful woman in the whole place?"

Pleasure curled through her insides. "You've got a big, steely pair, Mr. James. I like that."

Something hungry, predatory, flared in his eyes and he leaned over slightly. His voice was husky as he parried her thrust. "Do you? That's good, because I happen to like a woman who knows what she wants and isn't afraid to grab it."

"I'm afraid of very little," she said, eyeing him in appreciation and not bothering to hide it.

"And yet I sense you holding back with me."

"I'm careful in every aspect of my life. A little common sense is a good thing."

"Not when it interferes with the fun of living, I think. I guess I'll have to make it my mission to loosen you up, boss lady." Her brows shot up, but he didn't wait for a response. "Would you like to order something?"

You. Naked on a platter with an apple in your mouth. "What's Ethan's special tonight?"

"The duck over a bed of sautéed greens, with a mushroom wine sauce drizzled on top."

"Sounds fantastic. I'll have that."

"Wise choice." The man actually winked at her and grinned. "Ethan does get testy when the patrons don't follow his recommendations."

Damn the man for having the most alluring dimple on the left side of his mouth.

"Everything he creates is beyond compare. Our diners can't go wrong, no matter what they order."

"True. I'll let him know your choice." He waved a hand at her glass. "Another?"

She debated, then nodded. "I think I will."

He laughed. "So long as you're able to walk at the end of the evening, that's fine."

She barely managed to keep her mouth from falling open at his forwardness. If any other employee had made that remark, she would've reprimanded him. When it came to Gray, however, she couldn't be upset when his playfulness was edged with genuine concern. "Thanks, but I'll be fine. I won't be behind the wheel and I only live five blocks away."

"But you could stagger in front of a tour bus," he said innocently. "Then who would sign my paychecks?"

As she opened her mouth to retort that he wouldn't have to worry about that if he was no longer working here, she was shocked when he turned his back and simply walked away. The arrogant bastard just left her sitting there, his carriage and attitude screaming that he wasn't the least bit intimidated by her position as owner. Any of the others, save Ethan, would bow, scrape, and stammer in her presence. But not this man.

That damned confidence she couldn't resist. Somehow, in the space of a couple of weeks, the prep chef had honed in on her weakness and filleted it like a sea bass in Ethan's kitchen.

The second drink and her duck were delivered with a flourish, but with no further sign of Mr. James. It surprised her to realize she was disappointed. That small exchange had left her feeling more charged than she had in a while. Almost like she'd been awakened from a deep sleep.

Her meal had never tasted better, and she wondered whether a certain sexy prep chef had anything to do with that. Thoughts of him replayed in her head as she ate, and by the time she was ready to leave, she found her eyes straying toward the doors to the kitchen. Was she really so eager to get another glimpse of the man? *You're the boss. Just go in there and check on things. You don't need an excuse.*

When she was finished, she did just that. But only because she needed to close her office and retrieve her purse, she told herself. Mr. James was hard at work chopping vegetables when she walked through, and he barely acknowledged her with a nod. There was no cocky grin this time, no heat in his gaze. No familiarity. But then she caught Ethan observing him and not bothering to hide it, so that made sense. The chef was his boss as well and was much more stern and scary than Anna. No way would anyone in his right mind invite a tongue-lashing from Ethan.

Grayson James, on the other hand, could give me a tongue-lashing of a different sort. A very welcome one.

Good God! Annoyed with herself, she went through some paperwork and studied some orders for fresh meat and vegetables. Then she left twenty minutes later, locking her office and passing through the kitchen without letting her attention stray to the object of her fantasies, and took the elevator down to the lobby.

Fatigue dragged at her as she pushed through

the revolving door, and she suddenly wished she'd called a cab. But that was ridiculous for a mere five-block walk, even this late at night. At least the city never really slept, and there were cops on almost every corner this close to Times Square.

That's what she told herself, anyway, as the bright lights of her restaurant's block gave way to the lengthening shadows of a residential area with fewer people about. Though she was tired, her senses were on alert for any movement. Any person who didn't belong.

So she was jolted with terror when a hand grabbed her arm and yanked her into an alley between two apartment buildings. "Hey!" she yelled. "Stop!"

Another shriek was abruptly cut off by a palm clapped over her mouth as she was pulled backward, farther into the darkness. The hand was covered by a ragged glove with the fingers cut out, because they were digging into her cheek.

Every horror story she'd ever heard about women being abducted and assaulted flashed through her mind, and she exploded in movement, fighting him like a wildcat. Twisting and bucking, she managed to make him lose his grip for a moment—just long enough to sink her teeth into the side of his hand as hard as she could through the glove's material.

"Ahhh! Fuck!" Jerking his hand away, he

shoved her back into the side of the nearest building, then spun her around and pushed her face-first into the bricks before she could glimpse his features or clothing. "Scream or bite me again and I'll snap your pretty neck! Got it?"

She nodded, heart slamming against her rib cage. "Wh-what do you want? Money? It's in my purse."

"And where's your purse?"

She jerked her head as much as she could in the direction they'd come. "Over there. I dropped it."

"Hmm. Maybe I'll go back for that," he said in a low voice. "But I'm thinking the real prize is right here in my hands. Begging for a piece of this." As emphasis, he ground his groin into her ass.

"Y-you don't want to do this," she said, breathless with fear. "Someone will come and you'll be caught. Just take the money and go."

"Nobody's coming. Why can't I have both?"

"People live here. You don't want to risk jail."

"As if guys like me care about getting sent to Club Fed. Three squares a day, exercise, reading, and TV. Hell, I could even study for a trade, which is more than I get on the street."

"Please," she begged as his hand began to creep under the hem of her blouse. "Don't—"

Just then, the man's weight vanished from her back. Before she could register why, she heard a vicious curse and the sounds of flesh hitting flesh.

Spinning around, she spotted two men bounce off the wall and into some garbage cans, sending the receptacles flying and causing a loud clatter. In the dim light, she could barely make out a large man punching a slightly smaller man. The more slightly built one was dressed in a hoodie, the bigger one in jeans and a T-shirt.

She had to do something. Get help before her rescuer got hurt.

Just as she was about to turn and run, the attacker shoved the bigger man away from him and fled. He was fast, booking it down the alley and skidding around the corner. Gone, just like that. The bigger man stood under a sliver of moonlight, chest heaving, his tense stance suggesting that he was tempted to give chase. Instead, he faced her and took a couple of tentative steps.

"Ma'am? Are you all right?"

His voice was so familiar, but she was badly shaken. She could hardly think straight as she replied, "I feel sick."

"Here, let me help you." Taking her gently by the hand, he led her out of the alley, stooping to grab her purse on the way and hand it to her.

"Thank you," she said.

"You're welcome."

Tears pricked her eyes, a testament to how frightened she'd been. She hadn't cried in years, since she'd finally learned to swallow being a disappointment to her mother.

Her rescuer urged her back onto the sidewalk, under a streetlamp. Then he turned to speak but stopped, mouth hanging open. "Anna! I mean, Miss Claire," he corrected himself. "My God, I can't believe it's you. Are you sure you're okay?"

"I— Mr. James," she stammered in surprise. "Yes, I think so."

As if to reassure himself, he stepped close and took her hands in his, rubbing them as though to ward off a chill. Then he turned her a bit and inspected her from every angle.

She gave a watery laugh. "Really, I'm fine." Except for the nausea, which threatened to upset her dinner.

"You don't look fine," he replied, eyeing her with a concerned frown. "Just to be sure, I'm going to walk you the rest of the way home."

"Oh, that's not necessary."

He shook his head. "I insist. Which way?"

"No, I mean it's really not necessary because I live there." She pointed to the building on the corner.

"You're kidding! That's where I live, too." He smiled. "Then it's definitely no trouble at all to see you safely to your door."

"I don't—"

"Please? For my peace of mind?"

He looked so handsome, so worried, that she had to smile back. "Fine. That would be nice. Thanks."

"First, though, we should file a report. I should've thought right away of calling the police."

She considered that, then blew out a breath. "I think that'll be a waste of time. I'm not hurt and he didn't take anything. I didn't even get a look at him, so my input isn't going to help much."

"Are you sure? They can at least have it on record."

"No. Really, I just want to get home."

He hesitated, then relented. "I can understand that. Come on."

Tucking her hand in his arm, he escorted her the rest of the way to their building and inside. As they crossed the spacious lobby, she briefly wondered how a lowly prep chef could afford to live in a neighborhood like this, where the apartments were so expensive. Then she remembered that he'd been a hotshot attorney of some kind, so that made sense. He'd probably socked away plenty before changing careers.

As they stepped into the elevator, his finger hovered over the number panel. "Which floor?"

"Six."

He smiled again, a blinding slash of white that made her knees a little weak. "What do you know?"

"You, too?" She blinked at him.

"Yep. I'm curious, though. How is it that the boss lady missed the fact that I live in her building, on the same floor?"

She shrugged. "I make it a point to memorize names and faces because I like my employees to feel as if they matter to me—and they do. But my manager, Jeff Wilson, does all of the hiring paperwork and tax forms, and he collects the employee information sheets we keep on file. If I need to know specific information about one of you, I can look it up."

"I met Mr. Wilson, but I don't see him around much," he mused. "He doesn't take a very active role on the floor."

"Because that's not what I hired him to do. He does most of the paperwork, ads, and marketing."

"So you can be among the people, which is what you enjoy most."

"Yes."

"And yet . . ." The elevator arrived at their floor, and they got off.

She stopped and faced him. "What?"

"I don't know if I should say." His gaze settled on hers, assessing.

"You can speak freely. You *did* just save my life." She grinned in encouragement.

He relaxed some. "It's just that you seem very reserved most of the time. Aloof. It's interesting to hear you say that you enjoy being around your staff and guests when you don't really show it."

She stared at him in surprise. "I don't? But . . . I speak to people all day. I ask them how they're doing, if their meals are excellent, what they're celebrating. Things like that."

"What about the staff?"

"What about them?" She started to feel defensive. "I ask them if they need anything, what I can do to help them. I inquire about any incidents that may have occurred, how the kitchen has been running, check on the special reservations to make sure the staff is prepared."

"Yes, you do. You're a good boss," he allowed.

"Why, thank you," she said dryly, giving him a droll look. "I'm so glad you approve."

He ignored her sarcasm. "But when was the last time you actually *talked* to any of them?"

"What the hell do you mean? I just told you I talk all day!"

"When's the last time you asked one of them anything personal?"

"Personal?" She was at a complete loss. "Like what?"

"Jesus." He pinched the bridge of his nose, then dropped his hand and regarded her in part amusement, part exasperation. "You know Brandon the waiter?"

"Brandon Gates. Of course I do."

"Right. But did you know his pet iguana died yesterday?"

Obviously one of them had been dropped on their head. And it wasn't *her*.

"So? As long as Ethan didn't serve it in the soup, what does that have to do with me?"

The bastard actually laughed. An honest-to-God laugh that made his eyes crinkle and her toes curl. Made her insides warm in the most pleasant way.

"Christ, you're so uptight, you squeak when you walk."

"What?" She gaped at him. "Listen, Mr. James—"

"I saved your life, as you pointed out," he murmured, moving closer. Reaching out, he gently touched her face with the rough pads of his fingers. "I believe we've moved on to first names, Anna."

Her breath caught in her chest, her nerves dancing at his touch. The hunger in his eyes, his nearness torched all of her arguments to dust. At five-eight she wasn't a short woman, but the top of her head barely reached his chin. That was a secret thrill of hers—a big, tall man surrounding her. Pressing her down, covering her lips with his.

He was so close, their mouths almost met. Then he stepped back, and it took her a moment to adjust. To realize he wasn't going to kiss her after all. Flushing, she attempted to cover her embarrassment by fishing in her purse for the keys to her apartment. Finding them, she gave him a smile she didn't feel.

"Well, Gray, I should get home."

She turned and started down the hallway and he kept pace beside her, apparently not ready to relinquish his role as her protector. Suddenly her ordered world had been unbalanced, not just by the attack but by Gray's nearness, and she wondered if that's what he intended.

At her door, she unlocked it and faced him. "Thank you for saving me. I can't imagine what might've happened if you hadn't been walking home right behind me."

The idea made her feel sick again.

"I'm glad I was there." A shadow passed over his face and was gone. "Let me come in? You've had a shock and I want to see you settled before I leave."

Settled. That would be the very last thing she would feel if she allowed him inside; of that, there was no doubt. Some force that obliterated reason and good sense had her opening the door anyway, stepping aside to welcome him to her home.

"Nice place," he commented.

"I imagine it's the same as yours."

"Just the floor plan." Looking around, he appeared impressed. "I definitely don't have your sense of style."

"I can't claim much credit, except for the colors. I picked those and then hired a decorator."

"I like the browns with the deep red accents. It fits you."

Curious, she studied him as she set her purse on the bar. "How so?"

"The browns are subtle, understated, and strong.

Alone, they might be boring to the eye, and then bam! The red is exciting. Just like those flashes of your true personality when you let them out, as you did in the hallway a few minutes ago."

"Seriously?" A laugh escaped before she could help it. "You are so full of shit."

"And like now," he said, looking smug. "*Miss Claire* would never have said that, but *Anna* sure did. I obviously know what I'm talking about."

"I don't know whether to be flattered or frightened by the armchair psychoanalysis."

"Flattered. What else?" Gesturing toward the couch, he ordered, "Sit down. What do you want to drink? Wine? Something stronger?"

Bemused, she did as he said—for the moment. "Isn't that my line? This *is* my apartment."

"You can offer one to me some other time." He disappeared into the kitchen and began to rummage around as his voice drifted to her. "You know, sometime when you haven't been attacked by a mugger."

The image caused her to shiver, and she unwillingly began to relive the encounter. "I'll just have some water. Get whatever you want for yourself."

In moments he was back, the sofa dipping as he sat beside her and twisted the tops off two bottles, handing her one. "I don't often drink this late at night. Gives me insomnia."

"Hmm." There was something odd about that man in the alley.

"Are you sure you're all right?" he asked in concern.

"He talked too much."

"What?"

"The mugger." Anna lifted her gaze to see Gray studying her, brows furrowed. "He was all talk. He never did much except push me around and scare me. Isn't that weird?"

Gray leaned forward. "What else?"

"He smelled nice, like he had on his best cologne. And . . ."

"And?"

She gasped. "The man wasn't armed! He didn't have anything in his hands."

"Are you sure? Could be that it happened so fast, you missed a small knife or something in his grasp."

"No, I'm positive. The mugger wasn't armed, he spoke articulately, and he smelled nice. Something is off about the whole thing."

"That is strange," he said thoughtfully. "You should be more careful from now on. In fact, I'll be walking you home for a while. Just in case."

In case the man returned. Fear overrode the inner whispering that it was smart to keep a distance from this sexy man, no matter how much she wanted him. "All right."

Their eyes met and a strange flutter of butterfly wings took off in her stomach. Gray was looking at her as though she was the answer to every

question he had, and it was wonderful. Confus
ing. Arousing.

"You're so beautiful," he said with reverence
touching her face with the pads of his fingers.

"I don't remember the last time anyone told m
that."

"You deserve to hear that every single day, be
cause it's true."

"Thank you." Drawn to him, she reached u
and traced his lips with one finger. "You're a ver
handsome man yourself."

"I wasn't fishing."

"I didn't think you were." She paused. "Wh
me?"

His face registered surprise. "Why am I inter
ested in you?"

"Yes."

"Besides your beauty, you're smart, successfu
Kind. I think you need to unwind a lot, and I wan
to help you do that."

God, he smelled good. Woodsy and manly, and
it made her body ache to be touched. Completed
"Then help me, Gray."

For a few moments he didn't speak. His han
covered hers and he waited, giving her time to voic
an objection. When it didn't come, he leaned ove
and closed the distance between them. Brough
their lips together, parted hers with his tongue.

His kiss was liquid fire. Slowly, he licked he
mouth, his sensual exploration sparking an elec

trical storm throughout her body. All thoughts of why it was a bad idea to see an employee blew to dust. Pushing into him, she sought more. Needed more from this man. It had been far too long since she'd come alive this way.

All too soon, the kiss was over and Gray moved back. Confused, she tried to pull herself together.

"Will you be okay tonight?"

Only if you stay. But of course she wouldn't say the words.

"Yes, I'll be fine." She forced a smile. "Go on, get some rest. You're on the late shift again tomorrow."

Rising, he looked down at her. He didn't seem eager to go—more like resigned that it was for the best. And it was.

"Give me your cell phone."

"Why?"

"So I can program my number in for you."

"Oh. Okay." Fishing around in her purse, she found the device and handed it over.

He punched a long series of buttons; then he handed it back. "Here you go. Call me if you need anything at all, Anna."

Her name on his lips, the intensity of his gaze made her feel like a wounded antelope in the sights of a lion. The thing was, she didn't want to escape.

"I will."

With that promise extracted, he gave her a

wicked half smile and walked out the door, shutting it softly behind him. Following him, she looked up and then stood gazing at the colors in her living room, trying to see them—and herself—through his eyes.

Brown for steadiness and strength, red for excitement. Being alive.

Somehow, it seemed he'd taken all of the red with him when he left.

Grayson closed the door behind him and stood in the middle of his sparsely furnished apartment, frustration and guilt riding him hard.

As he'd started getting to know Anna Claire over the past few weeks, he'd slowly come to realize she was nothing like he'd first assumed. He'd thought she was too straitlaced and wondered why she hadn't snapped like a brittle twig. Maybe a little stuck-up, too. But she wasn't.

She was driven, determined, smart, and sexy. Kind to her employees and patrons, yet aloof to the former, perhaps because she was their boss. The woman was complicated, and yet he felt he was coming to understand what made her tick. She needed to have some fun, enjoy life a little.

He intended to help her along in that area.

A knock at the door interrupted his musings. "You took a hell of a risk," he growled as he opened the door. "Don't you ever use your brain?"

Simon King strolled inside and faced him,

wearing a grin. "I changed clothes, and nobody saw me come here. It's not like she got a good look at me anyhow."

Gray rolled his eyes. "She knows something is off, you idiot. Once she calmed down and had time to pull herself together, she said you were too articulate and you smelled good. And it didn't escape her notice that you weren't armed."

The cocky grin slid off his face. Good.

"Shit. I didn't expect her to be so aware of those kinds of details. Most women wouldn't be when they're so scared."

"Anna's not most women, Simon." Gray sighed.

"Yeah? Well, at least we accomplished our goal," his partner pointed out. "You got invited into the lioness's den. The question is, did you get a free pass to go back?"

"Most likely. She's a tough one, but I think this was the edge I needed."

Simon considered that. Thankfully, he didn't mention just how far Gray might still have to go to capture their prey. "Did you get the trace put on her cell phone?" he asked instead.

"Yeah. I'll get the rest in place next time I go over there."

"Which will be when?"

"Hopefully tomorrow."

"It would be quicker if you just broke in and did the job."

"And more risky, too, in a building like this

with all the apartment doors facing the hallway
and no access from the outside. No, being invited
in is a much better scenario."

"All right. It's your call." Simon paused. "Who
do you like for this, partner? Honestly?"

Gray rubbed the back of his neck. "That's the
million-dollar question."

And that's why he and his partner were on this
case, and why Gray had infiltrated the staff of Floor
Fifty-Five. Several of Anna's employees were running drugs, using the restaurant as a cover and
base of operations. His job was to learn the names
of everyone involved, how and where they were
hiding the drugs—and whether Anna was in on
the scheme.

Lowering himself into an easy chair, he answered, "I'm the low man there, so working my
way into confidences is proving harder than I expected."

"Whoever's behind this is mob-connected, my
friend. They're going to be suspicious of anyone
new and it will take too long to earn their trust, so
forget making buddies. Just find the evidence and
get out."

"I have to tell you, my gut says Anna's not involved."

"You sure that's not your dick doing the talking?"

Despite the seriousness of the situation, Gray
laughed. "Not at all."

"That's what I figured." His partner shook his head. "Be careful, okay?"

"I wouldn't be anything less."

But after Simon left, he couldn't help but think *careful* wasn't going to be a word that applied at all where Anna was concerned.

Also available from

J.D. Tyler

Hunter's Heart
An Alpha Pack Novel

Wolf shifter Ryon Hunter is visited by a beautiful spirit
with an urgent message: "Help me...I'm alive." It's wildlife
biologist Daria Bradford, using a rare Psy gift to call for
help. Finding her mortally wounded in Shoshone
National Forest, Ryon knows that she is his destined
mate but is afraid of what she will do if she finds out
what he is—or what he had to do to save her life.

**"An exciting series that will have readers
glued to the pages and wanting more."**
—Fresh Fiction

Also in the series
Black Moon
Savage Awakening
Primal Law

Available wherever books are sold or at
penguin.com

facebook.com/ProjectParanormalBooks